by the time you read this

by the time you read this

lola jaye

AVON

An Imprint of HarperCollins*Publishers*

This book is a work of fiction. The characters, incidents, and dialogue are drawn from the author's imagination and are not to be construed as real. Any resemblance to actual events or persons, living or dead, is entirely coincidental.

HarperCollins books may be purchased for educational, business, or sales promotional use. For information please write: Special Markets Department, HarperCollins Publishers, 10 East 53rd Street, New York, NY 10022.

FIRST AVON PAPERBACK EDITION PUBLISHED 2009.

Interior text designed by Diahann Sturge

ISBN 978-0-06-173383-3

09 10 11 12 13 WBC/RRD 10 9 8 7 6 5

For Heaven's Girl

acknowledgments

I'd like to thank God; Mrs. Sheila "Nanno" Graham for her belief in me; Nathan "Piza" Thomas for being my rock during those early days; Simon "Stewy" Trewin for being the perfect muse; Claire "Tha Editor" Bord for being absolutely on my level (not sure if that sounds like a compliment!); Judith "Tha Agent" Murdoch for not dissing me at Winchester and Karen "Kazzarino" Tester for reading the very first scribbles of Kevin's Manual.

Plus, I'd also like to send a shout out to EVERYONE who has played a part in the production of my book: family, friends, ice cream makers, colleagues, HarperCollins staff, ... you know who you are, but for the benefit of everyone else, pop your name in the space provided!

And enjoy the book Daddy Ted . . . I'll miss you forever.

prologue

It was like someone had just doused me in ice cold water and I couldn't stop shivering.

It was my birthday.

And he was going to let me know that this was it. It was over. A period of eighteen years snuffed out just like his life had been.

Don't get me wrong, this wasn't about a boy meets girl scenario. It was more than a friendship too. More than a mediocre fleeting love. In fact, more than anything I had ever known or wanted to know in my entire life.

This had been about my dad.

Deep breath.

I bounced on my childhood bed, placing the velvet lid back onto the box and pressing it shut because I knew I wasn't ready yet. I couldn't do it. Not now, not ever.

I stopped shivering, opened the lid again and slowly brushed my fingers across the surface, my eyes squeezed shut, multiple intakes of breath, hoping I could freeze frame this moment forever. But I was a grown woman after all, with thirty full years of experience. Of life. And yet here I was behaving like the teenager I used to be, not wanting or unable to see that I had to get that message from him. That very last message, or else it would have been for nothing. And worst of all, I'd be letting him down.

And I could never do that.

But for now, before I could even think of opening the box again, before I could begin to go through the process of thinking about where I was going or what I was going to do with the oncoming void, emptiness and sorrow, I needed to look at where I'd been. Where we'd been. Together.

And how it had all begun that miserable, lonely morning of my mother's wedding.

the manual

Mom's marrying some prick she met down at bingo. Apparently they fell in love as he called out "Legs eleven" in a smoke-filled hall in Lewisham, packed with bored housewives ticking off paper boxes. Eyes down, cross off a number and another, until some wailing overweight woman shouts "House!" to anyone who gives a damn. I hate them. I hate bingo. And sometimes I hate Mom. But most of all, I hate *him*. For ordering me about, telling me to call him Dad, for pretending to *be* my dad and, most of all, for not *being* my dad.

You see, my dad's dead.

Some illness I couldn't even pronounce finished him off about seven years ago in 1983 when I was five and he was thirty.

But we don't talk about that.

We hardly even talk about *him* any more, really . . .

Sitting on the edge of the bed, Doc Martens feet swinging in time to my croaky hum of the *Brookside* theme tune, I shook my ridiculously ringleted hair that had taken ages to style and stunk of Dax hair grease and let out an exaggerated puff of air. I was fed-up. Almost a teenager, yet there I was clad in a frilly yellow dress that allowed me to resemble a pavlova. I wished I could just disappear. Maybe travel down the rec with Carla—my best friend—or change the habit of a lifetime and happily start some homework, complete with the seven dwarfs' whistle. In fact, I'd do almost *anything* to avoid this crappy, stupid, pathetic "wedding of the year."

"Lois!" Mom called in a squeaky voice.

"What?" I replied with a sigh, my eyes darting to heaven.

"Excuse me, young lady?"

"I mean, yes, Mommy?" I replied in the cutest little voice I could pull off.

The door to my PRIVATE (couldn't she read the sign on the door?) sanctuary swung open. "Are you ready yet, Lois? We've got to be at the registry for eleven and it's already nine forty-five!"

I checked out my mother in her wedding gear, glad she looked almost as tragic as I did. Thick blue eye-shadow in a tug of war with an off-white, two-piece mess with puffed sleeves. Puffed sleeves! It was 1990! Who *did* that any more? The silver shoes didn't help matters either, along with the backcombed hairstyle, perhaps more at home on a schizo poodle!

"I'm nearly ready," I replied sweetly, but with a spot of annoyance lurking round the corner. I swung off my bed, quickly locating the pink dolly shoes she'd bought just to humiliate me that little bit more. I didn't care about most people, but Carla and her brother Corey would be at the wedding to witness my shame and that just wasn't fair.

"You look so adorable!" gushed Mom, and for one ridiculous second I convinced myself she was going to cry.

"Er, thanks?" I mumbled, pulling off my worn DMs to slip into the dolly shoes, my little right toe recoiling in instant pain as it connected with the hard plastic. Only last week, I found out my right foot was longer than the left. I'm totally deformed!

"Come on then, let's go, Lois." I ignored the invite of Mom's hand as it came at me like a weapon. "I don't want to be late for my big day, now, do I?"

This summer was one of the hottest on record, which I could believe if my dress, currently sticking to me like flies to dog poo, was anything to go by. The heat rash that ensued meant that I scratched and tugged the dress all the way through the vows and exchanging of rings. Mercifully, the service was short. Unfortunately, the reception (held in a restaurant that stank of disinfectant) lasted a lot longer than necessary. Boring stories floating around the room like confetti. And what with the kisses, hugs, dull speeches and hard squeezes from sweaty relatives I'd never even set eyes on before, things grew shoddier by the millisecond. Worse still, Carla remained cocooned between her dad and brother on a table miles from mine. It was a total nightmare of a day, growing extra tragic the minute Granny Morris drew what little strength she had to shove me onto the dance floor for a slow dance! Eeek/Eeew! The experience of dancing with Granny Morris reminded me of one of those horror films Mom wouldn't let me watch, but I'd catch next door with Carla and Corey—only much, much worse.

I had finally managed to escape another "I remember

when you were a little girl" tale, about to join Carla and Corey in sneaking outside, when out of the shadows of balloons, streamers and "The Birdie Song," a new guest appeared.

She was beautiful, with thick black braids cascading down her slimline back like a glossy rug. Unlike Mom's attempt at fashion, this lady wore a simple flowery shift dress and plain rounded hat that looked a bit like a full moon on her obviously gorgeous head. She smiled at me and, instantly, my mood lifted.

She walked toward me and I realized it was my Auntie Philomena—my *real* dad's sister. Her showing up was a massive surprise, especially as I hadn't seen her in ages. So instead of running outside to, I dunno, argue this week's top forty with my friends, I stood before this glamorous aunt of mine, waiting for something intelligent to pop into my head.

"Hello, Lois."

"Hello," I replied, sounding like a total geek.

"You look lovely."

I stared at her full lips, which looked pilfered from some unsuspecting model in a glossy magazine, and I began to wonder, did she act like him? Laugh like him? Think like him? I could only remember a handful of things about my dad. Stupid stuff, like the tiny mole just under his right eyelid.

"Auntie Philomena?"

"You remember me, then? I really wasn't sure if you would. I'm glad, though. Really pleased."

"No, well, I don't remember you THAT much . . ." I said, annoyed. Of course I remembered her. Unlike Dad's younger sister Ina, Auntie Philomena called me up a few times a year—mostly birthdays and Christmas. She even sent the odd hideous blouse, pictures or a lump of spice cake wrapped securely in tin foil through the post, when I'm sure a visit would have been more hygienic? But, apart from Mom making me travel up to Granny Bates once a year, I didn't really have that much full on contact with my dad's side of the family. And I was okay with that. Really, I was . . . I am.

I crunched a knuckle.

"I'm sorry," she said.

"For what?" I shrugged.

"For not being around much. I live pretty far away. And the kids . . ."

I stifled a yawn, the frilly fabric of my ridiculous dress beginning to irritate the tops of my knees. She beckoned me outside away from the crowds—and, thankfully, away from the sight of Great Auntie Elizabeth swinging larger-than-average hips to "Let's Twist Again."

The only bench we could find was soiled with bird crap, though it didn't concern me, as it would probably improve the look of the dress anyway. My mind did begin to wonder what Corey and Carla were up to, though.

"I need to talk to you," said Auntie Philomena, who on closer inspection had yellowing teeth.

"Talk to me? Me? About what?" I raised my voice in that high-pitched manner that made me sound as if *I really wanted to know.* And I didn't. Not really. Okay, maybe a little bit, then. Especially as the only time a grown-up ever wanted to talk to me was to ask about my homework (teachers) or nag the fun out of me (Mom, teachers).

"I have something for you, Lois . . . And it's really, really important."

"Right . . ." I sat on my hands, believing it could stop me from exploding. I wasn't good at this patience thing that grown-ups always spoke about.

A wave of fear washed over me, especially as she began to look at me weirdly, before her manicured fingers began squeezing my hand so tightly I thought she'd break the left metacarpus (I'd learned that one in biology a week earlier).

She continued, "It's something we should have told you about a long, long time ago . . ."

We? Okay, the woman was freaking me out now. My mind glossed over a number of likely scenarios: genetic disease; Public Enemy splitting up? The possibilities were endless and I'd had enough of this guessing game. I JUST WANTED TO KNOW.

"Is it about my dad?" I asked quietly, hopefully. A shot in the dark.

"Yes, it is." Auntie Philomena's mouth formed into an unusual smile. One tinged with sadness.

My mind started to wonder as suppressed joy threatened to leap from the pit of my stomach and out of my mouth like a mound of vomit. This was all too much. Something I'd dreamed of ever since I was a little girl. You know, *finding out he wasn't dead after all. It had all been some silly mistake after he'd contracted amnesia in the early hours of that morning, seven years ago. Of course, it would be difficult to piece together what occurred in the interim years, but after recently regaining his memory, Dad had set out to find us—his loving family—and finally succeeded today, the night of his wife's wedding! But seeing how happy she now was made him all confused, as he stood alone outside the number twenty-one bus stop located just around the corner from where Philomena and I now sat. He was too scared to talk to me—just in case I too had betrayed him.* Poor Dad!

"Lois?"

"Yes, sorry Auntie Philomena, you were saying . . . ? About my dad?"

My heart was ready to leap out of my mouth.

"I have something for you . . . a message . . . from your dad."

with stars on

I remember my dad lifting me up by his large hands and twirling me around in the air. Me, giggling with wonderful anticipation of the giddy feeling that would grip me, right before the remnants of my breakfast would start to rise in my throat.

"She's going to be sick, put her down!" Mom would shout. Spoiling the moment. *Our* moment. And that's basically all I could clearly remember about him. Oh, and the mole under his eye. The picture on my dressing table, and others banished to a small box in the loft, was all I had to help piece together the size of his nose, curve of his large lips, cute little button ears encased in what I could only imagine to be the smoothest skin I could ever wish to touch. I often imagined jumping into that photo, if only for sixty seconds—each one spent running my finger across the surface of his skin, the contours of his face, implanting an image in my brain that would live there forever and ever.

But I didn't have the power to jump into a photo.

And Dad wasn't alive again.

In fact, when Auntie Philomena left the reception I ran into the smelly toilets of that restaurant and cried. I continued to sob for the rest of the night, away from the noisy crowds and uncool music. And then again in my bed, still dressed in that awful frilly dress, dolly shoes banished to the ether. As usual, Mom didn't notice, she was too loved-up with the Bingo Caller to care. I wasn't even sure why I was crying because, as Auntie Philomena had put it, this was a *good* thing. Right? Like hearing a message from the grave. But I suppose that's what really bothered me the most: he was *still* dead. Lifeless. His ashes scattered in a foreign sea thousands of miles away along with old tires and rotting bicycles. He hadn't come to rescue me from my life of endless days at school, Mom's moaning and now a stepdad thinking he'd acquired the right to tell me what to do just because he was knobbing my mother.

Dad was still gone.

Philomena had handed me a crumpled old plastic bag like it was a pot of glistening gold; a perfect, divine specimen needing special handling. It was heavy, with something book-shaped inside. *Great,* I thought. Yet another book to read. So all I could do was chuck it on the floor among my Doc Martens, twelve-inch singles and one of the pink dolly shoes, staring at it from time to time with a cocktail of confusion, fear, excitement and sadness floating in the background.

Luckily, that weekend was spent with Carla while Mom and the Bingo Caller honeymooned in Cornwall. Although my best mate and her family lived only next door, same south London, same Charlton, it felt like a trillion miles away. And it might as well have been. Carla and her brother Corey were allowed to stay up late AND were allowed to eat ice cream AFTER nine o'clock. So, staying there was perhaps a great way of forgetting about Dad's "message" for a while and get my head right. But my head remained jumbled and I couldn't get it out of my mind, counting the days till Mom returned. And the minute the sickly newlyweds arrived back home, complete with their first all-shrieking, super-duper, mirror-cracking argument over what to watch on telly, I raced to my room, desperate to peer inside that plastic bag.

"Don't I get a kiss, young lady?" shouted Mom as I reached the top of the stairs—just outside my room and *that* plastic bag. My heart raced as Mom slowly climbed the stairs, moved toward me and smiled wildly to reveal her front gapped teeth.

"Sorry, Mom. Welcome back," I said, one eye on the door to my bedroom as she planted a wet kiss onto my cheek.

"Is there one for me as well?" said the Bingo Caller, opening the door to their bedroom. They couldn't have heard my silent toot as I replied, "Yes."

At last on my bed, I carefully removed the plastic and instantly clocked the ugly green notebook with the words *The Manual* written on the front in thick black ink.

Mom shrilled my name. "Lois!"

I quickly replaced the plastic bag over *The Manual*, stuffing it under my bed.

"What??!!" I replied, totally exasperated.

"Carla wants to know if you want to go to the sweetshop."

I clocked the piece of plastic poking out from under the bed. "Erm . . . yes, tell her I'll be right down . . ."

"What is she doing up there?" said Carla.

"Nothing! I'll be right down!" *The Manual* could wait another half-hour, right?

I waited impatiently as Mr. Tally, the bald man behind the counter, looked on as Carla picked out her ten penny candies. Mr. Tally had this annoying habit of watching us and ignoring the grown-ups who were probably busy out back, shoplifting a pint of milk (I'd never even stolen before, although Corey swiped a sherbet dip once).

"I think you've gone over," said Mr. Tally, and I wasn't sure why, considering he'd always tip the tiny paper bag out onto the counter and recount the contents anyway.

"How have I?" challenged Carla, today dressed in a pair of *very* ripped jeans. The door pinged as another young customer ignored the *"only two schoolchildren at a time"* notice slapped onto the glass door. "I've got a Flying Saucer, a Mojo, Refresher, whistle, pink shrimp and a Fruit Salad. How's that up to ten cents?"

I sighed and glanced at my watch. We'd been at this for ten whole minutes and I was bored. I had to get back to my bedroom and that plastic bag.

"The Jamie whistle counts for two pennies," he said.

"So I've still got three pennies then! Stupid!"

To save on time and aggravation, I picked out a ready-made bag, hoping it contained my favorites, and we headed toward home.

"Why don't we go down the rec?" asked Carla.

I opened my bag, relieved to find a white chocolate mouse. "I don't feel like it today. Let's just go home."

"You got stuff to do?" she asked with a look of utter disbelief. *As if Lois Bates would ever have anything exciting to do.* She had a point.

"So what's it like with the new pops?" she asked, her mouth stuffed with at least three items.

The white mouse and Black Jack currently being demolished in my own mouth nearly flew out as I shrieked, "He's not my dad, Carla!"

"Soooooreeee!" she shrugged, curling her lip like they did on telly. Actually, Carla could very well be mistaken for one of those actresses or models, anything she wanted to be. She was easily the prettiest girl in Charlton—no, make that south London—and even with short hair. Tall, slim, always wore the latest fashion, fun, but an absolute whiner if she didn't get her own way. I was relieved when she sucked on a gobstopper, leaving me to gossip about Sharlene Rockingham and whether Mrs. Codrington—our science teacher—used to be a man or not.

The hot sun shone above us, warming my insides like an electric blanket, and I could swear I felt Dad's presence. Like he was willing me to do it; just go home and open up that grocery bag, start acting my age and not my shoe size. I was a big girl now, after all—and, I repeat, *almost* a teenager.

I finally left Carla in front of her television and came face-to-face with the plastic bag in my bedroom. I discarded the plastic and the relief was instant—followed by a stab of fear. Puke tents were suddenly pitching themselves in my tummy as the plastic fell to the ground, mercifully covering the pink dolly shoe I now used as a pencil holder.

And there it was again.

The "something" my dad had left me.

The ugly green book, staring back at me.

The Manual

I opened the hard cover and immediately smiled at the first caption.

This is my (Kevin Bates's) manual to my daughter Lois. The love of my life.

I sighed heavily, dropping the book straight onto my toes, wincing as the pain shot upward. My body flopped backward onto my untidy bed, shoulders colliding with the one-eyed teddy, and a single tear poured from my eye like a waning waterfall. My chest heaved up and down with the force of a silent sob, not because it hurt (and it did) but because, after all these years, I'd finally heard from my dad.

And he'd just told me he loved me.

I made myself a cup of hot chocolate and placed it well away from *The Manual* and inches from Dad's picture. I sat upright on my bed, something that would please Mom as she was always going on about my *posture*. My face began to drip again. I wiped my eyes frantically and swiped at the snot with my hand, sniffing a couple of times, then stopped behaving like a wuss long enough to peep into the second page.

Rules of The Manual:

1. *You must only read each new entry on your birthday (from ages 12 to 30).*

2. *This is a private manual between you and me.*
3. *No peeping at the next entry!*
4. *You are allowed to look back at previous entries. Actually, I insist on it!*
5. *I've tried to be really neat, stringing sentences together in the right way, but if you spot the odd dodgy grammar or spelling mistake—just make sure you don't copy them next time you hand in your homework, young lady!*
6. *Under each new year, you'll see that I've pretended you'd actually be interested in what was happening in my world around that age.*
7. *You can look at the miscellaneous sections any time you like—if you think they'll help. I've cleverly placed these at the front, so you don't get tempted to peep at future pages!*

I frantically turned to the next page, heart beating forcefully under my T-shirt.

Hello Lowey,
Hope you're sitting comfortably.

I sat back against the headboard and shoved the one-eyed teddy onto the floor.

First off I have one thing to say.

I'm sorry.

I am so very sorry for leaving you. It was never my intention. You were only five years old at the time, remember? You probably don't, unless you're one of those rare and ultra genius kids, which I very much doubt considering the collaboration of the Bates/Morris genes (only kidding). One thing I totally saw, every time I looked at you, was this beeeeeautiful, vivacious, chatty, smiley little girl, who liked Cheese Doodles and running around the living room like a short-legged Olympic runner. This massive sports bag full of potential; a Motown lyric just about to be sung at an open-air concert to thousands; an unfinished portrait, waiting for that last flick of a brush to complete the artist's beautiful vision.

I wasn't ready to go, but I had to. And I'm sorry that by the time you read this . . . I won't be around anymore.

But this is your time, your beginning. And I want to guide you as best as I can on your journey. Be a father, a dad, a pops to you even though I'm not around any more.

Question: will you let me?

My sobs returned. This time, a little deeper.

Now, let's go back a bit.

I always thought I wanted a son first. To play soccer with, argue the mechanics of a car, play-fight and share my old toy race cars. But all that floated through the hospital window the very first time I held you as you tried to open your eyes, an hour after your beautiful mother pushed you into the world. You were so soft and you smelled so . . . oh, I can't explain it . . . you smelled all fresh, like the bubble bath section of the supermarket . . . like only a baby can. Damn, I was hooked and I knew as I looked into your eyes, I was finished. No longer Kevin Bates, sometime Jack the Lad, joker of the pack. But Kevin Bates, Daddy to Lois—and nothing would ever be the same again. I was in your power forever and ever. My little girl.

I turned the page, feeling sad. Then happy. Scared. Excited. This yo-yoing of emotion felt so strange to me.

I knew we were going to call you Lois.

Because a few weeks before your birth, I'd persuaded your mom to go and see Superman, where I had to summon superhuman strength to lift her out of that cinema seat! Huge! And that night on the way home from the theater, you kicked so much I thought I'd have to pull over and deliver you myself!

And even then, I knew. Had never seen your face, never heard your voice, but even then, I knew what you, Lois, would mean to me.

I stifled a smile. At last, explanation for my horrible and weird name.

While Philomena's kids were noisy, you were a quiet baby. Only really grizzling when you were hungry or needed a nappy change (two good reasons in my book!).

I loved looking at you. How your forehead would crinkle anytime you didn't get your own way or as you perched on your knees in front of the television deep in thought (something you certainly never got from me). How your eyebrows arched at the thought of something really important, like "Why does Big Bird have a funny voice?"

You, my baby, were a shy little thing. But on odd occasions you'd allow your mom and me the privilege of being a part of your world—especially if you needed our help for something really important, like whether or not you could watch Button Moon—or you'd ask for my opinion on one of your many artistic creations (like that drawing you did of the three of us, with rainbow Mohican haircuts).

Our times together were great, Lowey. Kissing you on the forehead as we slouched on the settee, watching The A-Team *(which, by the way, is the best show on earth). You'd giggle up at me and I'd feel this little lump in my throat as well as this surge of strength and then weakness for the cutest little girl I had ever seen. The way your eyes were so trusting as they looked to me—plain old Kevin Bates—for some type of reassurance that I'd always protect you. Be there for you. Comfort you.*

Wow.

And then I'd kiss you on the forehead again, Lois, just because . . . just because I could never resist that smile of yours. I'd like to think you'd still let me do that if I were there—you know, kiss you on the forehead as you snuggle up to watch TV. Or would you squirm away and tell me "I'm a bit old for that, Dad"? Well, you don't have a choice because I will be kissing your forehead every night before you go to sleep. For the rest of your life—whether you like it or not.

In a nutshell, I need you to know that your daddy loves you soooooo much. With stars on! And although I'm kind of gone, I will NEVER, EVER leave you. I'll be there with you, for you and around you. Don't ask me how, just know I will be and especially through this manual, which I hope you will keep forever and ever. And as well as your birthdays, I want you to open it up whenever you feel confused, lost, lonely or even happy! Yes, Lowey, when you are happy too.

I wiped the fresh layer of snot from my nose with the back of a trembling hand, and for a good ten minutes I didn't move or think of anything. This was all too much to take in. So unexpected. I suddenly felt ancient—at least eighteen. And while I ached to turn the pages, devour everything my dad had ever written to me, I knew doing so would mean nothing left for later. Next week. Next month. Next year. I needed this manual. I needed my dad and nothing would tempt me into jeopardizing any of that—even if it meant reading a sentence a day for the rest of my life.

I re-read that first page around a hundred times, ignoring Mom shouting up from the kitchen, "What are you doing in there, Lois?" and "Dinner's ready! Wash your hands first!"

I wasn't hungry for mere food, but sat down to the meal with the same old plates, same old knives and forks, same everything. Only *I* had changed. Something inside wasn't ticking the same any more. I'm not saying I was suddenly a grown-up. I just didn't feel like a little kid any more. And I certainly didn't feel like sitting at the table listening to the Bingo Caller and Mom talk about a load of terrible, while upstairs in a plastic bag was the bestest, most important thing I had ever read.

"The fish is lovely," enthused the Bingo Caller, carefully tucking into Mom's trademark snapper and rice.

"Our first meal as a family! Well, you know . . . since we

got married," giggled Mom, sounding like a little girl. Equally, the Bingo Caller gazed at her the way a toddler does at a lollipop.

"This is a lovely meal," repeated the Bingo Caller. Mom smiled, squinted her eyes, then dared to question why I chose to pick at the food.

"Nothing's wrong with it. I'm just not hungry, Mom."

"Aren't you feeling well?"

"I'm fine."

"Did someone upset you? Something happen when I was away?"

"Not really . . . No, nothing." I continued to pick at the food, just desperate for the sensation of my dad's manual against the surface of my fingers once again.

"Got a boyfriend?" asked the Bingo Caller, mouth full of fish.

I quickly and angrily shook my head in response. "Of course not!"

"You don't have to be rude, Lois. We just want to make sure you're okay," said Mom sternly.

"Sorry," I mumbled.

After dinner, I finally got the chance to escape. I turned to page five of *The Manual,* butterflies break-dancing in my stomach. It simply read:

> *As you read* The Manual, *always remember without doubt and without question, I love you . . . with stars on. Dad.*

I closed my eyes and grazed the top of my forehead with my index finger. An image of Dad gently kissing my forehead appeared along with this total feeling of calm replacing all the stuff I had to deal with at school, Mom remarrying . . . everything washing away like water down a smelly drain.

That night, just before dropping into the land of nod, I whispered:

"I love you too, Dad. Goodnight."

And I knew he'd heard.

try not to be a wimp

Kevin Trivia: *I scored a magnificent hat trick to clinch the county cup for my school.*

"What you're telling us is . . ." began Corey as a huge pink bubble grew out of his mouth like a balloon. Pop! "Your old man left you a book?"

I'd finally revealed *The Manual*'s existence outside Lanes Fish Bar.

"It's a manual, actually."

"So, it's a manual that follows your life?" asked Carla.

"Yep. Every birthday from age twelve until I'm an old lady of thirty."

"But you're twelve already!" said Carla.

"You're not listening. I only got it at my mom's wedding, so I get to read that entry and then every year until I'm thirty!"

"Oh, right," she replied with a yawn. I nodded my head as Carla scraped strands of silky hair around her perfect ear, which was decorated with a massive hoop earring.

"Bummer, Lo Bag, another book to read," said Corey, chewing furiously on the gum.

"Can you not call me that?" I asked—although I knew it was pointless, considering he'd been referring to me as "Lo Bag" since, like, forever. As I explained about *The Manual* AGAIN, Corey's index finger disappeared almost whole into his left ear as Carla stifled yet another yawn.

"He gives me advice and stuff . . ."

"So, what you're saying is, your dad tells you what to do even though he's dead?" asked Corey, eyes searching the street ahead for his friends who were meeting him in ten minutes.

"No . . . not really . . ." I replied defensively.

"Bummer," he added again anyway as Carla shook her head in apparent agreement with her brother. I sighed inwardly, disappointed that my friends found it so difficult to understand my new situation. But then, I couldn't really expect them to.

An offensive bang on the chip-shop window interrupted our conversation.

"Hey you kids, buzz off if you ain't buying anything! stop loitering!"

"Charming!" I said.

"Screw you!" shouted my friends as Corey placed two middle fingers firmly against the smeared window. Feeling a little left out, I spat a weak, "No, *you* buzz off!" in the proprietor's direction as I followed my friends across the road. My weak attempt at rebellion before the usual indignity of school the next day.

So the countdown begins. Bet you can't wait to officially become a teenager. If only you knew that one day you'll realize turning your clock back every winter is not enough. You'll want another five, ten, twenty years back soon. But I won't bore you with that right now, I may come back to it later. For now, it's my hope you'll manage to do ***one*** *thing this year you'll remember forever and ever.*

Can you think of anything?

Dad will give you a clue.

When I was twelve, I remember my dad taking me kite-flying for the very first time. It was a great day. The sun was shining brightly and I had to really squint as my eyes chased the red and blue kite floating in the sky. I was exhausted by the end of it all—so much so that when I chased the ice-cream van, I found I couldn't catch up. I was so angry, while my dad was in fits! But that was okay because I was out with my dad, being boys, being free . . . just me and him and away from Philomena, Ina and Mom. I've never forgotten that day—even now at my age—because it was one of the last times I really remember feeling like a kid.

I know we can't have those days together, but I really hope you and your mom have taken time out to make some lovely lasting memories of your own. Even so, I want you to make one more lasting memory this year.

Promise?

I searched my brain, tackling the events of the past year: Mom getting serious with then marrying the Bingo Caller; her constantly having a go at me; being marched up to the local market and suffering the very public indignity of picking out a "training bra." Frankly, it had been a terrible year, but I owed it to Dad to do "something to remember" before I hit thirteen.

I mentioned it to Carla that evening.

"We could go ice skating," she offered unhelpfully. Since getting her hair cut even shorter last week she'd decided to switch identities and was now all sophisticated—and stupid. I wondered what would happen if I took the scissors to my own mass of frizz. Nevertheless, I loved being around her and the family, as without them I'd be stuck at home with Mr. and Mrs. Boring. Popping round for Sunday lunch reminded me what a *normal* family could be like. Her mom was not only as beautiful as any movie star, she knew about stuff I cared about and dressed really good. Even Carla's dad was quite good-looking—if you liked geriatrics (he was at least thirty-five). And apart from Corey disappearing to the moon minus a return ticket, Carla mostly got everything she wished for—records, clothes, shoes. And, most importantly, I'd yet to witness a spat between her parents—unlike Mom and the Bingo Caller. I also wished to be as pretty as Carla—soft, spot-free skin with the slimmest waist, just like her mom—although possibly, all I had to look forward to in that department was "The Great Auntie Elizabeth Gene," but fingers crossed.

"How about ice skating?" she reiterated.

"We do that all the time!" I protested as Corey barged into the room for the fourth time that evening, baggy trousers hanging way below the waist and almost exposing the crack of his skinny bum, rolled up at the ankles and held in place with elastic bands. I'd seen the look on some guys down at the rec, but on Corey it just looked *stoopid*.

"What are you two *girls* talking about, then?" he asked.

"GET OUT OF MY ROOM, YOU CRETIN!" spat Carla as I took in the familiar scene of brother and sister mid-squabble. Corey was responsible for most rows, as he seemed to enjoy teasing his younger sister and behaving like the biggest idiot that ever lived. He also reeked of cigarettes.

"Lo Bag?" he said for no particular reason, flashing a dimpled smile.

"I said, get out of my room. I'm telling Mom!" said Carla, looking for something to chuck. These days, Carla and I were becoming more consumed in our own secrecy as Corey spent more time with "the boys." And since reading *The Manual*, I'd felt miles older than the two of them anyway. Things were changing between us.

Carla finally found one of her old teddies and launched it toward her brother.

"Cow!" he spat, reaching for the door.

That night, Carla and I swooned over a poster of Bobby Brown and practiced vogueing in front of the mirror, but not once did she ask me about *The Manual*.

I slipped back next door and into my room as Mom lay on the couch cuddled against the Bingo Caller, whispering sweet nothings. I changed into my yellow pajamas decorated with pink dots and pulled *The Manual* from its secret hiding place under the bed. The one-eyed teddy stared at me, like he had something to say, and I started to wonder if I was getting too old to have him on my bed.

You're in secondary school now.

A place where all the curly-haired kids want straight hair, the tubby kids dream of looking like beanpoles, and everyone is desperate to latch on to someone resembling a best friend.

This is fine, but having a bunch of other friends is always a good idea. At least I thought so when I was at school. In the juniors I had three good friends—one was good at Math, one great at soccer, the other okay at English. This all helped considering Math and English were my least favorite subjects!

When I got to secondary school, things were a little different. Just getting through the day without being called certain names was really important, and it didn't hurt to be around a bunch of boys who were feared, but the rules remained the same. So, now, what was his name . . . ? John or Johnny, I think? Now he was brilliant at both Math AND English. And there was Nick, who everyone was scared of (which obviously brought the name-calling down to a minimum). And then there was Charlie (secretly, my favorite best friend) who was basically good at . . . well, screwing around mainly.

Look at it this way: some will be good at geography, others good for advice. Whatever their strengths, I'm sure they'll make such a difference to your life. They'll teach you loads—good and bad. Believe me on that one.

But hey, perhaps there's someone you already hang around with and share secrets with. (Carla, maybe? You always seemed so close.) Whoever it is, never let her go. Best friends are a bit special and a bit rare—like sand made out of gold—and when you find a good one, keep her. Treat her the way you like to be treated. And always be loyal.

Admittedly, when you hit your teens, it may become difficult to keep up the loyalty bit as there's always this urge to join cliques. To branch out and experiment with situations that may not include your original friends. And there's nothing wrong with this (as long as it's good stuff), just try not to abandon your best friend in the process—she's the person who'll ultimately be there for you.

I'm basically trying to share the type of advice my old dad would impart as he smoked on a long pipe (okay, I'm fibbing about the pipe bit). His sentences would always begin: "Son, listen to me . . ." Most times I'd do so by rolling my eyes continuously around in my head until the onset of eye-ache. You see, he didn't always make much sense with his man-to-man speeches, but sometimes he got it spot on.

I don't doubt you'll meet a few more friends as you get older, and that's great, but the ones you can really, truly rely on, you'll be able to count them on one hand.

I hugged the one-eyed teddy close.

Then there are the not-so-friendlies.

Remember, Lowey, bullies are just wimps in disguise. You may think they're all brave when they confront you, shout a lot and basically frighten the socks off you. But with bullies, there's something about THEMSELVES they're trying to cover up by being horrible and mean to you. So, if you've inherited my gangliness, you're probably taller than a lot of the other girls and boys in your class anyway, which can help, but can also bring on the teasing. Or if you're anything like your mom's side—Auntie Elizabeth case in point—you're probably quite . . . generous around the middle and a little vertically challenged.

Actually, I was a cross between both sets of families: taller than all the boys in my class, not as slim as most of the girls . . .

The point I'm trying to make is, school can at times represent one big fat popularity contest, especially these days. I remember it well and it wasn't easy. I have to admit, being good at soccer was a bonus (especially as I helped win the cup). But it's just too early to see what you'll be good at, to make you less of a target. All I do know is that you'll be a beauty (inside and out) and this in itself might make you popular—or get you beaten up from time to time. Whatever you look like, there will be something that makes you stand out, and if a group of kids, or just one kid with a big gob, cottons on to this—you're in trouble.

Okay, now for the "try not to be a wimp" part.

LOWEY, DONT BE A WIMP!

If a real big bully has it in for you, never let her know you're scared. If she starts calling you names about the way you look, the color of your skin, the style of your clothes, just ignore her—this will hurt her more than you actually responding, as it will make her look and then feel a bit silly. If the situation calls for tougher action, then take it like a man and stand up to her (no, not by smacking her about the head with your backpack—however much she deserves it—and she might). Laugh her off or ignore her—she'll soon get bored. Let her know she JUST ISN'T THAT IMPORTANT in the grand scheme of things. You see, that WILL shock the crap—sorry, heck—out of her for sure. If this doesn't work, you can make a smart comment, just don't make the comment too smart, or she'll probably give you that beating after all. And if all else fails and she's still coming at you, turn and walk away. You may feel like a wimp for doing so (when in fact you're behaving like the BIGGER person), but it's the best way in the long run and just shows how unwilling you are to stoop to her low-down level. I say HER because if it's a boy then report him to a teacher straight away. No question about that.

I threw the one-eyed teddy across the room in frustration as I thought about Sharlene Rockingham waiting outside the school gates for me. Sharlene Rockingham, the thorn in my side. She'd started her vendetta against me all because she found out I hadn't cheered for her during sports day last summer. Admittedly, we'd never got on, but the constant snide remarks and dirty looks across the dinner hall were all leading up to something big.

Sharlene was the main reason I often fantasized about bad things. Like her death. Yes. I'd thought about her dying. Far from being a psycho, I'd never actually thought about HOW it would happen, or that I'd be the one to do it—only that when it did I'd be left to get on with things without wondering if she'd follow through with the promise of bashing my head against the science-block wall. I hated being a wimp about it, but not being part of the coolest crowd meant minimal back-up and a good chance of a kicking. Far from ignoring her, I made sure I put up a good-enough front by calmly telling her to "just buzz off" while pushing past and almost swallowing my chest in the process. To be honest I was kind of doubtful this piece of advice would work in the real world.

I read on.

I loved Phys Ed.

PE's one of those things you either love or hate. And yes, I was one of those morons who couldn't wait for Wednesday afternoon and a good session, rain or shine. Don't worry, Lowey, if sport isn't for you. Just remember it's rather pointless playing sick each week as you will have to go through PE eventually, anyway. So—and you're not going to like this—just get through it. Doing so will make you stronger, independent, a leader . . . or a shivering wreck. If, of course, you really are sick, that's different. By the way, your dad's not saying don't pull the odd sick day, just be smart and spread them out a bit—like twice a term—because teachers aren't that stupid.

I flicked back to the miscellaneous section of *The Manual* and soon arrived at a new and surprising heading. Why are boys such asses? I giggled at Dad's use of the word "ass" while hoping he'd have the power to at last shed some light on the opposite sex for me. An image of Corey in his big British Knight sneakers sprang into my head, basically because he was the only boy I spent time with—as Mom had put me in a girls' school.

Boys can be such asses, right?

Idiots, cretins, morons, this list goes on, I hear you cry. But that age-old question has baffled scientists for centuries—and you want ME to explain this further?

At your age now, males are at their most ass-tastic (okay, that's not actually a real word). They run around in packs, tease you for no good reason, they're lazy, moany and their feet smell like slabs of moldy cheese.

How do I know this?

Because I am one. A guy, that is.

Okay, seriously, Lowey, males do get slightly better as they age—a bit like a fine wine—but you'll have to wait until they receive that telegram from the queen (or, by your time, King Charles) to see any significant changes.

I giggled nervously at Dad's sense of humor, never realizing he could be so funny. In fact, Mom never mentioned anything about Dad these days, so obsessed was she with washing her new husband's graying jockeys, laughing at his unfunny jokes, kissing him full on the mouth—and right in front of me, as if I enjoyed bringing up my dinner. My mood, as always, lifted with joy at the thought of getting to know my dad, but was quickly replaced by a stab of sadness at the thought of the following week. My thirteenth birthday, and I'd yet to think of anything memorable to do while I was twelve. I searched my memory bank for something and then it came to me . . . Dad's manual. Hadn't my life changed since it had appeared? I no longer had an excuse to feel like a kid any more. I was on the brink of becoming a woman, and Dad knew that too. But most of all I didn't feel alone. And that had to be the best bit of all, no longer feeling lonely.

I reopened *The Manual*, pleased I hadn't let my dad down and thankful a new memory had been planted.

One I'd never, ever forget.

teabags bursting with hormones

Did you know . . . ? While England won the World Cup, Kevin scored (kissed) a girl for the very first time.

The morning of the Saturday before my thirteenth birthday, I peered out of the window to see the Bingo Caller helping Mom into the back seat of his car, her hand on her tummy. I went back to sleep and awoke to the sound of the front door being banged almost off its hinges. I smiled.

"Get up, you lazy thing!" shouted Carla as I opened the door. She was dressed in a pretty little baby-doll dress I could never wear, (not with my bandy looking legs) and huge trendy boots. "Change of plan. Your birthday party's gonna be at our house!"

Apparently, Mom had called from wherever it was she

and the Bingo Caller had gone and requested my thirteenth birthday party be shifted next door to Carla's.

"Charming!" I remarked.

"Is your mom all right? My mom wouldn't tell me what was going on."

"Probably had something better to do," I said, feeling a little put out, but hoping she had a good reason for her missing my thirteenth birthday.

Looking around next door's tiny kitchen—which was almost identical to ours, but filled with pictures of the family and with Corey's huge smelly sneakers by the entrance—it was clear a lot of effort had been made. Tiny cupcakes (soon to be decorated with hundreds and thousands) were baking in the oven; a wonky stool with dusty footprints was evidence of someone having placed colorful streamers on to the wall. A few friends from my school were invited (with Carla's help), along with Corey's friends, assuring a good turnout (even though I still doubted whether anyone would actually show up). Carla's mom forced a red bow onto my head, even though I'd insisted on wearing jeans and not a dress. But for once I decided not to mind because it was my thirteenth birthday. The biggy.

Mom rang just before the first lot of party guests arrived.

"I'm really sorry I can't be there, darlin.'

"So, why *can't* you come?"

"You know what it's like with flu. Thought I'd stay away so I didn't spread it around."

"The flu? I never heard you coughing last night?"

"It must have started during the, erm, night."

I shrugged off Mom's explanation. Besides, I had Dad now, who'd cared enough to write to me every birthday. "That's okay, Mom. You get over the *flu*."

"Really sorry, Lois."

"Don't worry. I have everything I need here," I whispered to myself.

"Never mind, though, your actual birthday isn't until Monday. I'll make sure I'm there for that. Okay, darlin?'

"Mom, I have to go now. People are arriving."

She started to mumble something as I replaced the receiver.

People began to trickle in quite slowly. And quietly. No one saying a single word. There was the odd sound of a leg tapping against a chair as guests basically gazed at each other, as if waiting for someone, anyone, to utter anything mildly witty. The silence was deafening and my life flashed before me—grand confirmation of my big fat L of a Loser status at school. But just as I thought the party was more than over, Carla's mom turned up the record player and began to move expertly to the fast melodies of "Motownphilly" by Boyz II Men, complete with subway dress and a group of lustful eyes belonging to Corey's friends. Soon, others followed. My initial fear of mass yawns and exits evaporated and I was free to find the bathroom to let out nothing but a sigh of relief.

I shut the bathroom door behind me just as Carla's mom, still on the "dance floor," proclaimed it was indeed Hammertime!

"Lo Bag, where have you been?" asked Corey, sounding like an old man. Voice all deep, as I shut the bathroom door behind me.

"In the John of course!" I shook my head to this silly question, itching to return to my guests and new friends."

"I . . . erm . . . wanted to give you your present."

"Your mom's already done that!" I replied. A roar of

laughter escaped from the living room and I longed to be among the joviality and not stuck with Corey the Moron outside the toilet.

"When?" he asked with a puzzled look.

"What do you think all this is about?" I said, gesticulating wildly toward my new pair of stone-washed jeans. "And the party!" The kid had been hanging around with his friends too long it seemed.

"Oh! So what did your mom get you?"

"A puffy coat! I told you she gave it to me weeks ago! Look, this isn't the time to annoy me, Corey!"

"I'm not . . . I don't want to annoy you. I wanted to give you this." He produced a square package hastily wrapped in what looked like Christmas paper. "Sorry, we didn't have any birthday wrapping left." He thrust the tiny item into my palm. "From me."

Before I could say thanks, he'd walked off. So I opened the present to reveal LL Cool J's "Mama Said Knock You Out" album on tape. Wow! My feet were already tapping to the beat of my favorite track. The one album I'd been after for months but Mom wouldn't let me buy (because it was rap music) and Corey had just handed it to me! Carla must have told him, I reasoned, along with wondering why Corey would save up his pocket money to buy *me* a present. The same Corey who up until about a month ago pulled my hair, farted in my face and called me all sorts of silly names. I thought nothing more as I rejoined the others on the "dance floor" and launched into Lois's very own awkward and stiff dance routine.

For the next week, I was on a high. I stood in the dinner queue, constantly greeted with invisible high-fives from girls who'd never even burped in my direction before. It would seem my party remained on the lips of almost everyone in my year, which unfortunately included Sharlene Rockingham, who cornered me behind the science block as I raced to Math.

"Why didn't I get an invite to your icky little party, then?" she asked gruffly.

"Why should I have invited you?" I replied. It seemed to slip out before I'd a chance to *really* think about it as Dad's advice pounded against the wall of my head, desperate to get in.

"You think you're better than me, don't you, Lois?"

"No," I moaned, a little cheesed off that my week of glory was about to be soured. I inched away, trying hard not to look like a "wimp" but without being too "smart" about things.

"I'm gonna be late, so I'll, er, see you . . ." I said pathetically.

Sharlene's eyes narrowed with evil. "Yep. You will."

On the morning of my actual thirteenth birthday, I opened up *The Manual*.

Happy Birthday baby!

You're now officially a teenager. From now on, every time there's a Y in the day of the week you'll be thinking "I'm not a child any more, damn it! I'm a grown-up!" while at the same time being scared to death (sorry) of becoming one.

I suppose you are a grown-up—almost. And let's just say, the lads will also be noticing how grown up you've become. They'll start staring at your chest whenever they speak to you for a start (I'll give you a few seconds to pick your jaw up from the floor in total embarrassment) . . .

Yes, I did feel a little flushed with embarrassment, but read on.

Actually, I'll come back to the boy bit later. (This is hard for me too, you know.)

Right now, let's go back to another subject.

Friends.

They're becoming more important to you now and you probably hate your mother.

Give her a break, though. Please. It couldn't have been easy picking up the pieces when I left. She'd never much liked being alone. It wouldn't surprise me if by now she's found another guy to spend time with. I expect that. Please don't give her a hard time for it, though, cut her some slack, Lowey. She's a good woman.

I slapped *The Manual* shut, remembering Mom's sudden bout of flu during my birthday party. I was still angry with her and no amount of words from Dad could change that. Part of me was pleased to know he forgave her for hooking up with the Bingo Caller, though, and perhaps I could try to like him . . . even if I did think the man was a Loser.

During the next few weeks, I attempted to be civil toward the Bingo Caller.

"Thanks for trying with him," said Mom, who'd obviously noticed the change in me. General politeness, helping to wash his car; I became the model stepchild.

"Thanks, Lois," he said one Saturday afternoon, right after I'd helped clear the shed—a job I'd been putting off for weeks.

"For what? It's only a shed."

"The effort you've made. Don't think it's gone unnoticed, because it hasn't."

I wasn't about to move in for a hug but did manage a quiet "Thanks."

But, of course, in true Mom fashion she had to go and spoil things one Sunday, right after I'd just reread some of Dad's entries.

Strike one: She entered my room without knocking.

"I'm really, really pleased you're both getting on!" she squealed as I discreetly slid *The Manual* under my bed.

Strike two: She sat on my bed—again, uninvited, and almost squashing the one-eyed teddy.

"I wanted to ask you something," she said.

She had a strange, overly smiling face that reminded me of those loonies outside the mental hospital two streets away from the dentist.

"Okay . . ." I urged.

"Things are a lot better between us all . . . you know . . . ?"

"They're all right," I replied, as my mind shifted to more important things, like whether Carla and Corey wanted to go down to the rec.

"That's what I thought. So I wondered if . . ."

"What?"

"If you should think about calling him Dad?"

Strike three.

"Lois?"

Silence.

"Lois?"

"I heard, Mom."

"How about it, then?"

Tempted to pour a whole tub of dish soap into my ear just to check I'd heard right, I replied with a calmness that contradicted the rage fizzing up inside of me. "I already have a dad."

"I know."

"Well then . . ." I jumped off my bed, not wanting to be involved in any segment of this pointless discussion.

"I know, but . . . and nothing would change that, I just think it would be nice."

My mother was obviously sick in the head. "Nice for who?"

"For you!"

"No, Mom!"

"But why?"

"I told you, I already have a dad!" I didn't want to shout at her, but she kept pushing. My stomach felt like a kettle just about to whistle. I needed her out of my room.

"Lois, no one's taking that away from you." Mom dropped her gaze. "But you were only little when your father . . ."

"Died. And I was five. So?" I stared at Dad's picture on my side table.

"So, I think it's important you have a father figure in your life like—"

"NO!" I roared, unable to take this garbage any more. I soooo wanted to tell her about *The Manual*'s existence in my life. How I was able to talk to my dad whenever I wanted. Have him beside me, just before I drifted to sleep, and under my pillow as I slept. He spoke to me through those pages, told me he loved me over and over again. I JUST WANTED TO TELL HER I STILL HAD MY DAD!

"Lois . . ."

"You think I don't know my dad, but I do."

"Lois, look—"

"I know him more than you think. We speak every day . . ."

As I trailed off, her eyes widened in disbelief.

"What do you mean?"

"Nothing," I replied, my body language willing her to get out of my room, my sanctuary, and away from any proximity to my dad's special manual.

"We'll talk about this another time," she said, calmly shutting the door behind her. I located *The Manual*, opened it, and swore as a stray tear plopped onto a page, blotting and smudging two precious letters of a word my dad would never, ever be able to write again.

I tried to ignore Mom and the Bingo Caller as much as possible while the weeks dragged by, only communicating by the absolute essential of words. So, for once, it was an unusual but welcome relief when the annual trip to see Granny Bates came around.

I used to enjoy spending time with my mom's mom, but that had been impossible since she'd moved into sheltered housing. Granny Bates, however, lived in Sussex and insisted I spent a week of my summer holidays with her at a bleak seaside house, with furniture more at home in a museum and surrounded by pictures of my dad, his school reports, soccer medals and any scribbles he'd presented her with as a child. What struck me was the absence of anything belonging to his sisters, my aunties Philomena and Ina. I never asked Granny Bates about this, though. In fact she hardly spoke to me at all, and I found the whole experience a bit like having a filling put in. I also missed Carla and Corey so much, especially as Granny's area was surrounded by sheep and old people! Luckily I had my Walkman and Corey's tape, which kept me sane while I sat opposite Granny Bates as she munched on the ginger snaps Mom always insisted I bring to her.

When I was younger, as long as I took my dolls or some books I could get through the experience without screaming, but since hitting my teens I was finding it increasingly harder to be around Granny Bates. I just wanted to spend time hanging around the rec with Carla and a few of my new friends from school. Sussex and Granny Bates now signified a total waste of my life, and I hated it.

"Gran, can we watch something else?" I asked. A tiny bit bored with the news program. Carla's mom had just got cable installed and I longed to flick onto something worthwhile, like *Yo! MTV Raps*.

"Your dad always loved watching the news."

Here we go again, I thought. That was another thing. Constantly comparing me to my dad. I wouldn't mind so much if I didn't feel she was having a go at me. Perhaps seeing me as not living up to what he was. I don't know. She was "pleasant" enough. I just felt that sometimes there was so much I didn't know or understand about the Bates family.

I stood up.

"Where are you going, young lady?"

"To my room, I might listen to my Walkman."

"You'd rather listen to that radio thing than stay down here with your Gran?"

"No, it isn't that . . ."

"You go off then. And keep the room tidy. It's Kevin's room."

She was almost raising her voice. I rolled my eyes again and headed for the room my dad hadn't even slept in before—Granny Bates had only moved to Sussex AFTER his death. Mad cow.

I spent the remainder of the evening staring at the ceiling, wishing my dad could rescue me. I opened up *The Manual* and picked up where I had left off.

So, instead of listening to your mom, you probably prefer to get advice from your friends. My best friend (as hopefully you still know) is Charlie.

Nope. Had never met him (at least I didn't remember ever meeting him). Seen a few pictures of him and Dad together though, but that was it.

When we were your age it was always about me and him. He once told me to stick my head down the toilet and let him flush—so I did. No, not really, but when we were thirteen I would have—if he'd asked. All I'm trying to say is, not ALL advice from friends is the right advice. Really think before you do stuff, consider who it may hurt (and yes, this includes your mom), then make a decision.

I'm not asking you to listen to every drop of advice given to you by an adult, no. Because, as you will soon find out, people (including myself) can at times talk a load of horseshit. But if you can, take note of older people. And when I say old I mean ***really*** *old. The elderly. They know stuff. You can almost picture the years of* *experience in their faces—and this can include the reality that life doesn't always go according to plan, no matter how efficiently you think you've planned it. Remember, they've seen it, done it, tasted it, felt it, experienced most of what you haven't yet. So try to cut them some slack when they have a go at you about things you may want to do. Their lack of support may just be a result of their own bad experiences while attempting to achieve something similar, and in their own special way they are merely trying to warn you against making the same mistakes. Make sense? You see, it's not always just another way to spoil your fun, however much you may think so.*

But for some reason or other, people won't be listening to them as much any more—so do the complete opposite to these "other people." Listen, absorb and plant at the side of your brain stuff you can use later on. It's so invaluable. Things my granddad used to tell me, I still use to this day. Of course your granddad is gone, but you'll hopefully have my mom and your other granny and granddad around to be getting on with.

One morning on the way to the supermarket, I decided to take in Dad's words and make an effort with my father's mother, by helping to carry the bags without being asked (I even carried more than was comfortable), and, back at the house, by packing away the groceries as she droned on and on about noisy neighbors and how she missed "back home" and wished she'd enough money to go back forever. I brought up the subject of Dad, hoping it would bring us closer together, I suppose. Instead, she remained silent, staring at me as if I'd grown a third eyeball.

"What was he like?"

Her face softened and I thought I saw a tear. "Your father . . . was the best son a mother could ever have."

She walked over to a picture of Dad and held it, running her index finger over his chin, up to his full lips and then to his mole. She stared at it for what seemed like ages.

I broke the trance. "You must miss him so much . . . like I do . . ." I know it was such an obvious statement, but I suppose I just wanted her to speak to me. For us to have some type of conversation. About Dad.

But my plan was—sort of—beginning to backfire.

"Of course I miss him. Very much. He was *my* son, my little boy. I miss him every waking moment of every day. My life seems to have stood still since that day . . . the day he went . . ."

She moved over to the old-fashioned glass cabinet. Among the porcelain figurines and a cloth map of Grenada was a picture of my dad. She picked it up.

"Me and his father always knew we wanted a good life for our children. That's why we came to England in 1948. I always made sure my little boy was safe. I could never rest when his father took him out. Never knew what they'd be getting up to. Climbing trees, running about. If he came home with a scrape, I'd immediately put the antiseptic on it. Make it clean. Then when he was a teenager, I wouldn't get a wink of sleep until I was sure he was safely tucked up in bed. I never stopped worrying about him. The girls, Philomena and Ina, never understood. Never." She looked at me blankly again, then turned to pick up Dad's picture. "Then he left home and moved in with . . ." she placed the picture back down again ". . . your mother. And that was it. Never saw him much after that. My son."

I wasn't quite sure where to go from here. So I said the first thing to enter my head. "Sorry."

"Sorry," she repeated blankly, placing the picture back into the glass cabinet.

Granny Bates seemed to shut down after that conversation. She'd say little words here and there, perhaps to answer a question to do with the whereabouts of the ketchup. It was as if an already dim bulb had blown—with no chance of a replacement any time soon. And I was quickly able to envisage the remainder of my "holiday" as something I'd rather not endure.

I rang Mom when Granny Bates was in the bathroom, telling her I was ready to hitch a lift home if she didn't get me out of here a few days early. She arranged for Carla's dad to drive over, while a silent Granny Bates sat in her rocking chair clutching a picture of my dad.

As I shut the door behind me, I knew I'd be in no hurry to see her again. Maybe I'd change my mind. Maybe I wouldn't. I couldn't have cared less. Okay, I did care. A little. For all her faults, she was still Dad's mom and I suppose I would drop her a line in a few months (groan). But I'd survived this long on my own and now, I had my dad constantly keeping an eye on me and really didn't need anyone else.

I was thrilled to be back in London with my friends, sleeping in my own bed and not having to be back at school just yet. My brief time away had seen a change in Carla. Her hair was a bit longer and she'd started to wear lipstick! Worst of all, she now had a boyfriend.

"He's over there!" she whispered, as we passed Lanes Fish

Bar, our old spot now occupied by a gang of spotty girls. Outside the alleyway stood a bunch of boys in back-to-front baggy dungaree jeans and identical orange sneakers with huge white tongues sticking out. They did look cool, I had to admit.

"His name's Darren!" she said.

The lovebirds caught each other's gaze and Carla ran over.

"Hi Daz," she said, all teeth and sloppy voice. I had never seen my best friend act like this before and it felt disturbing. The others were totally ignoring me as the couple lip-locked and Darren, or Daz, or whatever, stuck a huge furry-looking tongue into her mouth. It was utterly sickening.

Over the next few days it was "Daz this" and "Daz that" and, frankly, I was relieved when he dumped her for the school slut, exactly a week before the beginning of term.

My fourteenth birthday, which took place at the ice-skating rink, was a totally contrasting experience to my thirteenth—especially when Mom brought out this huge babyish cake complete with dodgy pink candles as my guests sniggered in the corner. I vowed never to have another birthday party again in my whole entire life, while almost bursting into tears on the spot and displaying my Mega Wimp side in the process.

Mom reckons I'm at a difficult age—I overheard this during a gassing session with Carla's mom over the garden fence as she put up the washing. Carla's mom lay on the lawn chair dressed in a teeny little bikini and looking quite gorgeous. Glancing at her and then at Mom sticking pegs into the Bingo Caller's revolting odd socks, I knew which mom was the trendiest. My mom knew zilch about being a teenager—how to dress, or who Kriss Kross were—and actually liked Take That! A difficult age? Me?

I did start to notice changes with my body. I had a shape that was catching up to Carla's but which I suspected would always be behind. And as for the other stuff, let's just say if it weren't for the awkward sex education classes at school, and Carla, I'd know *nothing* about THAT subject.

One morning I even woke to find that my tiny little ant hills had decided to grow into breasts. No longer a slave to the training bra, Carla and I got measured at Marks right away, only to discover we were in need of a 34B! And Dad was right, boys did start to change (not least when word got around that Carla was no longer with Daz). They began to sniff around Carla like dogs around a slab of ham. Plus they all sounded like freaks as every boy (except for Billy Turner) seemed to have picked up a new deeper voice that sounded like a cross between Corey's and Sharlene Rockingham's (she'd always sounded like a boy).

Miscellaneous: Hormones

Oh boy, I was dreading this bit, so let's just skip it until later, right, Lowey?

Oh all right, we'll do it now then . . .

I can safely say I've never been a woman so am unable to speak with any authority on the subject. Therefore, we'll just have to stick with the hormones of a teenage boy.

Have you read what I wrote about boys talking to your breasts? Well, hormones are the logical explana-

tion. If a boy at school asks if he can carry your back-pack, what he's really saying is, "I want to have sex with you." When he asks "How are you?," he's really saying, "I want to have sex with you." When he looks at you, he's more than likely thinking about . . . yes, you guessed it . . . sex. So my point here is . . . teenage boys are like teabags bursting with hormones. Once you dip a teabag into hot water what happens? It literally bursts (you'll get this analogy when you're older. Much older. For now, please beware, especially as by now you are drop-dead gorgeous in the making, even if YOU think you look like a giraffe in need of urgent dentistry). Just bending down to pick up a pencil will induce a craning neck in a boy. Or the way you purse your lips when you talk. Even a certain way of laughing will bring on something in these hungry little boys, so . . . I'm just asking you to be aware of it and remember, you're still only thirteen or fourteen.

Oh, and you're beautiful. Love you, with stars on. Dad.

Dad was so wrong about the boy bit (they only ever looked at me when Carla was within spitting distance) but right about the giraffe thing (although I'm inclined to go with anteater). The only boy who ever really spoke to me was Corey. But as I'd known him since forever, he didn't matter. Anyway, I'd come to terms with the fact that no boy would ever consider me girlfriend material and was content to live my love life through Carla anyway. As well as Darren she'd already been to the pictures with an older boy called Jake Saunders and snogged Colin Meek behind Lanes.

With her long legs and elegant haircut, it wasn't surprising guys found her irresistible.

Miscellaneous: Can't get a date?
Great!

No, not really, I know this is hard, especially if it seems like everyone around you has a boyfriend, is out at the pictures, holding hands, and buying sloppy-looking cards shaped like love hearts. But don't be in a rush. One day, someone will see how special you are, how great it is to be with you and vice versa. I never thought anyone would ever look at plain old me, but she did. Your mom did and what a stunner she is—proving the theory that there is indeed someone for everyone in this world.

When I looked at Gary Jones, Jake's best friend, I *felt* things. Like I wanted him to kiss me. But Gary, along with a host of other guys from Lewisham to Deptford, seemed to enjoy me invading their company as long as it was to discuss tapes and soccer. Nothing else. And I was okay with that. Especially when Gary and Jake once said they liked me because I was just like one of the lads, a comment which proved that one day I'd get a boyfriend.

Didn't it?

Miscellanous: Male friends 1
I bet you have a load of male friends. If not, then at least one. Someone you can hang out with, talk to? You make each other laugh? Discuss everything from school dinners to the state of the nation? This is all well and good, but don't expect anything else from this if you start to fancy him.

Boys want a girlfriend. Maybe not a pink-ribbon-wearing, frilly, soft, rose-scented little package, but a girl all the same (sorry!). Forget all this talk about them wanting to be with a girl who understands the offside rule, burps and leaves her hand down her trousers "because it's comfortable." Terrible. It's only natural for a bloke to be attracted to someone who acts like . . . well . . . a girl (sorry again!), who flutters her eyelashes, flicks her hair when she's embarrassed by a compliment and who'd never even dream of a burp or a fart.

So if you want one of your friends to ever see you as girlfriend material (and when I say girlfriend, I mean the holding hands, going to the park type) then try to be girly as well as (most importantly) yourself.

I decided to stop being friends with Gary and the others. No post-match analysis, no help with their homework and certainly no "women" advice. This alienation lasted a whole week, right up until Gary Jones commented on what a bitch I'd turned into, which stung like a fresh bee sting and I quickly changed my mind back to being me.

fact: humiliations will only get worse with age

Kevin Trivia: ***While men orbited the moon, looking for aliens, there were others on earth who publicly insulted some human beings over the color of their skin.***

Your last year of secondary school.

Your friends are probably talking about traveling, getting full-time jobs and/or changing the world . . . as soon as they "escape" the bars and locks of school. But Lowey, if you haven't decided to stay on at sixth form, please start thinking about it now. I'm not saying that by leaving school at sixteen you won't get anywhere (I did and I earn a very good wage as a hospital administrator), I'd just prefer you to have more choices and that means getting more grades. Please, think seriously about it, and in the meantime buckle down to some studying. Don't neglect your friends and boyfriend (if you have one. Please don't have one yet!!!!), just try to limit the time spent "hanging around" when you could be studying.

This is an important year for you.

Remember, your daddy loves you. With stars on.

By the time I was fifteen, three major events had occurred in my life.

I got asked out by a boy for the first time.

I became a revolutionary.

I got beaten up for the first time.

First, the beating part. Sharlene Rockingham finally got her way by pulling at my hair as I ripped her school shirt almost in half. A couple of slaps (from her), a few shoves and it was over. I gave as well as I got, but her bulk and my generous amount of "bone" would never be equal in any weigh-in. The clump of hair left behind on the playground floor looked suspiciously like mine as gasps and laughter increased among the assembled onlookers. It wasn't until we were standing sheepishly in the middle of Mrs. Codrington's office that I realized the front of my bra was actually showing, complete with ripped seam. Oh, the shame!

Miscellaneous: Humiliations

I've had my fair share:

- *Being beaten seventeen–zip at a soccer cup match.*
- *Spending a whole day at work with a piece of toilet paper attached to my trouser leg.*

- *Danny and Charlie pinning me to a shop window (blindfolded and naked) after my stag night, two hours before opening time.*

Hopefully, you won't be as lucky as me in the humiliation stakes. You might think your mom turning up at parents' evening wearing the most embarrassing floppy hat is the worst thing that can ever happen to you—but believe me when I say you ain't seen nothing yet. Humiliations have this unique ability to rise in number, with age. But how you deal with it will also change as you mature—an ability I hope you'll put to good use along with your ever-growing wisdom, experience, mortgage costs . . . well, you get my drift.

Two weeks of after-school detention was not a surprise. But the offer by Carla and a couple of reliable cronies offering to "deal" with Sharlene for me, was. Touched, I decided to let it go. I only had a year left at secondary school and getting good SATs had to remain my priority. Nothing else mattered . . . Oh, except perhaps becoming a revolutionary. Well, sort of.

One assembly, the headmistress announced the local council's plan to amalgamate our school with a rival comprehensive. The hall fell into a hush, as our minds contemplated what this meant. My own thoughts drifted to the next twelve months, possibly spent surrounded by members of the op-
[illegible]site sex—new boys, non-friend boys. And this new batch
[illegible] include *someone* mad enough to even glance my way.
[illegible]filed out of assembly that morning I could almost
[illegible]rgy around us, alive with titters, whispers
[illegible] turning against the new school.

"I can't believe they're mixing us with THAT lot!" spat Sharlene Rockingham, typically.

"Boys!" drooled Carla, almost licking her lips in happiness.

"Not everyone's a—"

"Just say it and see what I'll do to you! I'm not Lois, you know!" spat Carla.

Sharlene backed down as another girl spoke up. "This is what they want! Us fighting among each other. Well, you know what . . . ?"

"What?" we asked in surprised unison.

"We ain't gonna stand for it! Why should we?"

This question seemed to pump the now larger crowd full of adrenaline. So I thought it a good idea just to join in with it all.

At lunch, I followed Carla and a few others to the back of the science block.

"You know, we can't let this happen!" said one.

"No way. We've got to fight it!" said another.

"Too right! They can't amalga-wotsit us with another school, can they?!" added Carla, punching the air, the quickest change in opinion I had ever witnessed. I'd also never seen this side of her, or any of the other girls assembled on the wooden bench-cum-podium. They reminded me of check-coated old men on rallies, shouting at the television camera as placard-holding masses chanted and nodded their heads in agreement—the type of thing you saw on the six o'clock news and certainly not in my secondary school. Even after Mrs. Codrington shooed us all away, the meeting continued behind the gym block and by the next day even our Home Economics teacher had pledged his support.

What followed over the ensuing weeks were lunchtime "rallies" and meetings to decide how we were going to see off this threat to our education. My thoughts of handsome new boys became a sad but not forgotten memory as I joined the cause, secretly enjoying the togetherness. So, if this meant singing "We shall not, we shall not be mixed!" in the street, then so be it. If this meant welcoming Sharlene Rockingham into the fold, then so be it. We were a team, after all. Women, united in our quest to secure a good education for ourselves and future generations to come.

Lowey, if you're not prepared to fight for what you believe in, then you might as well pack up and go home.

When the head announced the amalgamation would be put on hold until further notice, I knew a bunch of fifteen-year-olds couldn't have swayed the minds of a selection of evil-doing council heads. But still, the taste of "victory" collided nicely with my taste buds: refreshing and unfamiliar.

But I was still glad to get back to normal, dodging Mom and studying for my SATs, which worked well until Mickey Mills asked me out one rainy evening as I stood outside Lanes chomping on a steak pie.

Now, Mickey Mills could hardly be described as handsome. Skinny, he resembled two legs sticking out of a neck and probably needed a bottle of Clearasil for his birthday. He wasn't cool, but at the same time held his own among the cooler kids at his school, commanding respect among the boys as well as having a small but creditable fan club among the girls. He dressed okay (even if his feet weren't in the latest Adidas). And he was mad enough to ask me out to see *Jurassic Park*, more to the point. I was quick to say yes, hungry for a morsel of what Carla and all the pretty girls at school had been consuming for years now.

Luckily there were no sex scenes in the movie, so I didn't have to check for any bulges in Mickey's trousers. Plus, I made sure I never bent over to pick up any popcorn (or pencils!) either.

"I . . . I really had a great time," stuttered Mickey Mills outside my house. If I really squinted my eyes and ignored the spots, he could almost pass for quite a good looker.

"Me too. Thanks for the ticket."

"Erm, thanks for the popcorn," he said. His faced moved in closer to mine and he squeezed his eyes shut like I did the last time I was constipated.

"What are you doing?" I asked.

He opened his eyes. "I was going to give you a . . . kiss?"

We stared at one another for ages before I moved in and planted a huge wet kiss . . . on his cheek.

"Goodnight!" I said, the key already turning the lock. My heart was racing as I shot up the steps with a great big smile on my face.

You may think you've found the best thing since, I dunno, video laser discs, but it's best not to fall for the first person to pay you any sort of special attention or hair compliment. There will be plenty of other lads who will comment on your lovely hair, sweet little laugh and your special ability to do fractions without a calculator (you can, right?). Besides, if he is truly "the one," then surely it's meant to be and you'll end up together anyway. Only, later. Much later. When you're, like, thirty-six? Okay, thirty.

I couldn't wait for school to start in just over twelve hours, so I phoned Carla right away with the news.

Mom appeared as soon as I replaced the receiver.

"You see each other every day and she lives next door. Why do you have to phone her? I'm not made of money, you know," she moaned, dressed in an old nightie and clutching a mug of cocoa.

"There's loads to talk about, Mom. You wouldn't understand!" I stressed.

"Did you have a nice time tonight?"

"What?" I asked coyly.

"I guessed you were meeting a boy."

I felt myself blush with embarrassment. "Just a friend, Mom."

"Corey's a friend. This was a date, wasn't it?"

Suddenly, I longed to jump into bed and escape this unwelcome interrogation.

"Not really. Mom, I'm really tired."

"Okay, love. But you know you can talk to me about . . . anything."

"Yes." I was already hiding under the covers.

"And feel free to bring him round. Perhaps I could make us all some tea. Snapper and rice?"

Knowing I'd rather boil my own toe, I nodded a quick agreement and raced upstairs to dream about Mickey rescuing me from a pack of green dinosaurs.

At school, Carla and I gossiped heavily about my date and then replayed it all back at hers that evening.

"This is sooo cool!" enthused Carla.

"I know!"

"You know what?" asked Corey, who since leaving school

seemed to have embraced maturity overnight. His walk strayed from anxious gorilla to masculine strut, and he now wore his jeans straight.

"None of your biz!" I said.

"Oh, go on!" he whined, sounding like a five-year-old all over again.

"Lois has a boyfriend!" blabbed Carla.

I stamped on her foot.

"Ow!'

"Who?" Corey asked.

"Why?"

"Want to see if I know him," replied Corey.

"You don't, so mind your biz!"

"I was only wondering . . . that's all!"

"Wondering what?" questioned Carla.

"If he's a jerk or not."

As soon as he left, Carla and I resumed our gossiping. It felt so great to have something in common with my best friend again. And as time went on, I began to enjoy this more than the company of Mickey Mills, who on closer inspection had really bad breath. I knew I'd never kiss him and was glad when he finally dumped me, citing my refusal to "french him" as strong-enough grounds.

there's a good way and a bad way to do it

Kevin Trivia: ***The best thing to happen to me the year I turned seventeen? Watching Pele's amazing opening goal against Italy. What a match!***

To leave or not to leave?

You probably hate school and can't wait to be released from the shackles of all those rules, not to mention the revolting school dinners. But please, Lowey, really think about staying on at sixth form or going to college. Get those extra grades. Remember, it's all about having choices.

Sixth Form College represented a change of scenery, and with it a handful of perks. Top of the list: no school uniform, plus daily access to some really cool guys. Not that any were ever interested in me. It had been and would always be my best friend Carla who enticed the hungry crowds. She'd grown into something quite special too—if you liked slim waists, large breasts and a sassy Jessica Rabbit walk just to top it all off. Even Mr. Tally had started to look at her funny as he weighed out a quarter bag of cola cubes. While I preferred to live in my jeans, Carla's Daisy Duke's (i.e. the tiniest shorts ever) seemed to be in constant competition with her bum cheeks, so it was hardly surprising when she got together with Antoine Richards, a smooth guy from the upper sixth, proceeding to spend most if not all of her spare time with him. Again, I got used to this and it failed to niggle away at me until I called round one day and Corey answered the door.

"She's out with some boy," he offered. I hadn't seen him in ages. Almost eighteen now, he seemed to be into more grown-up things like Art College and a scooter. He'd also grown a goatee and looked really impressive. And he'd been spotted recently with some blonde bombshell from the Hankle Estate. Not that I cared about that.

"This is the second time she's blown me off for Antoine!" I whined as we entered the lounge.

"What kind of name is that?" he asked, producing a box of cigarettes from nowhere.

"No thanks. Don't smoke."

"Neither do I, then!" he said, flinging the box across the room.

"She said she'd be home by six!" I continued pointlessly.

"I dunno why you bother with my sister."

I wanted to say, *because my dad told me to.*

Corey disappeared into the kitchen.

"Where is everyone?" I called.

"Mom and Dad are at the pictures. It's just me here." He reappeared with two cans as I parked myself in front of the telly as always. He threw a can of beer at me, which I failed to catch.

"Still can't catch, Lo Bag. Bad. Very bad indeed." He shook his head in mock horror and I gave him the finger. "So, how is you?"

"I'm all right."

"You still with that idiot?"

"You mean Mickey? That was eons ago."

"No one since?"

I ignored him and began sipping at the beer, which tasted absolutely disgusting (although I'd never, ever tell Corey that). "How are things at college?"

"I'm really enjoying my art course . . ." he began, smiling, showing off those dimples. As he spoke, I hoped he'd forget to ask me anything "profound." He attended Art College to study . . . art, I suppose, while I studied A-level English and Computer Science at the local sixth form. His friends were all arty folk, whereas my only friend was Carla. The more we chatted, the more I knew we'd hardly anything (except Carla) in common any more, and this made me a little sad.

"Music," he said with a smile.

"What about it?"

"You still into LL Cool J?"

"A little bit . . ."

"You remember that tape I gave you?"

"I dunno where it is now. That was ages ago."

"I always thought of you when I listened to track two. That was my favorite album."

"Can't remember that," I said quickly.

"Track two?"

"Yeah, well, it's probably in Mom's cabinet." I sipped away at the beer, feeling giddy as the fizz caught the edge of my tongue. I swallowed and, without warning, that feeling you get when you're about to choke your insides out made an unwelcome presence at the back of my throat.

"You okay?" he asked.

"Uh hum!" I struggled, trying and failing desperately to clear my throat. As things advanced up the embarrassment scale with cough after cough, Corey stood up, making his way behind me as I continued to splutter madly.

"Just let it out, okay?" His hands slapped onto my shoulder.

As quickly as it had begun, the throat tickle subsided and I attempted to regain some dignity and composure as Corey remained behind me.

"I'm okay now, really."

"I know, Lo Bag," he said, his hands kneading a tense shoulder. *My* tense shoulder. I automatically froze with the sudden intensity of this act, not wanting to move while wanting to turn around and . . . kiss him. All I could hear was his breathing because it felt like *my* breath had long since disappeared with the shock of it all. What to do? What to do? What to do, Dad?

"Turn around . . ." Corey's voice sounded different. Hoarse. Urgent. I stood up to face him and then it just happened. "It" being my lips connecting with his, followed by a beer-tinged tongue rummaging around my teeth like a penniless man digging for gold. I was wishing I'd brushed my teeth for the full three minutes that morning, and I also wished something romantic was playing in the background instead of the *Top of the Pops* theme tune. Looking back, it probably wouldn't be my most enjoyable kiss, but at the grand old age of seventeen, it was certainly my first.

Words failed me afterward. I'd just kissed my best friend's brother, for pete's sake!

"D'you want another beer?" he asked, all matter of fact.

So that night, we drank a little as we watched *EastEnders* on telly, and by nine p.m. hid the beer cans as Carla's mom and dad returned from their night out.

Dad had written something in the miscellaneous section about kisses, so as soon as I fled next door, heart racing with the intensity of it all, I dug it out.

Miscellaneous: Your first real kiss

I couldn't figure out where to put this, so I stuck it in the miscellaneous section (if I had my own way it wouldn't even be a section, because I'm not sure I want some guy kissing you). But if my dreams of you having kids and growing old with your family around you are ever to materialize, then a kiss is probably likely.

Sooooo . . .

Here goes (deep breath, deep breath).

Your first kiss.

You've probably just had it or are about to. All I can say is, it will feel . . . well, rather crap actually. The good (or bad) news is, it definitely gets better with practice. Because first time round you'll be all teeth and lip knocks. You'll be paranoid about your breath. Or this could all be my own experience, while yours, well, yours could just be magical. Like Cinderella's with her prince.

Remember to enjoy it . . . but not too much!

And I had.

I smiled and leaned over to my bedside table, the picture of Dad smiling back at me. I was almost too embarrassed to face him, armed with the knowledge that I had, at last, broken my kiss virginity.

I decided not to tell Carla. Not that she'd notice any difference in the way Corey and I interacted, because we waited until she left the room to sneak in a quick kiss. Gazing at one another across the dinner table as we tucked into Sunday lunch. Once, we even held hands under the tablecloth as Carla's mom talked lipstick colors. An exciting moment in time and one that made me believe all that fluff they sang about in songs. But then I'd go home, sit on my bed, one-eyed teddy by my side, feeling confused at why I was thinking about Corey in THAT way. I'd known him most of my life and seen him as nothing more than . . . well, my best friend's annoying older brother. Everything was weird now. Nice, scary, mad, exciting. But mostly nice.

"When did you start fancying me?" asked Corey as we left Lanes Fish Bar, carrying his family's dinner in two paper bags.

"I never did!" I protested.

"What? Never?"

"You're just looking for an ego boost."

"So what?"

"You're not getting one."

I felt a surge of delicious electricity as he grabbed my hand. "Go on, Lo Bag!"

I pulled my hand away playfully.

"I'm going to tell everyone about us," he said, and I thought I'd burst.

"Not today, though?" I wasn't quite ready for everyone to know about "us." Like *The Manual*, this was something for me that had nothing to do with anyone else. And I wanted to hold on to that feeling for as long as I could. Before anything had a chance to go wrong.

One evening, as Carla ice skated with Antoine, Corey and I lay on the sofa staring blankly at the television screen.

"Hello there!" said a voice. As we looked up, Carla's mom sprang into focus complete with a huge grin.

Corey and I jumped up simultaneously.

"Mom!"

"Relax, I've known for ages that something's been going on," she said, placing her sequinned handbag onto the settee, which was still warm with the heat from our bottoms. "Me and your dad aren't complete plums, you know."

I smiled with the relief of it all, finally free to tell Carla the truth. Hoping she'd take it just as well as her mom. I was in love with her brother so this felt like the right thing to do, and Corey seemed to be in agreement as he walked me next door.

"But let's just wait for now. Mom won't say anything."

"Why wait?" I said with pangs of paranoia. "Carla will be fine about it."

"Just give it till the end of the week, that's all."

We kissed on the doorstep. The most magical of kisses and one I wouldn't forget in a hurry, but for the wrong reasons.

. . . I know that you'll really like this boy, but remember to take things SLOW. I mean really slow, like a

snail in a pushchair being pushed by ANOTHER snail drinking his third pint. If he puts his hand in a place you don't feel comfortable with, tell him to get lost and that you'll tell your dad on him and HE IS WILLING TO HAUNT.

If he insists on taking things further too soon, he isn't worth it. No matter how much you like this boy, NEVER do anything you're not comfortable with. If he's a good guy, he'll respect you and your wishes. Remember my bit on boys, hormones and teabags? This doesn't really go away, sweetheart, so always have that in mind. Admittedly, when it comes to you, I'm absolutely no use in these matters . . . So it's probably better to talk to your mom about this stuff . . .

I tensed up at the mention of Mom, knowing I'd rather place toothpicks in my eyes than talk to her about Corey.

. . . She'll know more about this stuff than me. Or perhaps you can talk to your best friend about it. Whoever you have, please talk. It's a great way to see things more clearly.

That night as I struggled with homework, my mind was consumed with Corey. Things we'd do together. How he made me feel. Contrary to what Dad had said on the subject, being friends for so long had to count for something. And not having to sneak around any more would mean holding hands, being together . . . I wondered if I should just ask him out on a date. A proper date, to mark the very first day of going public.

Miscellaneous: Is it ever okay to ask out a boy?

Yes.

I think times have changed since my day (yes, you heard right—I'm sounding like MY dad!). But, remember, there's a good and bad way to do it and it can be a bit tricky. Just try to be subtle, and after you've got the first bit out of the way: i.e. "Would you like to go and see a film?," let the boy choose the film. Or if it's to a burger bar, let him choose which one. We do still like to remain man-like, you know. Nevertheless, don't listen to anyone who says a boy never wants to be asked out by a girl. That's complete and utter garbage! It's so rare for a girl to ask out a guy, so when you do, he'll be elated, trust me on that. Go for it, girl—he'd be mad to turn you down anyway!

Armed with a sudden bout of confidence, I called round at Carla's the next day, to be greeted by her very tearful mother clutching a tissue.

"Is everything okay?" I asked with a shot of alarm. My mind produced a horrible image of Carla or Corey lying dead on a slab.

"No!" she sniffed, followed by a loud blow of the nose. My heart rate accelerated as I entered the living room. Luckily, Corey was alive and punching the air while Carla playfully ruffled what was left of her father's receding hair. Nothing unusual there.

"Corey's been accepted to some fancy art college!" said Carla nonchalantly.

I turned to Corey. "Congrats!" I wanted to jump into his arms and plant wet kisses on every inch of his face. I contained myself.

"Cheers, Lo Bag."

"You must be so happy. I know this is what you've wanted."

"Yes . . . but . . ."

"Have you told her where it is?" sniffed Carla's mom.

"Don't upset yourself, it's for the best," offered her husband.

"Where is it?"

"Goddamn France!" said Carla.

I looked to Corey for some type of credible explanation, but all he returned was a lopsided, almost drunken smile, perhaps lost in a world of self-congratulation.

"France?" I willed the carpet to open up with a Lois-sized hole and swallow me into it, but of course it didn't. Instead I listened to Carla's mom crying at the injustice of it all, as I fought the urge to join her.

"That's great! Really great. I'm really happy for you," I managed to mumble instead.

"I'm sorry," he whispered a few moments later as I stood in his corridor.

"No big deal, Corey," I whispered back softly, before making my way home.

In my bedroom, I easily located the cassette Corey had given me for my thirteenth birthday and placed it in my portable cassette player. I pressed play and listened to track two of LL Cool J's album. "Around the Way Girl" flooded my earlobes.

My favorite.

do as i say, not as i did

Kevin Trivia: ***I truly felt I'd become a man after watching* Shaft *with Charlie at the Coronet. A classic.***

My baby's eighteen! Yeah! Even though you probably thought so five years ago, it's now official—you're a woman. How does it feel? Probably no different from yesterday, really. There's always this big build-up to your eighteenth, and when it finally comes around you realize it's just the day after you were seventeen.

Yeah, right!

This is MASSIVE.

A big deal. And I bet your mom's throwing you a huge party or you're going out with your friends for your (first, I hope) legal drink. Whatever you're doing I hope you mark it memorably, have loads of fun and don't get too drunk, okay?

Lois, now you are eighteen you have more power over what you do and I really hope you take advantage of this in a good way. Like, making sure you vote when it's time. None of this "it won't make a difference," upper teenage rebellion crap. In some countries people are still dying for the right.

And if you haven't already, get a passport, learn to drive and save a bit of money each month. You might be thinking "What's my old man on about?" but trust me, these will all come in handy one day.

The Sunday Corey's dad drove off with him in the passenger seat, and headed for Eurostar, the sky was full of the promise of rain. Carla's mom was dabbing at her own damp eyes as the car disappeared up the high street, past Lanes Fish Bar then the rec, our former stomping grounds. There was Carla, uncharacteristically upset at the departure of her brother, attempting to keep her tears locked until at least bedtime. Me, rubbing her back supportively as I waved him off, stiff upper lip, to the outside world merely wondering if the rain would hold off for another day, already "over" the departure of the first boy I'd ever kissed. Even my personal goodbye, the previous night during the hasty get-together Carla's mom had arranged, was calm and accepting of the situation. Corey didn't say much to me, busy with the rest of his family and assortment of invited friends, although he did manage something about keeping in touch. Writing. Which I dismissed straight away because as I said to the outside world—Corey included—I was already over him. Right?

"Be happy," I said, because he looked anything but. He was about to reply, I think, before his tearful mother whisked him into the kitchen for something to do with cake. Like my feelings didn't matter. Like *I* didn't matter.

As I said, I was over him already. Before that moment. Perhaps I had been on the day he kissed me for the very first time.

Not to worry, I still had my dad, stacks of coursework, driving lessons and thoughts of my future to be getting on with, which regularly alternated between going to university (no way) or securing a job with a half-decent wage.

I was already over Corey, I told myself again that night, as I sunk my tear-stained face into the belly of the one-eyed teddy.

I got a job working at Freeman Hardy Willis shoe shop in Lewisham. The hours were regular and I was given a twenty percent discount that seemed to excite Carla more than me. Admittedly, the days were tiring. Stepping up ladders to locate "Miriam in red, size five" during a hot summer meant regular contact with smelly feet and prickly customers. But the independence that came with earning my own money outweighed any amount of bunions and foot fungi, and soon even Carla was a slave to that thing called a "work ethic," getting herself a position with Marks a few doors down. We'd meet for lunch and ride the bus in together. And apart from launching into a progress report on Corey's eventful life in Paris (which I really didn't need, considering he'd managed one postcard since his departure) it was great.

Dear Lo Bag,

Paris is great. Such a beautiful city. You should see the art. I spent hours at the Musée du

Louvre the other day. Wish I could move in! The Arc de Triomphe is also a wicked piece of architecture.

Hope everything is cool.

Take care,

Corey x

After a few months and the day of my nineteenth birthday, I was promoted to supervisor at the shoe shop and Carla announced her resignation from Marks, citing severe boredom. Although there was never any fun in tearing down defaced pictures of myself produced by colleagues jealous of my swift promotion, this wasn't what forced me to leave . . .

. . . this is the BEST time for you. No responsibilities, young and free. Get out there, Lowey, and explore, travel. Need help on where to go? Close your eyes and think of a sky and you lying under it—what would you be wearing? A (baggy) bikini? Fake fur coat with a woolly hat? Where are you, Lowey?

Visualize it.

Are you barefoot lying on a beach or trekking a dusty route near smallish mountains in thick hiking boots? Africa, Asia, Americas, Himalayas? You're at an age when you're probably broke, can't afford much, but ironically it's also the best time to travel (don't worry, there will be times when you are older, but the freedom you have right now is priceless, you'll see). If you're at college or university, there's always half-term. Get a Saturday job, save up, but just go. Anywhere. See the world. Discover how others live. There is so much of this universe to explore. You know, I always told myself I'd travel when I got my gold watch and retired. Me, you and your mom backpacking in Australia or something. We'd even talked about it a few times and I also liked the idea of going on safari in Africa before your mom quite rightly reminded me of my phobia (yes, your dad has one) of cats. I had to remind her that BIG cats were different to those small ones that roam the high street at night, squealing and scratching everything in sight. They're different; big cats are manly cats! I'm digressing. Bottom line is, I had the dreams to travel and . . . well, we all know what happened to THOSE dreams. It didn't happen then and probably isn't about to happen now. I used to have this weird and basically unfounded thought that I had loads of time left at my disposal . . . well, more fool me.

Growing up seems to happen in half a heartbeat.

Tomorrow's not guaranteed, so live today. See the world.

Apart from that trip over as a child, I only got to go to Spain for my honeymoon and I so regret not traveling more when I had the chance. So do as I say, Lowey, NOT AS I DID.

"I can't believe she's leaving a good job to gallivant around America for three months!" whined Mom to anyone who'd listen. Carla's mom was at our kitchen table painting her nails a bright red as Mom prattled on and I made a pot of tea, my mind wondering about what the next phase of my life would hold.

America.

Although this wasn't the land I envisaged once I closed my eyes, it was the most affordable thanks to a charitable organization called Jump America that made it possible for students and young people to "explore" America. They'd fix me up with a three-month job too, and all for the price of a subsidized ticket, with food and lodgings thrown in. I posted my application, knowing I'd be turned down anyway, but hoping for one summer not filled with Mom and the Bingo Caller alternating between *Terry and June* and Kathleen Turner and Michael Douglas from *The War of the Roses.*

"I think it's a great idea!" chipped in Carla's mom, blowing on her newly painted red nails as Mom and I sat in her kitchen.

"Thank you!" I replied gratefully.

"If I hadn't met the love of my life and had the kids so young, I'd have done the same. Traveled. That's why I'm so pleased that Corey's doing it—even if it has ripped my heart out."

I lowered my eyes at the sound of Corey's name being mentioned and Carla's mom smiled a knowing smile in my direction, acknowledging our "little secret." I really wanted Mom to acknowledge my dad by recalling their plans to tour Australia, but all she did was nod her head and pretend to admire her neighbor's newly painted nails.

When my letter of acceptance had arrived, the shock was instant. I then went on to change my mind a million times, alternating between staying and going.

"But I had loads of stuff planned for us," whined Carla. And, admittedly, the guilt waded in, evaporating as soon as I heard Mom and the Bingo Caller having a row in the kitchen. I wavered again when Corey was mentioned, who by the sounds of it was having a ball in Paris.

But I wanted a piece of that.

Dad was right.

have life will travel

Kevin Trivia: ***I was going to get a tattoo, which was all the rage, but at the last minute I "remembered" I had to go and pick up my mom's laundry. That's my story and I'm sticking to it . . .***

Among the confusion of delayed flights and changes to departure gates announced by a generic voice on a loudspeaker, I was still convinced I was doing the right thing. I just knew.

"I feel like I'm losing another one!" wept Carla's mom as we hugged. She smelled of citrus and was wearing a tiny spotted red miniskirt, which even at her age turned heads for the right reasons.

"Take care of yourself," I said, ruffling Carla's hair. The generic voice mentioned another delayed flight to

Washington. I was off to New York and my flight was leaving on schedule according to the display screen.

"Bye, Lois. Bring me back something nice, eh?" said Carla.

"Like?"

"I dunno . . ." She actually scratched at her beautiful head like a cartoon character, but without the huge question mark hovering above.

"Well . . . ?" I said with mock impatience.

"Sneakers?" she said as an afterthought. Her beautiful face then sprang out a mass of tears and sniffs. I couldn't remember ever seeing her cry like that before. Not even when Corey left. Corey, who'd sent a grand total of two postcards and not bothered once to pick up the phone to call me.

Mom appeared. "I've bought you some hard candies for the journey. They'll help with the ear popping."

"Thanks, Mom."

"Take care. Make sure you eat properly. Not too many hot dogs. And you call me as soon as you get there."

"Yes, Mom, I will," I said, actually meaning it. I noticed how haggard she looked and silently cursed the Bingo Caller for putting Mom through the daily ritual of an argument. Only last night I'd caught the tail end of a huge row over something that Mom "needed" and the Bingo Caller replying heatedly with something about "risks." With a sincere kiss on her cheek, I mumbled goodbye, hugged Carla and her mom once more and slid my pull-along through to the Departure Lounge and into the unknown.

Searches, passports and a boarding gate followed. Apart from one trip to France with school pre-Eurostar and a flight to Barcelona a few years ago with Carla's family, I should have been nervous at the thought of my first trip alone. Even more so as I strapped myself into the seat, with any remaining thoughts of England and Corey wafting away with the candy floss clouds. But the line between nervous and excited had been crossed, and after the first in-flight meal I drifted off into a welcome sleep to dream of Dad and how proud he would be of me at that precise moment.

As the bus moved away from the airport and headed toward our hotel in Manhattan, I was astounded by how different and unusual everything seemed. Huge roads, huge cars and traffic lights with "Walk" alerting pedestrians to cross. Every corner you turned, shops. So many different places to eat. A man walking his dog; an old lady pushing a wonky cart. Everyone pushing forward.

The driver announced "Welcome to the Big Apple" and the bus full of those inches away from an adventure burst into rapturous applause.

I had never felt happier.

I knew I wouldn't be making enough money that summer to sample much of New York's delights, but just being a part of something only ever glimpsed on TV shows would be enough. For now.

Jump America placed me and a few others in a swanky Manhattan hotel, throwing in a hearty breakfast of pancakes and waffles the following morning. Naively, perhaps, I assumed the remainder of my three months would be spent identically—in pure luxury on the edge of a fast-paced metropolis. But the next day we were ferried by an incredibly hot coach, over the Hudson River and into New Jersey. Which was hours away from New York and its striking skyscrapers. Instead, I was faced with the stench of cow manure and masses of greenery. A tiny woman with the teeniest glasses perched on a button nose, and a pair of khaki shorts that sat just above her knobbly knees, walked toward me as I got off the bus.

"Well, hi there. Welcome to our farm!" she squeaked, as if announcing my million-dollar win.

"Thank you," I said as the driver dumped my cases beside me. I struggled up the endless "driveway" as she babbled in a Michael Jackson on helium voice. The history of the "farm" (a lump of wood set in a trillion acres of nothing) was that it was home every summer to around a hundred kids sent over by their parents. Summer camps were really common in America, but as she showed me around what was to be my home for the next three months, my heart sank a bit.

The "dorms" were dark, functional, and the bed felt like the bark of a tree against my backside.

"That okay for you?" she squeaked.

"Yes. Thanks." I stifled a yawn.

"You're the last to arrive," she said in her high-pitched voice as I opened my suitcase. "I'll leave you to unpack, but make sure you're downstairs in fifteen to eat dinner."

I gazed around my new surroundings: simple décor and a light musky smell that I was sure would soon begin to irritate me. I lay back on the world's most uncomfortable bed and looked to the ceiling, noticing at least two cracks. I pulled out *The Manual* from my hand luggage and, hugging it close to my heart, I instantly knew I'd be all right.

Actually, I was wrong.

The first morning was awful. I had to stand up among twenty or so others and say my name, my favorite animal and why I'd chosen to come to summer camp. Some of the answers (especially from the Americans) were so detailed, so "feely," I felt totally embarrassed with the clichéd "spreading my wings" bit. Worse still were the introductions to the children, ninety-nine percent of them rich brats whose parents had dispatched them to the camp for a bit of peace—and I was soon able to see why. The constant bickering and tantrums the camp "counselors" had to deal with were endless. Luckily, my unique role was confined to the admin office, my days spent away from the mayhem, answering calls, placing orders for food, that type of thing.

From the nineteen or so camp counselors the only two that I bonded with were Greg from Bolton and Erin from Seattle.

Two weeks into my stay, Greg and I were on washing-up duty.

"Is this all you thought it would be?" he asked, in that weird northern twang I'd quickly grown used to.

At first a bit stunned at this question, I gave it some thought as I scrubbed a pot. "Not really. For a start, I hadn't expected all the cleaning! But it's all right!" Actually, if I were honest, I'd been having the time of my life while at the same time secure in the knowledge I was following Dad's advice by doing stuff many people my age (scrubbing pots excluded) only dreamed of. And hey, at least it was an *American* pot. Plus—and I hated to think it—Carla's absence had given me valuable space to obsess about what I wanted to do with *my* life. The job itself was eight to five in the office and evenings spent helping out the camp counselors, which at times meant trying to decipher the rules of softball and roasting marshmallows—s'mores—with the kids on an open fire.

"You're quite funny," said Greg, drying the last pot, which effectively was my job. He'd really begun to grow on me and I loved the way he asked me about my feelings and in turn was really passionate about stuff like politics and whether the National Lottery had bred greed among the social classes. I thought he was what Carla would term "deep." He wasn't particularly good-looking, but that didn't matter, as his smile felt genuine, warm. A bit like Corey's but minus the dimples.

"Lois . . ."

"Yep?" I replied, crouching down to place the pot in the cupboard.

"I—" he began as Erin appeared.

"Hey, hurry up you two! I'm gonna read the kids a story in five," she said, all blonde hair and teeth. I imagined Erin to have won a dozen or so beauty pageants in her time.

"Do we have to listen to another tale of blood and gore?" I mock whined.

"No, this one's a love story," she said with a cheeky wink in my direction. "See you guys later!"

Before I had the chance to process Erin's wink, she left.

"I like you, you know, Lois," said Greg.

"I like you too." I folded the *huge* towel on the edge of the *huge* sink. Everything was *huge* in America.

"You're different," he said.

"So are you. In fact this whole experience is different!" I enthused, gesticulating wildly with abandon. I suddenly felt so free, so happy to be standing in a large American kitchen washing and drying for a bunch of people I hardly knew. It was the one place I wanted to be out of anywhere in the world at that moment and that time. Greg turned to me and placed a soapy hand on my chin and I didn't mind.

Not for one moment. And that's when he did a really weird thing; he moved his head toward me and planted a huge wet kiss on my lips. I was surprised at first because it felt strange. Not as lovely as with Corey and no tongues, but so comforting.

"Sorry . . ." Greg shot back as if electrocuted.

"No, it's okay," I said, a smile spreading across my face.

Mornings were always hard to wake up to. Exhausted from the night before. Up at six. Preparing breakfast with Chef for the kids. Helping to prepare "fun" activities like canoeing and basketball for an array of superbrats used to getting their own way (I knew if I ever saw a kid again, it would be too soon) and then back to the office job, delivery men and invoices. But by the end of the first month, the farm became home to me—Erin and Greg a huge part of my circle of friends. Unfortunately, I didn't get to see as much of America as I'd hoped. My one day off a week was spent traveling by Greyhound bus to New York for window shopping and a burger.

"So you really like Greg, huh?" asked Erin as we relaxed one evening after a grueling day canoeing with thirteen teenagers including a premenstrual drama queen. Greg had snuck back to the storeroom to fetch snacks.

"He's okay . . ." I drawled in embarrassment. I fingered the postcards I'd written the day before. One to Auntie Philomena (it felt rude not to, even though I'd only heard from her about twice a year since Mom's wedding), one to Granny Bates (it felt like the right thing to do), one to Mom and one to Carla "and family." And yes, that included Corey.

"Are you over him then?" she asked sheepishly.

"Who?"

"The one with the American name who lives in France!"

"Corey? I am soooo over him it ain't even funny!"

We straightened up as Greg returned with cookies and potato chips.

"So, I was saying," he began as Erin tore open the cookie packet. "It's all a government conspiracy to enable control over the masses. We're slowly becoming a big-brother nation. We'll get it in England soon, you'll see."

I stuck a cookie in my mouth, gazing at Greg. Half the time I wasn't sure what he was talking about, but it sounded important, plus he made me feel things I hadn't felt since being with Corey.

I barely had time to read *The Manual*, mostly too tired or too busy having fun or laughing off the thousand or so comments regarding my "cute li'l accent." One night, though, for the first time in about two weeks, I realized I'd missed it. I missed hearing from my dad. So, in an oversized "I Luv NY" T-shirt, feet tucked under me as I sat on the bed, I brought out the familiar green manual, ready to sink into the words, laugh, maybe even cry at whatever my dad had to say to me. Five minutes in, a knock on my dorm door interrupted our moment.

"Who is it?" I asked.

"Me. Greg."

My tummy muscles squinted in response to his voice. I shaped strands of hair into place and slid *The Manual* under my pillow.

"Come in."

Greg was in a pair of boxers with nothing on top. Tufts of

hair poking out of a very skinny chest, knees almost as knobbly as the director's. He sat beside me and immediately started to kiss me, this time a little more passionately than the first time. I didn't know what to do or say, so just went along with it because it felt nice. But when I felt something hard pressing against my thigh, and noticed a tent pole of an erection staring back at me, I knew I needed Dad's help.

"Greg," I said breathlessly.

"Yes?"

"Can we just talk?"

"Course we can."

That night I ended up telling him all about Corey, while he spoke about an old girlfriend he used to date back in Bolton.

"Well, if you ask me, Corey's an idiot. Letting you go."

A part of me wanted to defend Corey. "Well, it's all ancient history now."

"At least we agree on that." There was a moment of silence before Greg moved in for another kiss.

I turned away. "Sorry . . . I'm a little tired." And scared and confused and awkward and naive. "Almost twenty years old and a virgin!" I wanted to scream, but kept quiet as he made for the door flanked by an air of disappointment.

"Okay, Lois, I'll see you in the morning, then."

I flipped back the pages of *The Manual* a few years.

Miscellaneous: Saying "no"

That boy you like has finally seen sense and asked you out. You've been seeing each other for a bit now, been

out a few times, you're in his bedroom kissing and he wants to take things a little further. What do you do?

My advice: DON'T DO IT! DON'T DO IT!

Okay, I've just made myself a cup of strong tea laced with a little brandy, taken a deep breath, and here's Kevin Bates's advice to his daughter about sex . . . But you're five years old??? I know, I know, by the time you read this you won't be. It's just hard for me, okay? And even harder knowing I won't be around to vet any of your boyfriends, give him the evil eye, pull him aside as you leave to prepare fresh lemonade and threaten to break every bone in his arm if he EVER lays an unwanted finger on you. There, I think I've got things off my chest for now. Time to get serious. I can do this.

Yes, I can do this. Yes, I can do this. I was a child of the Woodstock era, after all. I even think if I'd lived in America I probably would have gladly viewed this landmark spectacle (from a respectable distance, mind, and merely for research purposes).

Now, back to business.

Before you're alone with your boyfriend, make sure you've already mulled over in your mind what you will and will not be agreeing to. Forewarned is forearmed. So, hand-holding: yes. Any other "touches": no. It's always a good idea to let him know about these limits too, in advance. Say, on your second date, or the minute you catch that questioning "gleam" in his eye. Don't be afraid to tell him quite clearly "No, I don't want to have sex with you." Then you can start getting all 101 reasons off your chest like this: Reason 49: I don't feel ready. Reason 100: I have a dad who will haunt you every day for the rest of your life.

It's probably a good idea to strengthen the numbers by stopping the kissing and physical stuff altogether. Yes, scrap all of it. And if he doesn't respect your decision you know what you have to do: walk out of the door. I'm ashamed to reveal this now, especially to my daughter, but I once said the following to an old girlfriend: "If you loved me you'd let me, you know . . . go all the way . . ."

She said: "I do love you. Do you love me?"

I said: "Of course I love you. More than anything. That's why I want us to do this."

But she hit back with a nice verbal left hook: "If you love me, Kevin Bates, you'll wait for me . . . Right?"

Good point.

I was confused. How would I know if it was the right time? If Greg was the right one? Was I in love? Had I felt it before? My mind rewound to an image of Corey. I pressed erase.

When I first met your mom, she was standing outside the chippy wearing this flimsy little miniskirt and high-heeled boots. I had this really bad afro, a more freshly electrocuted look than the Jackson Five. But this didn't matter, because when your mom looked at me I thought my heart would pop out of my chest (actually, something else wanted to pop out, but because you are and will always be my little girl, we'll call it my heart). I was THAT happy.

When she agreed to go out with me, I knew I was the luckiest man on earth. You should have seen my grin; so wide it almost split my face in half. And when she agreed to marry me, I felt all high with pride and happiness that this beautiful, intelligent woman wanted to spend more than her spare time with little old ME. I was certainly NOT the handsomest man ever to walk the earth, definite future hair loss (thanks to my old dad) and at times (especially after a pint) the social skills of a baboon; but she still wanted ME. And I loved her back. So very much. And when you were born it felt like I'd just scored the winning goal at the World Cup. I finally had everything I wanted. What I'm getting at is this: whatever anyone says, loving someone and having someone love you back can be one of the most beautiful experiences you could ever hope to be a part of. And to deprive somebody you love of that just isn't on. So, if in the future your mom does find love again, don't deny her this. Support her. Don't hate the guy (while acknowledging that no, he'll never be as strong or as good-looking as your dad) and please, please don't give your mom a hard time because . . .

I slammed *The Manual* shut and chucked it onto the bed. I'd been searching for answers about ME and being in love, not Mom. I needed Dad to tell me what I was feeling about Greg. Was it love? Should I lose my virginity to him?

I lay on my bed, just thinking. Counting the cracks in the wall.

At around midnight, Greg called my name softly from behind the door and I asked him in.

"Just wanted to see if you were sleeping," he said.

I sat up. "Not yet."

He took my hand and kissed it. A tiny gesture that at that precise moment—miles from home and away from everything familiar—meant so much.

And that night I made love for the very first time.

* * *

Losing my virginity sparked a change that is hard to articulate. I hadn't felt like a child for years now, so it wasn't so much that. It was more a sense of well-overdue rebellion, or perhaps it was just not having to live in the shadow of Carla any more. I was *me*, Lois. A little wild. Out of control—well, sort of. A whole year below the legal age of consent in America, I was now regularly drinking cans of beer (even though I hated the taste) and for the first time in my entire life I felt "special." Everywhere I went, people commented on my accent, the way I walked. As if England was some faraway land full of princes, horses and cucumber sandwiches.

One night, having confiscated a bag of weed from one of the kids, my rebellion was inches away from being elevated to a level I'd never even dreamed of.

"We could tell the director . . ." offered Greg, as we stared at the tiny bag and its promise of unknown possibilities. Not to mention sickness, addiction, suspension, a disgraced flight back to England . . .

"Or we could just smoke it, right?" added Erin, which surprised me. Wouldn't it stain her lovely white teeth?

"When . . . I mean . . . what if the director found out . . . ? Isn't there a smell?" I stuttered, not used to the particulars of such an operation. I'd only ever tried smoking cigarettes with Corey.

"Don't be a git, Lois. If we smoke it outside—after the s'mores roasting—we'll be fine," added Erin using my tutorship of British words way out of context.

That night, after the kids were supposedly tucked up in bunk beds, but more likely engaged in something illicit, Erin and Greg finally lit the joint.

"Try it, it's good!" said Erin, just before placing the joint to her mouth. She inhaled deeply and I took the "joint" from her, holding it awkwardly and clearly with the wrong fingers. Luckily, both of them were obviously too stoned to notice as I wrapped my drying lips around it and took a long and deep drag, feeling the smoke tickle my nostrils.

"Suck in!" encouraged Erin. I did as told.

"Don't forget to exhale!" said Greg, and as I did they both fell into hysterics. It wasn't *that* funny. Neither was the way my throat burned, which led to a fit of coughs, quickly reminding me of my first ever puff of a cigarette. I took another "toke" to make them happy before lying back and allowing them both to get on with the laughter that now racked their bodies.

Miscellaneous: Sex, drugs and rock and roll
I'm not naive enough to think you'll never come across some of life's darker sections. Life isn't all yellow daisies and rainbows, however much we wish it could be.

So, whether they're offered to you or they're just something "new" and "exciting" you feel has to be tried for the sake of it, decisions regarding sex and drugs made in a split second can change your life forever. So take time to really think about what you are doing. Because, whatever you decide, there are definite consequences. Hopefully, your personal values, what you've read in this manual and your own beliefs, will be of some benefit in knowing how you should handle things like sex and drugs. But just remember:

- *Stay focused on what you want out of your life.*
- *Drugs: users are losers!*
- *You may want to think about the pill.*

- ***Blues, Motown and rock and roll all came before the noise that is pop.***

That night, while everyone slept, I sneaked into the kitchen and devoured half a portion of blueberry pie, left over from dinner.

I hated blueberry pie.

A week before my return flight, I learned the news of Princess Diana's death. I'd been in America almost three months, and the moment Erin rushed into my room to tell me was the first time I'd felt this silent pull to go back to a place that had never really felt like home.

"I can't believe it!" said Erin as we assembled for our usual midnight feast.

"Me neither!" I replied numbly. Although hardly a royal watcher, I knew Mom would be upset. Not to mention Carla, who once modeled her short haircut on Princess Diana's. I called Carla that night and she confirmed the story was true. Apparently, the television and radio stations were showing nonstop coverage. Programmings were canceled, people were openly crying in the streets, strangers who'd never even met her. I couldn't quite get to grips with what Carla was saying but could be sure of one thing—two young children were grieving the loss of a parent, and that I knew all about.

"I can't believe it!" I said on the phone to Mom.

"No one can. When are you coming home?"

"I thought I'd already given you the date?"

"I have it. I just want you home. All this business, it makes you think . . ."

"I know."

And I did. But I had a matter of days left of my contract and felt it was important to honor it. I finally got off the phone to mom (who had now convinced herself she was about to lose me to the "wilds" of America) and went to find Greg in the grounds. He was sweeping up dead leaves, an early sign that fall was looming.

"Hey, Greg!" I said, momentarily startled at how American I now sounded.

He dropped the rake. "Lois."

I enveloped myself into his arms and sniffed his aftershave. You see, I knew. I knew that soon I would never see this man again. The first man I had ever had sex with. Perhaps a man I could have really loved.

"You okay?" he asked, as I came up for air.

"Yes, Greg." And I was. Because at that moment I had accepted our fate. They always leave you in the end. Corey had. So, moving on from Greg and the farm was something I had probably begun to do the moment I arrived. "Why wouldn't I be okay?"

"Even though I don't agree with the royal family as a concept, I think it's tragic what happened to Diana."

"I know. And it feels really strange around here. I mean, earlier, some of the kids and even the director offered their condolences to me. It's all a bit odd," I said aimlessly.

"Have you spoken to Cody?"

Realization. "You mean Corey. And no, why would I?" I replied, a little too defensively, perhaps.

"He's in Paris too, right?"

"Right," I sighed. Greg was deep, yes. In tune with my feelings, yes. But he was still a man with a slight jealous streak and at that moment I regretted being so open with him about Corey.

I looked up at Greg and decided to lie. "I haven't even thought about Corey since coming here. But hey, thanks for reminding me . . . !"

The last week of my Jump America experience came all too quickly. Erin was first to leave, and as she left for the plane trip to Seattle I listened to her empty promises.

"I'll write! And do you have email?"

"No, I don't." Email was confined to Sixth Form College and no one I knew even owned a computer.

"Then we'll write. Promise?" she asked, her beautiful face longing for a response.

"Promise," I said emptily. As we exchanged addresses, I so wanted to believe that we would speak again, but it was hard. In my life, people had a habit of saying one thing and doing another.

A few days later, Greg followed. And as we kissed on the steps, a cab waiting to dispatch him to the airport, deep down I knew this was definitely and without doubt the end of Us.

"I'll write," he said.

"Me too."

"Love you," he said awkwardly.

A pause followed. I suppose this was my moment to say it back. Solidify the last three months of our bond. But the words did not even float around my tummy, failed to even bubble to the surface of my mouth. Instead, I decided to quote a scene from that lovely movie *Ghost*, which the three of us had watched on video the night before.

"Ditto."

I felt this flurry of excitement as his taxi moved off into the distance, because soon it would be my turn. I was going back to England. My home. And I couldn't wait. I couldn't wait for everyone to glimpse the new me and, quite bizarrely, I wanted to clutch onto the collective feeling that currently gripped the nation in regards to Princess Diana's death. I wanted to be a part of that, of something, however strange that sounded. And the first person I wanted to see was my mom.

I felt pumped with a strange exhilaration as I stepped off the flight that afternoon. As always, the clouds were gray and a cold breeze gripped me immediately. But I was home. As I walked past WH Smith, many newspapers and magazines emblazoned with images of the princess caught my attention. The gloom was everywhere, in the atmosphere, the gray skies, and in the faces of everyone I saw. In keeping with the new, independent me, I was keen to make my own way home and hoped the last bit of money I had left was enough to use a minicab. I was shattered, wanted a bath and needed my mom.

The motorway was surprisingly clear. Passing through Knightsbridge, in the window of Harrods, a huge picture of the princess and Dodi Fayed decorated with flowers, a sad reminder of the events of the past two weeks.

"Did you hear the news over there?" asked the cabby. He hadn't asked where I'd traveled from but I suppose that was irrelevant. Not being in England at such a time would always be seen as being "over there."

"Yes, I did."

"Terrible. So terrible," he said, shaking his head.

"I still can't believe it."

"You see someone almost every day, on telly, the papers . . . and then they're just taken away. Just like that . . . It's like—" the cab turned a corner. "It's like you think they're gonna last forever. Know what I mean?"

"More than you think."

We made it back into Charlton—home—and I hadn't enough money left to tip him. And then I remembered this wasn't America.

Turning the key into the lock, I immediately dumped my bags in the hallway and followed the sounds from the kitchen. Mom and the Bingo Caller stopped mid-sentence as I opened the door.

"Hello there, Lois! I could have picked you up!" said the Bingo Caller, to which I nodded my head sincerely. Mom had her back toward me, her hair more curly than usual and, slowly, she turned to greet me.

"Lois! Come over here and give me a big hug!" she enthused, with a big gap-toothed smile. At that point, surprise rushes of emotion made me want to squeeze my mom really tight and let her know just how much I'd missed her. So I moved forward, arms outstretched before I felt all my excitement hitch a ride straight back out of my body.

"What's going on?" I asked, pointing to my mother's tummy.

"Oh, that . . ." she replied with a straight smile.

"Your mother's seven months pregnant," added the Bingo Caller.

"Pregnant?"

I wanted to vomit, scream and pull each hair out of my head.

Pregnant?

At her age?

With the Bingo Caller's child?

I sat down to steady myself.

My mother was pregnant. My mother was pregnant. My mother was pregnant.

"You okay, love?" asked Mom.

Pregnant. I kept repeating this to myself like some weird mantra, thinking if I said it enough the reality of it would disappear. I managed to push myself out of that kitchen and over to the phone, which, thankfully, remained in the same spot near the banisters, but not before muttering some excuse about jetlag.

"Yes, your mom's up the spout. Now tell me about New York! The blokes. Did you go to Saks? Did you get me some sneakers? Well, actually, I would have preferred make-up, but anything will do."

"Why didn't anyone tell me?"

"About?"

"The pregnancy?"

"Your mom told me not to mention it. She was worried for a start—you know, what with being in her mid-forties."

"It's disgusting."

"My mom thinks it's sweet," she said absently.

My mind remained a mish-mash of nothingness as Carla prattled on.

My mother was pregnant.

"Are you listening to me?" she snapped.

"Carla, the world doesn't revolve around you, I've just found out my mom is pregnant!"

"And I've just found out my mom and dad are getting a divorce."

"What?"

"You heard."

I lay back on my bed, mouth freeze-framed to "open," unable to recognize the world I'd stepped back into. Princess Diana was dead, Mom was pregnant, and Carla's parents were getting a divorce. I'd never even known anyone to get a divorce before. This world called England felt too alien to me and I suddenly longed for the simplicity of the farm and Greg's fingers on my chest.

That night, even *The Manual* failed to offer me the comfort I craved.

believe in yourself

Kevin Trivia: ***Your mom originally fancied Charlie when we first met, two days after my twenty-first. Said I was too much of a "show off." Me?***

Miscellaneous: Siblings

Your mom always wanted a large, large family and I was up for it too. Producing a soccer team of my very own (male and female)—the Waltons of South London, if you like. What I'm getting at is this: your mom might decide to have another child. Or two. I don't know how old you'll be if and when this happens, but I really hope, Lowey, that you'll be mature enough to deal with it and not a) dunk its head in the toilet on a regular basis; b) dye his/her hair green just for laughs. (Charlie did that to me once. Not a good look.) I want you to remember that although she or he may not be a part of me, she'll still be a part of YOU. By all means there's nothing wrong with allowing them to do a few chores around the house and then claiming the credit, but it's also up to you to look out for them, listen to their fears and be the big sister I know you can be. And if you become as close as Philomena and me, then you're sorted. But don't worry if you're not. Ina and I were never close. Even now with the diagnosis and that, I have yet to see her, and on the phone things still feel a bit strained between us . . . but that's another story. Having a brother or sister is great because being an only child can be lonely and I don't want that for you.

But I was happy being "lonely."

Had been most of my life, anyway (apart from having Dad's Manual of course). I wasn't about to allow this child's imminent arrival to change *anything*. His or her impact on my life would be that of a feather dropped in an ocean. Never mind the constant banging as the Bingo Caller fixed up a cot in the spare room, or produced two rows of shelving over the old chest of drawers. I repeat, Mom's kid would be making absolutely no impact on my life whatsoever.

That was until she arrived one morning in full screaming glory, wrapped in a pink and white blanket and plonked into my arms, uninvited.

We were at the hospital.

"Isn't she beautiful?" gushed the Bingo Caller as I gazed down at my so-called "sister," looking a bit alien-like with her tiny head snuggled against my tummy, the blanket making my skin itch.

My arm began to ache. "Yes . . . she's, erm . . . lovely."

Amid gushes of pride and Mom informing anyone who'd

listen just how painful the twenty-hour labor had been (and surprisingly more eventful than my thirty-hour one), my desire to escape grew stronger by the minute. But I was trapped. Forced to hold the pink and white blanket, inhale that disgusting hospital smell, while the world and his dog (minus Corey) popped in to have a look at a kid who, on closer inspection, resembled some sort of nocturnal garden creature—all wrinkly skin and oblong-shaped head. What can I say? The Sprog was nothing special, but for some reason Mom, the Bingo Caller, everyone, thought otherwise.

"She is just like you!" gushed my best friend, as the male nurse did his party trick of fluffing Mom's pillow at the same time as staring adoringly toward Carla. Even with the Sprog in her arms, she was beautiful. Her once short cropped hair now running down her shoulders, shrouding large red lips and eyelashes as thick as falsies. She'd also grown a few inches thanks to the skyscraper-type heels she now insisted on wearing. Although she'd always been beautiful, she was now "supermodel wife of a rock star" beautiful. Cow.

"You think so?" gushed Mom.

"No, I'd go for her dad. His eyes for a start! Just like Corey and his—" said Carla's mom as the room switched to mute, except for the sound of the male nurse still fluffing Mom's pillow, his eyes now resting on Carla's mom's bosoms. The choice of two sexy women, way too much for him, clearly. A picture of Greg and Corey flashed in my mind and I smiled with the knowledge that at least two men on this earth had found *me* sexy.

"It's all right if you mention Dad, Mom!" said Carla.

She'd taken the split very badly and in part blamed her mom, which surprised me. Carla's mom had been very clear about things: the marriage had run its course, the kids were grown and it was time to live again—something like that anyway.

As everyone chatted names and diapers, I planned my breakout.

"Mom, would you like me to get you anything from the house?" I asked, buttoning up my coat as the child stirred slightly in Carla's arms. "Mom?"

With her lips cracked and smelling of stale sweat, I had never seen my mother look happier. "No, love. I have everything I need right here." She smiled at the Bingo Caller, who in return planted a kiss onto the thick clump of hair caked to her forehead.

"See you, everyone," I sang. But I was answered by silence, as all eyes remained transfixed onto this little bundle that stirred in the arms of my best friend.

I slipped away, angry for feeling the way I did. I wasn't a kid any more, I was pushing twenty-one, and yet . . . and yet . . . Mom, the Bingo Caller—and now their offspring—still had the power to encourage general feelings of shittiness to materialize. I returned home, located *The Manual* and reread the section on siblings.

It didn't help.

The Sprog cried constantly. Two a.m., six a.m., with Mom as she breastfed in the kitchen, me wondering if it would ever be possible to drag myself out of bed in a few hours for one of the five job interviews I had lined up. The first was for a PR firm as an office manager, which I had absolutely no chance of getting, what with being under-qualified, under-experienced and five years under the age limit.

Apply for a couple of jobs you have absolutely no chance of getting.

Why?

You might actually get one of them.

Plus it's always wise to get in as much experience with interviews as you can. And if you don't get the job, write to the company and ask them if they'd be kind enough to post you reasons as to why you didn't get the job. It could be you were under– or over–qualified (yes, I've heard that one), didn't answer certain questions the way they would have liked, anything. It's always good to know, so you can prepare for the next one . . .

The interviews went well and, slowly, my confidence grew. Of course, I began to apply for somewhat realistic posts, using (and exaggerating) my office experience in America and my brief stint as a supervisor at the shoe shop. Meanwhile, the new addition to our household may have taken up most of Mom's time, but she was still able to snatch moments in which to whine about my lack of attention to the Sprog.

"You know I've been busy with the interviews. Don't you want me to find a job?"

"I'm just saying, you could give her a hold once in a while," she ventured, ambushing me between the wall and her entire bodyweight, complete with babe in arms. "She doesn't bite!"

"I know that!" But as I looked down at her, nothing really stirred within me. She was some kid who just happened to be related to me slightly. She didn't particularly look like anyone familiar and, lucky for her, the Bingo Caller needn't be mistaken for her real dad any time soon.

"There you go!" said Mom in triumphant tones, as I placed my arms around the little body, which had really grown since our last encounter. She still felt so fragile, so soft, reminding me of the Tiny Tears doll I'd begged Mom to buy me, but which had somehow ended up in Carla's Christmas stocking instead. The Sprog smiled, and Mom took this as confirmation that we were the best of friends.

"See, she loves her big sister, don't you my sweet little darlin?' Lately, Mom's voice could switch from "mildly intelligent woman" to "squeaky children's television presenter" in seconds. I gazed down at the child, complete with counterfeit smile, wondering just how long was appropriate to stand cocooned between a wall and your mother. As a small cry escaped the baby's mouth, I sensed it was time to hand her back.

But when the crying continued an hour later, as I attempted to scan the job papers, things became a little clearer for me. And when the crying woke me up at around two a.m. and then again at six, I knew what had to happen around here. So I waited another three hours before lifting my tired body out of the house and went straight into the Job Center, where I located a full-time job, applied and was told I could start right away. As unsuitable as the job was (stacking shelves in a huge superstore during "twilight" hours but paying much more than the daytime wage), it eventually allowed me to gather a deposit and two months' rent on a two-bedroom apartment with Carla—who'd been itching to move ever since her parents had divorced and her father had moved to Barcelona.

* * *

During my last night at home, I peered into the Sprog's cot, watching her chest move up and down, her tiny eyes closed to the world around her. By now she was cute(ish), large curls dominating the Winnie pillowcase found in Mothercare as Carla and I shopped for our new home. And not for the first time, I tried so hard to feel "it"; this unconditional love Dad had written about in *The Manual*. This feeling you were supposed to feel toward small babies related to you by way of genetic accident. As always, nothing came. No swishes of love. She was just a kid. Just like I'd been to Granny Bates, Auntie Philomena and Auntie Ina. Being tied to someone by blood didn't guarantee anything. I gently placed a finger on the Sprog's forehead. "Goodnight," I whispered gently, knowing she could be anyone's kid lying in that cot.

Anyone's.

Carla and I settled into our two-bedroom apartment overlooking a mangy, often noisy old park, home to twice-weekly unauthorized bonfires and a rainbow of graffiti. Still, it was in Greenwich, almost kissing the border of Blackheath. Far enough away from Mom (a short bus ride away) but still close enough to roots planted by my dad. And I needed that familiarity.

Along with the less than flash scenery, the dreary inside walls of our apartment sometimes reeked of damp, but none of this mattered. Carla and I were two young women armed with the freedom to do what we liked, when we liked. New Jersey—or at least the experience—was still reverberating through my body like aftershocks of an earthquake and I couldn't wait to replicate my experiences. All change. Time to start handling *my own life*. Which unfortunately meant managing bills, home cooking and lugging bags of laundry two streets away to the launderette.

At first I loved living with Carla. But after a while, say, like a WEEK, some of her attributes began to grate on me. For instance, her general laziness in regards to hygiene, an inability to pick up after herself and her constant bitching about my choice of television program. The most exasperating had to be the sound of her and Fred (new, rocker boyfriend) having sex in the room next door while I attempted something resembling sleep after a long overnight shift at the superstore. A pattern I'd hoped had been left at Mom's, thanks to a screaming baby. Still, every now and then I pinched myself, just to remind me that I was away from the chaos and unwanted family portrait scenes of my previous life, which had to be a good thing.

Of course, I'd visit Mom's for some Sunday dinner (often armed with a bag of washing). Aghast at how the once spotless house I grew up in had become increasingly untidy, with toys and diapers strewn about and all to the soundtrack of a crying baby. I'd load the washing machine as Mom or the Bingo Caller cradled the Sprog while whistling the theme tune to *Coronation Street* (which, apparently, she loved). Then I'd disappear next door to Carla's mom, returning just in time for the final spin. One Sunday, Carla's mom was out so I had to stay at Mom's and sit through the Bingo Caller playing "daddy," watching his daughter intently as if trying to sink into those tiny little eyeballs, his face lovingly contorted into something I would never again see in my own dad's eyes. This made me sad.

"Are you all right, Lois?" asked Mom, making me jump. I pulled out the last of my underwear.

"Why shouldn't I be?"

"You were looking at your sister and—"

"No I wasn't!" I snapped. Horrified to feel a tiny stream of water trickle from my left eye, I quickly removed it with my fist.

"Love, I know we haven't had a chance to have a chat since you moved out. Or even about America. So much has happened . . ." said Mom, now at the table, watching me with that same "Do you have something you want to tell me, young lady?" look I hadn't seen in years.

"Yes, I know, Mom."

"Go on then," she urged.

I smiled. "I'll start with Carla, shall I?"

"Uh oh. What's it really like living with your best friend?"

"She CAN be a bit messy at times."

Mom scurried around for the biscuit tin and dipped in with a silent invitation for me to join her. As I hadn't much planned until evening shift, I sat on the chair opposite, my bum immediately squashing a rubber duck.

"Your sister, she loves that thing."

"Really," I said dryly.

"Tell me about America."

"That was an age ago, Mom." A time I replayed in my mind nightly. A time permanently etched into my psyche, my being, my everything. "I can hardly remember much about it."

A flicker of my own guilt surfaced as her expression switched to that of expectation. It wouldn't hurt to tell her *something*, however small.

"Okay, if we want to get all dramatic about things, it was the summer I finally came of age, if you like."

Mom threw me a look that said, "I'm not sure what you're on about but because it sounds mildly important I'll at least *try* to understand." So I began. The Empire State Building. The bratty children. Erin. Greg (censored, obviously). The director's knobbly knees. Learning to survive on my own. The s'mores. The housekeeping. The lovely weather. The brown bear droppings outside my dorm window. Dancing around a campfire.

"It sounds lovely."

"It was."

"Did you meet a young man?"

"No," I said quickly. Mom narrowed her eyes in mock disbelief and I burst into uncontrolled fits of giggles. I felt myself relax as the powerful but steadied patter of tiny feet entered the kitchen.

"Ohmigosh!" screamed Mom, standing abruptly as her biscuit toppled to the ground. The Sprog teetered forward and then backward like a malfunctioning Duracell bunny, finally landing bum first onto the feet of the Bingo Caller (who'd suddenly appeared from nowhere).

"My baby just walked! Ohmigosh, I can't believe it!" she screamed again, flapping around like a chicken on E.

"Get the camera!" she shrieked.

"She'd done the odd step a minute ago, love. So I brought her in to show Mommy!" sang the Bingo Caller. I smiled obligingly as the Sprog flatly refused to perform any more, judging by the sudden downward turn of her lips and scrunched forehead.

"Come on, Flower!" said her father, blowing a huge raspberry into her stomach and whisking her into the air, much to Mom's horror AND delight.

The Sprog struggled in her father's arms.

"I can't believe it!" reiterated Mom, trembling hand to her mouth.

"That's my girl!" added the Bingo Caller.

"Say hello to your big sister Lois," said Mom, calming down slightly.

"Hi there . . ." I offered uncomfortably. She gazed toward me blankly, before burying a head of curls into her father's chest.

"She's just shy around you, that's all. Needs to get to know her big sister, don't you Pooky Poo?" The sight of my mother ruffling the Sprog's hair was enough to make me heave and leave.

"I'd better be off, Mom. Leave you . . . guys to it."

"Why not stay for dinner? She might do a few more steps!" said Mom hopefully.

"I've loads to do. Maybe next week?"

Once outside, I was able to breathe evenly as I spotted Carla's mom walking through her front door. Three-inch red heels and a skirt to match.

"Hiya!" I sang.

"Great to see you, darlin." My own girl seems to have forgotten where I live. Come on in!" she beckoned.

Inside, she attempted to fix her already neat hair. "I'll get us both a stiff drink and you can meet Calvin!" she enthused. How sweet, I thought, a dog for company.

"Nothing too strong for me," I said.

She placed the drinks onto the coffee table. Three drinks.

"Calvin!" she called, just as one of the best-looking, tallest men I had ever had the good fortune to rest my eyes on strutted into the living room dressed in tracksuit bottoms, a white T-shirt clinging to an abundance of hard body. Admittedly, it took a while for my jaw to ascend into its rightful place.

"Lois, this is Calvin."

"Hello."

"Hi." He extended a large hand with neat nails.

"My boyfriend."

Did I mention he had to be about my age?

"Nice to meet you . . . erm . . . Calvin . . ." I stuttered. His hand felt cold to the touch, but as we shook, his eyes remained transfixed on Carla's mom.

She smiled shyly. "We met at the gym."

Thankfully, my look of surprise was taken the wrong way. "Hey, at my age it isn't easy staying this trim!"

Calvin turned to her. "You don't need much help, babe. You're perfect."

"Thank you, darlin,' she responded with a wink, as something told me that new drug Viagra wouldn't be needed any time soon.

Over a few glasses of fizzy wine, Corey was mentioned—due back for a holiday next week and flourishing in France—along with a brief innuendo about how much he'd *love* to see me. But after about thirty minutes of gatecrashing this two-person orgy, a hasty maneuver toward the door was imminent, and I was sure I could hear the pinging of a bra strap as soon as the door shut behind me.

My little girl's twenty-one.

Twenty-one!

I can't quite believe it. Also, it feels so strange because, well, I'm only thirty, so to have a daughter of your age feels quite overwhelming. I often wonder what you look like now. Long or short hair? Would you like soccer or prefer tennis? Back in a minute, sweetie, just need a second.

Sorry about that. Just went and had a manly . . . soak of the handkerchief. I think I got a bit emotional there. Now where was I?

Yes.

Believe the hype. Twenty-one is a definite coming-of-age thing. It finally seems acceptable—at least by society's standards—to leave childhood behind (but you try telling that to me and Charlie. I think we remained twenty-one—at least I did, right up until I said "I do" to your mom. But, from what I've seen, men take a lot longer to mature than women anyway). Anyway, enough of the boring stuff, you go out and have a drink, party all night, be young, but at the same time don't forget to put on your sensible hat ready for Monday morning . . .

Happy twenty-first birthday, my love.

Actually, my twenty-first birthday was spent at Mom's, watching her coo over the Sprog as she attempted to dish up a collapsed birthday cake in the shape of the number twenty-one. Carla's mom, Calvin and Carla popped round, but mainly, it seemed, to also coo at the Sprog. I was surprised but pleased with the arrival of a card from Carla's dad, via Spain, but shocked (and pleased) when Carla arrived with a huge bunch of flowers and a tiny pink message that simply read: "Happy Birthday Lo Bag x."

"All I got was a crummy key thing for my twenty-first. He obviously lurrrves you!" she mocked as I feigned indifference while the inside of my tummy did back flips. I guess I really didn't have time to process Corey's gift, because just as I was making to leave Mom's, Auntie Philomena showed up, again totally unexpectedly, just as she had at Mom's wedding nine years ago.

The years had been kind to her, but perhaps the Caribbean sun had more to do with that than anything else, as she had moved to Carriacou with her family almost two years ago.

"Happy birthday, Lois!" she said as we embraced. She handed Mom a package as we congregated in the kitchen. "Nutmeg bread," she said.

Mom smiled a stiff thanks. "I'll make some tea, shall I?"

"Thanks, Auntie Philomena. But you could have sent the bread and card through the post!" Wouldn't be the first time, I thought.

"Haven't been much of an auntie, have I? It was important I did this."

Mom cleared her throat (in sarcasm, I think) as she busied herself with the cups.

"I owed it to Kevin to come and see you on your twenty-first."

To hear my dad actually mentioned by anyone was a shock. It was as if, for a few short seconds, he was alive. Perhaps sitting in a café in Catford or something.

"Have you seen Gran?" I asked, remembering the last time I'd spoken to Granny Bates. A strained phone conversation.

"Yes, I stayed with Mom for a couple of days. You are my last stop before going back home."

Mom placed two cups of tea on the table. "I'll leave you two alone . . . go and see to Abbi."

I suspected Auntie Philomena would be okay with this.

"So, Lois, it's your birthday. Twenty-one. So, first off . . . happy birthday!"

"Thank you," I replied. No hugs or stuff—because it wasn't like that between us. However, Dad had loved her, even trusted her to give me *The Manual*, and this knowledge was enough for me.

Her smile straightened. "I have something for you, Lois."

I held my breath, remembering the last time she'd said that to me.

"A twenty-first birthday present."

She reached into her bag and retrieved a tiny package wrapped in colorful paper.

"Open it up then," she said, surprisingly more excited than I was. I unwrapped the package carefully as bits of color soiled my fingers. The paper seemed old. "What is it?" she asked impatiently. Inside, was an oblong-shaped camera.

"Kodak Tele Ektra," I read from the side. I opened it up.

"A camera. That's nice," said Auntie Philomena, shaking her head slowly and smiling. It was then, I knew.

"Is it from . . . ?"

"Kevin, yes. Made me promise to give it to you on your twenty-first."

My heart rate accelerated. "He never mentioned it in *The Manual*." I thought back to the way I'd carelessly unwrapped the paper. My dad had wrapped this with his bare hands, and if I'd known I'd have unfurled it in private. Savoring every moment. Searching the two strips of film for any signs of my dad: stray hair, the smell of his favorite aftershave, any trace of DNA I could find to link us together.

Having Auntie Philomena round on my birthday was great. Receiving the camera, wonderful. But finding a ream of 110 film still inside was a breathtaking, scary and absolutely, without a doubt, exciting surprise.

Of course, I rushed to the drug store and paid extra to get the film developed that day. I stood outside the drug store a few hours later and opened up the rectangular package. Twelve snaps. Five of me as a young child, in dresses I could barely remember. Hair in tiny, fluffy pigtails. Sitting on the floor, twirling like a ballerina, standing by the bathroom sink. Some of the furniture I recognized as still in Mom's house today but unfortunately now occupied mostly by people my dad wouldn't even recognize.

But it was the remaining seven pictures that would render me catatonic for hours. Eyes almost stapled to a set of prints taken just months before my daddy died.

Me sitting on my dad's knee, cupping his face with my little hands. Me, Mom and Dad sitting on the settee. Mom pretending to look annoyed as Dad and I giggled at something I have no way of remembering. Other pictures in similar guises, but, basically, Dad and me together. However, it was the last picture on the film that finally made me cry: it was of Dad, only half his face visible, the remainder obscured by a thumb. My thumb. I could tell by the amused yet forgiving look on his face. His little daughter attempting to take a picture, not knowing it would be the last one she'd ever take of him.

I cried. I cried. I cried.

I placed the picture of me and my dad under my pillow and kissed it before I went to sleep. Like *The Manual*, I found a way for the camera and the pictures to fit neatly into my life, finally framing the distorted picture of Dad and placing it on my television, pride of place where I could glimpse it every day. Ready to share that moment with the world. Of course Carla did question its artistic credibility, especially as there were a lot more clearer shots of Dad. But in all honesty I didn't care what anyone thought—*I* knew what that photo represented to me.

I returned home from another night shift at work to find Carla sprawled on the floor of our apartment, eating a bag of chips on the carpet, face transfixed by the television. Dad's incomplete photo intact.

"What are you watching?" I asked with zero interest.

"I taped that show *Sex and the City* last night. It's so dirty and it's great. Wanna chip?"

"No thanks, it's eight o'clock in the morning!" I replied, the vinegary aroma colliding happily with my taste buds.

"I was out with Fred all last night at a gig. I just got in an hour ago myself. Don't feel like sleeping yet."

I moved into the kitchen as her voice followed.

"I've got some news, Lois! I'll tell you after the show," sang Carla.

The sink was full of dishes and I wondered what she did all day to warrant such mess and why she never felt the urge to just . . . clean up? I sighed heavily as I hunched over the sink.

"You don't have to worry any more," said Carla, emptying the contents of her plate into the bin. A solitary chip traveled down the side of the bin and onto the floor and I waited to see if she'd pick it up.

She turned to me. "You'll be rid of me soon."

I bent down to do what I always did—pick up after her.

"I'm moving out. Fred's finally seen sense and realized he can't live without me, so he's asked me to move in."

At first, Carla's words were like the sweetest composition in my ears. Carla was moving out. No more mess. No more slouching. Oh, but then again, no more rent—however small and random her contribution. *Damn it.* And as much as I hated to admit it, I would miss the girly chats, regular TV analysis and that sweet smell of dewberry.

"How am I supposed to pay the rent?"

"Er, I dunno . . . find another roommate?" She opened the fridge door and retrieved a can of cola. Her shoulders sagged. "I am sorry, babe. Really. It's just I think . . . no, *I know* Fred is the one. I know he is and I don't want to mess this up."

I almost begged Carla to stay, at least until a replacement was found. But apparently Fred was off on tour in a few weeks and her plan was to spend as much time together as possible in the meantime.

If my experiences with Carla had taught me one thing, it was to forget about a replacement roommate and somehow find a way to take care of the bills myself. This realization suddenly brought with it the need to find a long-term, full-time job. My evening work was no longer enough to sustain me.

An advertisement in the local paper promised the world as well as a $30,000 salary. I didn't even have an interview, just a handful of questions over the phone about my knowledge of the Internet, a shuffling of papers then an excited, "When can you start?"

In the plush waiting room of I.T.T. Enterprises, all I could think about was having the apartment to myself and perhaps being able to save some cash.

"Lois Bates," said a voice. I stood to attention and patted

down my creasing trouser suit, picked up in Lewisham's indoor market.

"Hello."

"Hi there. My name is Kenneth Rig. You can call me Ken. Thank you for getting here on time. Time is of the essence in this business. And thank you for choosing to work in the world's fastest growing industry—the Internet."

Ken led me past the receptionist, through a side door, down some steps and into a darkened basement-type area. Gone, the plush furnishings and thick shag-pile carpets.

"It's a little dark in here, so mind your step, Ms. Bates."

Ken opened the door to a huge room, which I suspected hid a secret sweatshop history. Endless rows of tables, chairs, phones and people (mostly women) yapping into concert-type earpieces.

"What you see before you is the 'operations room.' Look around you, Ms. Bates." Ken raised his hand like a magician in white gloves. "Here we call our customers, make orders, arrange deliveries and such. We also have a team operating outside. Their role? To get the products noticed. Make the sales. We call them the Ground Force Operations Unit."

I smiled good-naturedly at Ken. The man was a bit of a twit, but I had to remain focused on all the money I could make out of this "operations unit."

Ken showed me the fire escapes, loos, and what to do in the event of a code blue (i.e. if Callee is hesitant about going ahead with the order).

"Do you have any questions at this stage, Ms. Bates?"

"What type of Internet products will I be selling?"

Ken's face lit up like a set of Christmas-tree lights. "Don't worry, I'm coming to that *right* now."

He was thrilled to introduce me to I.T.T. Enterprises' top three sellers, placing the items on the table as I tried to ascertain what they actually were. I could just about identify the computer mouse.

"Keep in mind that this is only a mere fraction of the goods we sell. We have a huge range sold over the Internet and in our catalog."

"The mouse is quite cute," I said unnecessarily.

"Cute? Cute? This is not just any mouse!" His voice raised itself a few hundred decibels. I'd definitely entered weirdo territory. "This, the Slazoo, is *only* our third biggest seller. The Slazoo not only works as a mouse but also a hand massager. Now you can be relaxed as you surf!"

I grabbed hold of the next item—a watering can—wondering what the heck it had to do with computers. Sprinkle while you surf?

"What you have there Ms. Bates is the IU. Our number-one seller."

I fingered the contours of this strange item.

"It allows you to sprinkle while you surf."

"That's what I thought!" I said with intellectual pride.

"Our Internet urinal."

My hands shot away.

"Don't worry, it's not been used," he giggled like a schoolgirl. "You have to remember the Internet is taking off in a big, big way. Chatrooms, dating sites—it's not often convenient to leave the computer at regular intervals. I myself can stay glued to mine for hours at a time."

My third day into the job and I hadn't sold a thing. The Operations Room buzzed with activity, though, as the general public were routinely persuaded to invest in everyday essentials such as The CiggieSurf Cigarette Holder—smoke while you surf!

"This job is crap. I'm only doing it while I study," Jan informed me. She'd been at I.T.T. Enterprises for six months and sat opposite me with a fluffy pink animal stuck to her headset.

"Have you ever earned five hundred quid in one week here?" I ventured, knowing full well what the answer would be.

"You having a laugh? I make about fifty to a hundred quid if I'm lucky. Sometimes, nothing."

"Tell me about it!" added Preethi, a newer girl.

"Ken thinks this shit is all part of the Internet revolution. My arse! The real money's in setting up a website with a great idea or becoming a certified engineer. That's what I'm going for. In a few weeks I'll *really* be earning at least thirty grand and that's after only a few months' studying."

I urged Jan to tell me more about becoming a certified computer engineer, which she did. And by the end of my first week I'd made zero pounds at I.T.T. Enterprises but gained enough information to help me with the next stage of my professional life.

keep moving

Kevin Trivia: *Most fave record bought in 1975? Minnie Riperton's "Lovin' You"—for your mom, of course.*

Inching toward the millennium, I made major decisions. My life would become a whirlwind of work, work, work.

I now worked full time as an office temp with an agency and spent Thursday evenings and Saturday all day stacking shelves at the superstore to make ends meet. And not forgetting three evenings a week at a "virtual college" in Lewisham—namely, a shoddy airless room stacked with rows of computers teaching the fundamentals of Information Technology. But I wasn't complaining. Yes, I was exhausted, but egging me on from behind the scenes was my dad's belief in me, pushing a hidden drive never tapped into before which fueled my desire to succeed. So while Carla partied with her "soon to be a rock star" boyfriend, I worked, studied, slept and ate. Of course, Mom would ring to complain about my lack of interest in the Sprog, something I allowed her to think because that's what she did best—thought the worst of me. Then again, even if I wasn't working such long hours, I doubted whether I'd be so quick to see the Sprog anyway. It felt easier to feel this way about her after all, as the Sprog wasn't *really* my sister.

Carla continued to follow rocker Fred (who I suspected to be a good old-fashioned Home Counties lad with a suspiciously middle-class upbringing) like a lovesick puppy, moaning about my membership to the "beige cardie brigade"; her constant "you're only young once" speeches escaping too freely from her Plum Delight lips. And when this prompted a tinge of self-doubt to ping its way into my head, all I needed was the pages of *The Manual* and immediately I would hear the voice of my lovely dad.

Such determination meant I finished the course within eight months and, true to Jan's words, I'd landed two job interviews within a week.

Miscellaneous: The BIG job interview

That all–important job interview.

The biggie.

The job you feel you've been waiting for all your life.

The one that'll lift you onto the first rung of the ladder, that'll, in turn, change your life forever.

You're a little nervous. Perhaps you're sweating more than usual. All semblance of common sense and knowledge having legged it out the window ages ago . . .

I smiled.

You'll want to make a great first impression. Only natural. But when you get ready for that interview, don't overdo the make-up and hairdo. Just be neat and not too overdone. Who likes an overcooked roast? Okay, bad example.

I peered into the mirror. Apart from lip balm and a dash of eyeliner when looking a little tired, I rarely wore make-up. My hair spent most of its life bound and gagged in a hair band.

If you turn up cheerful, with bags of confidence and smiling (but not in a deranged way), you'll stand out loads more than the other wannabes (unless, of course, one has a skirt barely covering her bum and the interviewer is a lecherous old git). Here are a few pointers to think about when you are in front of the interviewer:

- *He's human, just like you are.*
- *She doesn't want to see your baby pictures.*
- *She doesn't need to hear you let out wind.*
- *He doesn't want you to give the impression you are actually after his job.*
- *She will not wait while you dash to the pay phone to call your best friend for the latest soccer score (Charlie).*

- *She will not be influenced by a rush of compliments ("Love your hair! The color really suits you!!" won't give you any extra brownie points).*
- *No matter how mind-numbingly boring the interview (and there'll be some) never, ever yawn. If you try to stifle one, you'll just look like you're trying to swallow a mouse. Just try your best to get plenty of sleep the night before.*

My first job interview after leaving school was my absolute worst. Not because I messed up on any level—I read up on the company beforehand, wore my best suit, brushed my teeth, combed my hair and didn't wear any make-up(!). However, as soon as the interviewer laid eyes on me, let's just say it was obvious he'd made his mind up about me from the start (based on what he thought "people like me" were like). He wasn't hiring.

I know/hope things will be different for you.

So, just carry yourself with loads of confidence as you walk into that interview. Bearing in mind that confidence stems from deep inside; down past the ribcage and somewhere among your decaying breakfast, lunch and dinner. And I hope by now you have loads (confidence, that is, and not decaying food) and that this comes across as so, and not as arrogance. Because there's a thin line between confidence and arrogance in the eyes of others. A very thin line.

Also: Trying on a dozen outfits, bathing in a sea of dodgy aftershave, practicing best lines in front of the mirror with a hairbrush "microphone," blowing in the palm of your hands every twenty seconds to test toxic breath levels . . . all sound like preparation for a hot date to me.

And perhaps it wouldn't do you any harm to look at it that way. Just make sure you don't end up looking like someone with the initials SDP (Saddo Desperado Pratt) tattooed on their arm. A clued-up interviewer will spot the SDP tattoo straight away. They've been through dozens of interviews before. They are pros. You're just . . . desperate. So fool them into thinking you're confident, efficient and the ONLY person for the job. Let them see OCFTJ (Only Candidate for the Job) spelled out on every inch of you. But again, WITHOUT coming across as arrogant, because, as I said before, there's a thin line . . .

PS: While we're on the subject of tattoos . . . NEVER, EVER GET ONE please, honey.

The interviews went better than expected. I remained calm, focused and never once asked a silly question (if we ignore the "do you have any toilets?" remark). The only negative theme that seemed to pop up was my age. At twenty-two, had I gained enough experience to take on a well-paid IT role? Being reminded almost weekly of the country's IT shortage I knew age wouldn't really be a factor in their decision and decided to dazzle them with a slick sentence about being "eager and keen to work my way up."

Within a week I was offered two posts and decided to go with the company paying a grand less than the other. An exciting PR firm up west as opposed to the dreary property development company. Besides, the $22,000 salary felt like a lottery win anyway.

The morning of my first day at work arrived in no time. Recalling the trendy-looking interviewer dressed in Prada glasses, surrounded by a huge atrium reception slap bang in the middle of trendy Soho, thoughts of Lois Bates not being good enough, trendy enough or pretty enough began to tiptoe into my head. My wardrobe was a mixture of out-of-date market wear. My only business suit was a crease-fest from a Finsbury Park wholesaler's kind enough to open to the public on a Saturday. My shoes were aged, complete with an ever-expanding hole in the right heel. But, peering into my full-length mirror, I could see the outfit had actually come together quite nicely. The trousers would have to be pulled in at a later date, as I appeared to have lost weight over the last few months. Turning to the side, I saw a noticeable bum curve and smiled shyly. A pair of straighteners borrowed from Carla had tamed my unruly mane, completing the look.

With a few minutes to spare before I had to leave, I pulled out *The Manual* for a final rush of support.

Miscellaneous: That new job

Your first day at that job you've been after for ages. First off, I'm so proud of you. I knew you'd do it. Second, calm down! It's only a job and you will be alive at the end of it (okay, I'll stop with the death jokes). Just remember, you DESERVE to be there just as much as anyone else. You've earned your spot fair and square, kiddo.

Take in everything during this introductory period at your new job. Learn what you can about the company, your immediate colleagues (work stuff, not who they're messing about with), soak up the atmosphere, ask questions if you need to. Now's the time to do it, as you'll just sound a bit dumb if you do it later. For example, I waited two weeks to find out my supervisor's name once, and in another job it took me three whole days to realize I was sitting at the wrong desk. Okay, you'd never be as dumb as your old dad, but you see where I'm going with all of this.

Work's a bit like school I'm afraid, only this time you CHOOSE to be there (or are forced to, to pay the bills). Like school, you'll have the hierarchies, the nerd, the pretty girls, the studs. Same ol' same ol' I'm afraid. You may even need to go back over my school advice from time to time. Office politics, an unavoidable old chestnut that I can go on about for ages, but I won't.

You may also have what I like to term as an Office Husband, who everyone will think you're secretly having a relationship with. You'll go to lunch together, sit together in meetings, argue about television. And it'll feel comfortable, nice, cozy and, most importantly, without threat. There's nothing wrong with this as long as he doesn't start getting ideas. If he does, you'll have to deal with it ***really*** *sensitively as, remember, you're in the workplace.*

Of course, if he gets offensive you report him or, failing that, refer to the "How to make a man temporarily helpless" section of this manual.

Then there's the office best friend. The girl/boy you'll share a lot of things with, may even have after-work drinks with, but that's where it all ends. S/he will never see the inside of your home and you probably won't socialize outside of the work domain. One of you may suggest it one day, but you'll also find a way to wriggle out of it somehow. I don't think real life and work should EVER mix. And yes, this applies to boyfriends too. If in doubt, remember this question from your old dad and always answer it:

Would you ever s in your own back yard?***

Okay, you would if the toilet was blocked, your neighbors were all out and you'd had a really dodgy omelette the night before. But you get what I'm trying to say, right?

"They have the best omelettes here. But apart from that, the food's not great in our staff canteen. Most of us use the cafés and bars around the area, because they're much nicer," explained the PA assigned to show me around. I compared her trendy get-up of designer jeans and heels to my crumpled old suit. "It's lovely here in the summer, though, the sun floods in from the wall-to-wall windows."

The cafeteria housed a collage of primary colors against the backdrop of natural light, the aroma of fresh coffee and croissants flooding the atmosphere. My tummy gave off a slight rumble in protest as we moved on.

The conference rooms housed arty collages surrounding solid oak tables and crisp leather chairs, and I was equally impressed with the corridor, water cooler and the shiny brass handles on the door leading to my office.

"And this is you!" announced the assistant, opening the gold-handled door. The least impressive of all the areas I'd seen, judging by the dark and gloomy room with two old computers dumped in a corner, and the sound of garage music coming from one of the three functioning PCs.

"Hello," said a nerdy-looking man with scruffy, shoulder-length hair. "I'm Keith, but you can call me Keitho." He spoke in an American/Australian twang I'd never heard before.

"Nice to meet you," I said with a nod of my head. Mainly because his fingers seemed permanently attached to the keyboard.

I was then introduced to Jamie, who immediately reminded me of Erin. Blonde hair, big boobs and beautiful.

"Hi there. I'll have to catch you later, just had a call out," she said quickly, with a wink. Apparently someone in Accounts couldn't reboot. As she shot out the door, the last member of the team introduced himself.

"And I'm Matthew, but you can call me Matt," said a most beautiful specimen of a man. Definite office spouse material. Dreamy eyes that I could gaze into all day long.

"And your name is?" inquired Matt.

"Huh? Erm . . . Lois," I felt myself blush.

"As in Lane, right?" chipped in Keitho, briefly looking up from the keyboard.

"Yes. I was named after her, so my dad says."

"Far out!" exclaimed Keitho with maximum enthusiasm.

"You have a friend for life there. Sci fi and comic freak is our Keitho!" said Matt, smiling to reveal a perfect set of teeth to complement those sparkling eyes. Matt was possibly the best-looking man I had ever met, after Calvin (or even Corey—as much as I hate to admit it).

I followed Matt and Jamie to lunch in the colorful cafeteria as Keitho manned the calls. Jamie was a listener while Matt could talk all day. But I didn't care. He was just so good-looking. Like a movie star trapped in an IT nerd's body. By five thirty I'd answered my first call out with Matt "supervising" and I'd fallen marginally in lust with him.

Giving up the evening job left me free to relax at the weekend. Much needed, considering the amount of time spent socializing after work with Matt, Keitho and Jamie. My life soon became a whirl of trendy cocktail bars, one in particular, on the corner of Old Compton Street, that served the sweetest (if not the only) Blue Lagoon cocktail I had ever tasted. A life so unreal, so new, I thought I'd burst with the excitement of it all. I also uncovered plenty about my new workmates. Matt was single and lived with his mom in Bow. Keitho was nearing the end of his five-year work visa from New Zealand, with hopes of finding a "desperate-enough English girl" willing to marry him before the immigration deadline. Jamie was single but in love with a mystery man she'd "never, ever" reveal the identity of. Matt and Keitho had placed bets on our very old and very married MD, while I figured it had to be a friend of the family.

The job itself wasn't the most taxing or exciting (Employee: "My computer won't work!" Me: "Er, perhaps if you switched it on?"), but with it my confidence grew, as did my bank balance and a desire for a brand-new wardrobe of clothes, especially as I'd dropped a dress size.

I was now shopping in Covent Garden, unafraid to spend $60 on a pair of shoes, haggling with intolerant wholesalers was distant memory dust. I was also now unafraid of the trendy wand, happy to dress my age and skip the "beige cardies." Even Carla, who I hadn't seen for some time, noticed when she came round to invite me to one of Fred's gigs—which I declined, of course, gigs not really being my scene.

However, now I didn't have an excuse not to venture back into Charlton to see Mom and her child, which I managed on a monthly basis and was something I got through mostly by clock-watching. Then, on one such day, I ran into Corey.

"Lo Bag!" he enthused, scooping me into his strong arms.

"I thought you were still in France!"

"I'm back for a bit. Sometimes you need your mom's cooking."

"Your mom's roasts *are* legendary . . ."

Then, silence. I couldn't think of one word to say to break it.

And then he spoke. Quietly. "It doesn't take that long to get here via the tunnel, you know. *Either way.*"

I ignored the insinuation. "Look at you!" I said in over-exaggerated tones. I pulled at a tuft of his hair that had grown into a fashionable but lazy style, the baggy jeans and holey T-shirt telling the world "I'm so cool."

"You look great!" he enthused, shaking his head slowly and, I think, appreciatively. He held out his arms and I felt a blush as he scooped me into them for a second time. Even though I'd fantasized about Matt nonstop most nights, in reality I hadn't felt a man's body against mine since Greg two years ago, and it felt good. Corey felt good.

"You've got to come in! Mom's out with Calvin. We can catch up and you can tell me what my sister is doing with that idiot Fred, the wannabe rocker who speaks like he has a plum in his throat!"

I followed Corey into the house with a strong sense of déjà vu.

"So, what do you think about your mom and Calvin?" I asked.

"I try NOT to think about them, if you know what I mean."

I laughed nervously. "I meant with him being so much younger and that . . ."

"Well, Dad's living it up in Barcelona . . ."

"How is your dad?"

"Opened up a bar and everything. I went to see him a couple of weeks ago. He asked about you, wants to know when you'll come and visit."

"Really?" This surprised me.

"Of course! You're like one of the family. Seriously, though, if my mom's happy then that's cool. I just hoped she would have found someone a little bit older than me, you know?" He pulled a cigarette box from his pocket and offered me one.

"Sorry, don't smoke."

"Don't be, it's a filthy habit and I should have remembered you don't smoke," he said, lighting up. "My sister tells me you're a top executive or something."

"Hardly. I work in computers."

"Say no more, Lo Bag. Supposed to be good money in that. But I got to say, you surprise me."

"Why?" I raised a newly plucked eyebrow.

"I saw you doing something more creative, I suppose."

"What, like you?" I laughed.

Corey remained focused. "I can see how it could be tempting. Some of my friends have jumped onto the computer bandwagon, becoming certified engineers and kissing goodbye to a serious future in art. Not me."

"So, you think I've 'sold out' then?"

"I didn't say that, Lo Bag. I just believe we all have a creative side. Mine's art, Mom likes sewing things, Carla . . . well, Carla just likes to sit and gaze into the eyes of her boyfriends." We both laughed and Corey's dimples sang out to me.

"And what's mine then?"

"I dunno . . . you tell me."

I remembered my twenty-first birthday present. The joy

at seeing the pictures for the first time. My dad and me in various poses. Together. Captured in film for the very last time, and yet—forever.

"Maybe I haven't found it yet. Sorry . . ."

"Lo Bag, I don't judge anyone. You're just doing what you feel you have to do. And there's nothing wrong with that."

As we continued to "catch up" I perspired uncomfortably into my crisp white shirt. Especially when he looked at me, perhaps in no particular lustful way, but in a way my body seemed to respond to. I'm not sure if this had something to do with my "drought," as Carla liked to put it, or just the familiarity of the whole situation, but after over four years of being apart "it" was still there . . . this thing. This thing I couldn't articulate. This thing that had existed between me and Corey ever since he kissed me in this very living room after my beer-choking session.

"You look really lovely," he said out of nowhere. I wasn't sure where to look. His lips, his chest, further down . . . I felt like a little kid, merely on the brink of adulthood, unsure of how to say or do anything that would seem remotely adult. He moved over to me, slowly, and I knew what was going to happen, because it had happened before. Our lips connecting. Slowly at first, and then moving with a hunger that needed immediate gratification.

Upstairs in his room, his fingers moved without guidance. Unbuttoning, removing, burying themselves in places I'd only allowed Greg to explore. I thought I'd explode as his tongue made quick circles on my lips, brushing against my teeth, teasing me with every short stroke. A rush of heat moving up inside of me, appearing out of my mouth as words. "I want you."

"Are you sure about this?" he said huskily.

I was sure.

"You okay?" asked Corey.

"Yep." It just seemed right, lying there together. Corey lit up a cigarette and held it to me. I didn't think twice as I took it from him.

"Just like old times, right?"

"Tell me about it."

"You okay?" he asked again.

"Yes! Stop asking me that." I passed the cigarette back to him.

"Always away with the fairies, you. Even when we were kids."

I smiled as he kissed me so tenderly on the forehead. So soft, so loving. And I wanted to stay there with him forever, but at the back of my mind I knew he'd be off back to France soon. I had to prepare myself for this inevitability. Him leaving me again. So that's what I did.

"Where are you going, Lo Bag?"

"I really have to go," I said, jumping into my clothes, one eye on the clock.

"But what's the rush? Mom won't mind seeing you here. Trust me on that one."

"You have a great trip back to France, you hear?" I neared the door.

"But I'm not going back until next week. We could—"

"See you!" I sang, halfway out of the room. I exhaled deeply, shutting the door behind me.

It was better this way. Yes, we could have met up again. Talked some more, had a nice time together. But then he'd be back on the Eurostar within days. Away from here. From London. From me. I wasn't about to put myself in the firing line only to be shot down. No way.

Corey left on the Friday according to Carla and by the Saturday I was sitting alone in the apartment as I did most weekends. I didn't mind as not going out drinking like many people my age meant I got to save cash (although I did make an exception on Millennium Eve by buying a bottle of champagne which I hardly touched and left for Carla).

Another Saturday at home and the sun shone furiously outside as the sound of children playing loudly annoyed the crap out of me as I tried to concentrate on a videotaped recording of *EastEnders*. Thanks to a small pay rise, I now had all the mod cons I desired, including a tabletop washing machine, which meant fewer trips to Mom's and the Annoying Sprog's. The phone rang. It was Carla.

"Fred's got a record deal," she said.

"That's great!" I replied, flicking the pause button.

"And he's dumped me."

"Oh . . ."

"Said it would never work, now that he's about to become a big star." Her voice faltered and I knew she was in pain.

"Sorry . . ."

"Can I call you back? I've just got to finish putting a hammer to this crappy guitar. I'll call you back, okay?"

I smiled, re-pressing the pause button. Although I was

sad for Carla, her situation just proved my theory about people.

The phone rang again, but this time it was Mom. My body tensed up, preparing an invisible riot shield for the onslaught of strained conversation regarding my lack of visits, eating and sleeping habits and whether I had enough soap powder in the house—but this time I couldn't have been more wrong with my mundane predictions.

"It's your sister."

"What about her?" I groaned. Last month Mom had phoned to boast about the Sprog's obvious genius tendencies, following a quick completion of the puzzle I'd bought her for Christmas. The Sprog said this; the Sprog did that. Boring stuff that only a real sister would appreciate—and I wasn't her real sister.

"I . . . I can hardly say this . . . I can't . . ." said Mom.

"Mom, what is it?" I hit pause on the video.

"She's gone missing. She's gone missing!"

The police had been called.

Mom had last seen the Sprog playing in the back garden as she prepared vegetables for dinner. The phone had rung and Mom had launched into a long conversation with a friend, only to return and find the toddler had disappeared.

Carla's mom and Calvin jumped into their car, while Carla and I ran round to the neighbors' houses, screaming her name. We searched around the rec, under trees, shoving hastily photocopied pictures into the path of anyone within eyeshot, as well as in Mr. Tally's shop window and telephone boxes. We begged passers-by for a snippet of a sighting, anything that could lead us to her whereabouts. I then heard a whisper about the police visiting the mental care home up the high street but refused to let this news penetrate. Likewise when I heard they were considering searching Blackheath Common.

An hour passed.

We retraced our steps. Covered old ground. Communicated by cellphone—the first time I was able to justify the fact I'd actually bought one.

Two hours.

No sightings.

Three hours.

No news.

I was now left with a new, horribly unbearable nagging thought: that this little girl wasn't coming back. I was totally bewildered as I watched my mom unravel, almost disintegrating right there in front of me, inconsolable at the loss of her "miracle child." Her husband was unable to offer any useful words of comfort, as he himself looked riddled with fear. The Sprog wasn't even three yet. Too young to hold a conversation and too incapable of finding her way home. What if she was hurt? What if someone had hurt *her*? I tried to remove such echoing thoughts from my head and my heart, but failed miserably. Bad things always happened. People left, went away and *never* came back.

I crumpled her photocopied image in my hand, unable to fight a searing ache that appeared from the tips of my toes to the very last strand of hair on my head. Huge, angry tears appeared. *Please don't let anything have happened to her,* I begged. *Not to my little sister. Please.* I remembered what Dad had written about siblings and knew for sure that as of the summer of 2000 I loved her. I loved my little sister Abbi. She was a terror, screamed a whole lot when unable to manipulate her own way, lugged around a smelly knitted donkey, its ear shoved up her nostril (and which she refused to sleep without), and the trickle of snot that always found its way into her mouth—let's face it—disgusted me. But she was Abbi. Forget all that stuff about her not being my sister. Of course she was my sister! Mom gave birth to her. We had the same blood running through our veins, just like me and Dad, and I loved her. Loved that smile. Her cheeks. Those ringlet curls, that lovely doe-eyed smile. A stunning child mostly seen in the pages of catalogues advertising mini parkas and pink lace-up shoes. What a beautiful child. So beautiful, I had even managed to convince myself that Mom's and the Bingo Caller's genes could not have produced this little girl. That when Mr. and Mrs. Beautiful came back to reclaim her, complete with Volvo and golden retriever, we'd all be devastated. And she'd be gone forever. So I had decided that I would never *truly* love Abbi. Never truly embrace that sweet, adorable little girl.

And in some ways, this had made real sense—But now it just sounded childish, ridiculous and above all, cruel.

I paced the streets of my youth again. Lanes Fish Bar, the rec, fearing the worst possible conclusion. I was too late with my declarations of love. Too late.

Abbi was dead.

Too late.

Her tiny little body cold against the harsh elements.

Too late.

My tears arrived in abundance again, this time accompanied by masses and masses of guilt.

I walked slowly back to the house, my head bowed, and willed myself to turn the key in the lock. It was then I heard the crying and so braced myself for the inevitable, for more tears, more sorrow. Abbi was dead. Gone, just like Dad. And I had to be strong again.

I shut the heavy door behind me.

An obvious crowd had gathered in the kitchen. Everyone's back was toward me as I opened the squeaky kitchen door.

"L . . . Lois!" screamed my mom as the crowd split, revealing her swollen, tear-stained face to me.

"Mom?"

"L . . . look . . ."

"Mom?"

"She's back!" wailed Mom, in her arms a disheveled but alive little sister.

"Sprog!" I raced over, collecting her from my mother. Abbi raised her eyebrows in surprise at my current level of fuss. She wriggled a bit until someone handed her the knitted donkey, whose ear she placed firmly into her nostril. I think the room erupted in laughter, but I couldn't hear a thing. I just wanted to smell her, rub my fingers into each curl and, most of all, I never, ever wanted to let this child go again.

Apparently, Abbi had crawled through a hole and into the garden next door, belonging to an elderly couple who'd not long moved in. She'd fallen asleep behind their rose bush, and apart from a few thorn pricks was relatively unharmed as she lapped up the attention from me and half the neighborhood.

* * *

That year, Abbi's return was the best birthday present I could have wished for or needed. My birthday message from Dad was very simple:

> *You've seen a lot of changes in the past few years. Done a lot of growing up, traveled, I hope, and experienced new emotions. Keep growing. Never look back and just keep moving.*

take a risk

Kevin Trivia: *During that mad heatwave of 1976 I decided it was time to pop the question to a certain lady . . .*

Mom kept saying how pleased she was that things were now back to "normal" after the Abbi incident. But I knew different. Things had changed between Abbi and me—or at least, *I'd* changed toward *her*. She was still the noisy and lively little girl she'd always been, but as she got older, I really allowed myself to experience and, I suppose, enjoy her.

"Happy birthday!" sang Abbi as she shoved the ear of her donkey up her nose. I swiped the last piece of soggy toast from the kitchen table and smiled my acknowledgment at Mom's effort toward my birthday breakfast, twenty-four hours before the actual day. A huge fry-up complete with fairy cakes (courtesy of Abbi) and a magnificent masterpiece of an oil painting (again, courtesy of Abbi). Carla and I were off to Barcelona for the weekend to see her father, take in the sights and, most of all, have a well-earned rest. I was exhausted thanks to the demands of my job and constant study to keep up-to-date with ever-changing IT trends.

"I bought some Marmite in for you!" said Mom.

"I don't like Marmite any more, Mom!" I protested as Abbi jumped onto my knee, wriggled about, then leaped off again, but not before trying to carefully place the rancid donkey into my mouth.

"Abbs, sit still!" chastised Mom.

"Lois eat donkey!"

"I'm really not happy about you flying."

"I'll be fine!"

"Just because that millennium bug didn't happen last New Year's Day doesn't mean it couldn't happen any time now. I don't want your plane getting into all sorts of trouble."

"Mom, I'm in IT and I know that that's not going to happen. It was all a mix-up." I sometimes thought my mother assumed I typed letters for a living.

"If you say so," she conceded.

Carla's dad greeted us at the airport, clearly repressing his enthusiasm, while the two of us found it much easier to let go judging by the squeals of happiness at the sight of real-life palm trees.

"I'm just glad you could come out and fit me into your

busy schedule. I hear you're some big executive now, Lois!"

"I don't know who told you that!" I laughed.

"Corey."

I tried not to look away at the mention of Corey's name. But flashes of our last meeting popped into my head, before I could banish the memory into the secret compartment marked "don't go there" in my head.

Carla's dad hadn't changed much, apart from wisps of gray strands in his newly acquired beard and a slight paunch which stretched his shirt ever so slightly. I wondered if he knew about Calvin.

"Come on, girls, let's get you back to the apartment and I'll show you around."

Carla's dad had opened a bar in Castadefells, a small seaside town, and lived nearby in Gava Mar in a small, tastefully decorated one-bedroom apartment.

"Hope she's cut out the snoring, because you'll have to share an airbed!" he said as Carla threw him an evil look.

Placing my pull-along case beside a glass cabinet containing pictures of his children, I was surprised to see one of myself with the others, standing by the rec, mud on each of our shoes. I must have been about eight years old. Three years after Dad died and there I was, playing with my friends.

"I'll leave you girls to freshen up. I've left the address of the bar. Take a taxi and come meet me later?"

"Okay. But just for a bit, though, Dad." Translation: Carla had no intention of spending more than the required time with her father. She had other plans, which perhaps included hooking up with as many Spanish men as possible to fill the void Fred had left behind.

"You are so boring!" she whined when I requested a quick snooze after returning from the bar and a very long walk up and down Las Ramblas.

"I'm just a bit exhausted! We only flew in this morning."

"On a two-hour flight!"

I kicked off my sneakers.

"We've got to sample the nightlife, and I don't mean Dad's old-biddy bar either. Apparently that big shopping center we went to turns into a huge multiplex nightclub after about ten. So if we leave soon, we could make it for twelve . . ."

My eyes widened in horror.

Remember to find the time to have fun, Lowey.

And so I did. If you call "attempting to breathe inside a club thick with cigarette smog and fending off any drunken reveler who thought it their right to air-thrust behind you on the dance floor" fun!

Outside, away from the crowds, Carla slipped her swollen feet out of her red stiletto shoes and placed them neatly together, next to my sensible footwear of rounded-toe slip-ons. As we sat on the pavement, the cool night air instantly dried the beads of sweat gathering beneath my blouse.

"Don't you ever get . . . lonely?" she suddenly asked.

"Nope," I said abruptly and quickly took another sip of my drink as one more drunken reveler shot out of the bar and staggered toward Carla.

"*Guapa!*" he sang.

She rolled her eyes slowly and with exaggeration, then turned her back to the man. "As I was saying . . ." she said.

"And as I was saying, no, I don't get lonely."

"But you live in that apartment, all alone."

"So?" For one horrible second, I thought she was angling to move back in with me.

"I can't even remember you with a guy—"

"Yes, I know, I know . . . but take it from me, I really am not lonely. I love my life . . ." I caught the expression of pity etched onto my best friend's face. I knew she'd never truly understand me. No one did, except my dad.

"Why?"

"Why?"

"You heard!"

"Carla, I like my own company. I know you moved straight back in with your mom after splitting with Fred, but that's you."

"This isn't about me. You're only twenty-three, yet you act a bit like a pensioner. I've even had to drag you out today, otherwise you'd have slept the whole damn time. Need I go on?"

"Go ahead," I encouraged. So Carla continued her assassination of my life. My "obsession" with work. Hardly ever going out to clubs, sticking mainly to the after-work crowd of Keitho, Matt and Jamie. My lack of experimentation with "club wear," metallic make-up or hairstyles. I let her finish, too tired to argue. Besides, I'd never felt the need to explain myself to anyone.

"And . . ." continued Carla, sipping on her cocktail, eyebrows scrunching as if thinking of what to say next. It came. "I'm glad we did this. Came to Spain. I mean, apart from seeing the old man, it's good for us to . . . I dunno . . . clear the air and do stuff together."

We were so different. Our lives were clearly shifting toward opposite destinations.

"I'm glad too. It's actually nice not having to think about the stresses of back home."

"Oh, like, what key to press on the computer?" She snorted at her own unfunny joke. However, unbeknown to her or anyone, my stress levels had actually increased recently, thanks to Mr. Purvadis, my landlord, informing me he wanted to sell the apartment.

"Oh, just buzz off *por favor*!" she spat at the guy who still lingered around us, clearly thrilled at the shape of Carla's *trasero* in that tight-fitting dress.

My tummy muscles tensed when she predictably leaped onto the subject of Corey. Whenever Carla and I attempted to bond he'd always pop up.

"I knew about you two." She sipped her drink. "You and my brother."

Perhaps it was the hint of neon light shining on the side of her face, but she suddenly looked evil.

"Did you think I was an idiot and wouldn't find out?"

"Who told you?" My voice quivered slightly.

"Mom let it slip one day. You know how she can never keep anything to herself. I was so peeved that you didn't tell me, you know, then. But now I'm grateful."

"Because?"

She sipped at the cocktail. "You and my bro—yuck!"

"Thanks."

"No problem. For what it's worth, I think the slut actually liked you."

"Yeah, right!" I said nonchalantly, as I took another sip of alcohol.

"And you obviously liked him, too."

"That was then."

I disappeared inside the bar, returning ten minutes later with a plate of *patatas bravas*.

"I think you still carry a torch for him," she said, dipping into the plate of food. I had hoped she would have forgotten the conversation, but alcohol, it seemed, made her sharper than ever. I shook my head, hoping she'd change the subject soon.

"I've met someone," she finally said.

"What's he like?"

"A city investment banker, I kid you not! And, more importantly, Rob's the absolute love of my life . . . I hope. Why d'you think I haven't even looked at another bloke since we got here? I know it sounds weird, but every time I look at Rob, I just get this urge . . ."

"To ravish him?"

A giggle.

"To just get married and have his babies."

"Is that all you want out of life?"

"What's wrong with that?"

"Nothing, but you're only young."

"I can't believe YOU of all people are saying that. Like you even act your age!"

I ignored that. "What about getting a job?"

"I have one at the lingerie shop on Oxford Street. Well, I *did* anyway . . . But that's beside the point."

That comment further alerted me to our differences. There was I, loaded with ambition, wanting to pursue the highest level work-wise, when all Carla wanted to do was bake cakes.

"Drink up then, there's so much more booze to get through!" I said, with as much fake enthusiasm as possible.

The remainder of the break went well, with visits to the beach and a trip to Barcelona Zoo. But very soon I was back in England, facing some major decisions.

Mr. Purvadis had been gracious enough to give me three months' notice on the apartment, by which time it would definitely be going on the market. I consulted the miscellaneous section of *The Manual*, hoping Dad could impart words of inspiration. Something or *someone* led me to *Risks.*

> *Go on. Take a risk from time to time. Nothing life-threatening or unsafe, but with things that perhaps have the power to propel you closer to what/who you want to be. Am I making sense? Probably not. I'll give you an example. No, I can't. Sorry. I've always played it safe—and look where I am now. I so wish I had taken a few small risks. I won't tell you what they were, Lois, because it just feels too painful to write them down. Sorry, babe, I'm just having a bad day.*

My dad had obviously been on a downer. The pain and regret seeping from the pages was so real and vivid. I had to do something—I couldn't let my dad down—I just wasn't sure what.

At work, I couldn't escape this nagging feeling. Even Keitho's shenanigans with his chatroom buddies didn't have its usual power to lift me. It wasn't until about a week later, sitting in the staff canteen, that the answer to the question finally became clear.

I was going to buy my apartment from Mr. Purvadis.

A risk.

What with Carla telling me what an idiot I was to "tie myself down," it still felt like the right thing to do. Even the Bingo Caller echoed caution, prattling on about the 1980s property crash. But I knew that for the first time in my entire life I was living in a place that felt like home, and if I lost money in the process, so be it. Besides, I was going to listen to my dad.

Try not to allow anyone's opinion to dictate how you see yourself.

Plus, I needed a home . . .

"I'd never buy a apartment," offered Jamie, filing her nails while ignoring an incoming call.

"Me either!" agreed Keitho as Matt appeared from a job.

"Don't listen to them, Lois. Keitho's a drifter and Jamie's waiting for her secret lover to buy her a love shack!"

Jamie threw him a sharp gaze.

"Thanks, Matt!" I said sincerely. He threw me a sweet smile in response and, not for the first time, I felt myself blush like an idiot.

Working late soon became a regular occurrence and something I didn't mind, especially when it was just Matt and me. It was easy to get through the time, laughing and joking about nothing much in particular.

"That's me done for the night," I said, switching off the computer.

"How many 'Have you switched the computer on?' questions have you actually asked today?" queried Matt.

"Just two."

"A slight improvement on yesterday. Our call outs would halve overnight if users just remembered to switch the damn thing on before reporting a problem!"

I smiled. "But then we'd be out of a job!"

"Didn't think of that. You up to anything tonight?"

"A bit of study. Television. And you?"

"A beer by the TV sounds good."

Part of me wanted to say more, to leap out of this sea of small talk. But my nerves won over.

"Goodnight then, Matt."

"Night."

I turned to the door.

"I'm leaving myself in thirty minutes," he said. I wasn't sure if that was an invitation.

"Okay, well, I'll see you tomorrow, then."

"You will. Bright and early."

I pretended to search for something in my pocket.

"Looking for something?"

"Just my subway card."

"Come out with me at the weekend, Lois."

I thought he'd never ask.

"I can't believe you're going out with Matt," said Jamie as she tapped at the keyboard. As always, the radio sang and phones rang off the hook in the background. The daily soundtrack to my working life.

"It's just dinner!"

"But without the rest of us . . . That's what I'd call a date."

"If it turns into something more . . ." I began, before trailing off. It suddenly felt strange revealing personal details to someone other than Carla.

"So, what are you wearing?"

"Trousers and a top."

Jamie scanned my comfortable trouser and shirt combo. "So, he's going to see you just like he does every day. Nice . . ." she said teasingly.

"What . . . what do you think I should wear?" I asked shyly. As if in the presence of a master, desperate for her to share her words of feminine wisdom that would ensure I didn't make a total mess of my date with Matt.

"I suppose I could wear my nice jeans . . ."

"Let's go shopping!"

I hated shopping at the best of times and failed to see the glee that obviously gripped Jamie as she announced her intentions. But I reluctantly agreed, because, as Jamie put it, she'd known Matt for years, and knew what he liked and disliked. She'd be the perfect style adviser, apparently.

That night I gazed into my wardrobe. At the high-necked shirts. The odd pair of trendy jeans, but nothing you could call overly sexy and sophisticated. I was plain old Lois Bates, Kevin's daughter, trying to make her mark in this world. I sat on the end of my bed (which hadn't seen any action during its lifetime) and sighed inwardly. The thought of going out with Matt filled me with excitement but also with fear. I reached under my second pillow and picked up *The Manual*.

* * *

"This is going to be great!" sang Jamie as we walked up Oxford Street on Saturday. It felt strange spending time with her outside the office, away from the others. And as we bonded over coffee, she told me about her family, namely her mother.

"Boyfriend after boyfriend that one!" she said with a slurp of coffee.

"It must have been hard."

"Kind of . . . yeah!"

"So what about this mystery man of yours then?"

"What about him?" She looked down at her empty cup.

"I'm not asking you to tell me who he is."

"Good, because I won't."

"Is he married?"

"Single."

"Older?"

"Same age. And that's it. Come on, let's hit the shops!" Which I did, though secretly I was longing to be back at home snuggling on the sofa with a steaming cup of tea. Jamie skipped and dragged me along to an endless array of clothes shops and department stores.

"I'm not sure about the dress . . ."

"But it's lovely, Lois." Jamie fingered the tiny backless black dress I suspected would fit Abbi.

"I'm just not sure it's really me. It's a little short . . ."

"Matt will love it," she teased with a wink.

"You think so?"

Five minutes later Jamie and I stared toward the same mirror.

"You look stunning. I told you!" she said. I stared at my reflection and, surprisingly, didn't mind what was staring back at me—a mature, twenty-three-year-old SEXY woman. I had to rub my eyes just to see if this *was* really me, while Jamie released my frizz from its ponytail and piled it on top of my head, allowing various curly strands to tumble toward my cheeks as we both stared at my reflection. The dress clung to my curves very flatteringly, making everything look . . . rather good?

The two of us stood there staring at the mirror, and suddenly I wished this moment could be caught on camera. And although this would never be one of those ugly duckling to swan stories, I did feel a little sex-kittenish if I do say so myself. Watch out, Matty, I thought. Perhaps it was because I'd never been called "stunning" before, or because I was exhausted, or because a part of me wanted to please Matt, but I ended up paying for that backless dress with only an ounce of trepidation. I also bought (with Jamie's insistence) a pair of red "take me against the wall" killer heels I couldn't envisage ever being able to walk straight in.

The last stop was the make-up counter of a department store. I wasn't sure about the lipstick—bright blood-red and certainly not right with my coloring—even though Jamie assured me it was this season's shade and the assistant couldn't have cared less enough to offer an opinion. So I settled on buying my first ever foundation along with the lipstick.

Miscellaneous: Make-up
Your mom was never one for war paint—although she did like to roll on a bit of lipstick during our early dates. I suppose what attracted me to her in the first place was her natural beauty. And that's what will get you noticed

by the right boy. It's such a myth that men prefer you to pile it on. Less is more.

You're probably thinking all those girls at school with the shorter skirts and the brightest red lipstick will get all the guys' attention. Erm . . . okay, they probably do . . . erm . . . as I said . . . talk to your mother about this one . . .

I turned the page, realizing that Dad had written this Miscellaneous entry for my teenage years, because right now it wasn't making much sense.

I moved on.

Miscellaneous: First dates

First off, I hope this date wasn't influenced by his looks. So what if his teeth weren't as crooked the day he asked you out—even Quasimodo had a good heart. Give him a chance whatever his race, dress sense, height, job status. If you stay focused on the wrong things, you could let a good man go. BUT—bad breath? No exceptions.

So, some male has finally come to his senses, noticed what a rare, precious diamond you are and has asked you on a real date. Or perhaps you've followed the entry on asking a boy out (this wouldn't surprise me, considering how assertive women are these days: have you seen the Blondie video?).

This may sound old-fashioned, but don't wear anything too sexy. A skirt up to your armpits may thrill a man gazing at a magazine, but on his arm he wants a classy, attractive woman. And no, I'm not saying that because you are my little girl. Okay, maybe I am, but depending on what age you are reading this, you may or may not have already worked this out for yourself: men are very visual creatures and he'll merely absorb what he sees. So, giving him a certain impression early on perhaps isn't the best thing to do.

Also, don't go for any wacky hairdos (I remember the beehive!). And don't overdo the perfume. I don't know about him, but I have a very sensitive nose. I remember your mother almost killing me with her overpowering scent when we were out in those early days. She always thought I had a cold because I kept sneezing into her soup.

Turn up on time and get all that "fashionably late" crap out of your head (newsflash: he'll hate it). And if he's the latecomer (assuming he doesn't make a habit of it), be cool and don't nag the bloke—there'll be plenty of time for that later on in the relationship.

So, what do you talk about?

Sports are always safe bets with guys. So ask him about his hobbies and interests (without sounding like the world's biggest snooper). But if he doesn't LIKE soccer, make your excuses and get out of there real quick as it's clearly an emergency! Please. That's all I ask of you, dear daughter.

And DON'T UNDER ANY CIRCUMSTANCES bring up the following on your first or any other date:

- *how much he can potentially earn, minus tax*
- *swear words in other languages*
- *kids' names*
- *your dinner.*

Don't worry if the conversation dries up midway. If you're right for each other, there shouldn't be many silences, and if there are they will be comfortable ones. Ones where you won't be nervously thinking of what to say next or filled by mounting dread at how badly the evening has gone. They will be just like the ones me and your mom enjoyed.

Also, look out for wet patches under his arms—this is probably nerves. However, if it still happens by the second date, feel free to ask him about any possible medical conditions. And, lastly:

- *trust your instincts*
- *don't let him sweet talk you into doing things you feel unsafe doing*
- *carry extra cash*
- *if Richard Gere walks past in a pair of tight, stripy shorts, simply IGNORE.*

I know you don't need me to tell you the next bit, but I will anyway because I'm your dad: a film, grub, concert, flowers, drinks, cab home, anything paid for by a boy doesn't mean you have to pay him back in kind . . . if you know what I mean. And if you don't—great!

Lastly (and this is it—I promise!), don't forget to just be yourself.

Being myself was harder to achieve than I'd imagined, especially when teetering on three-inch heels, my little toes killing me as Matt moved in for a hello kiss on my cheek.

"This is lovely," I said, shrugging off my coat—to reveal the backless dress. As well as being half naked, it still felt strange being with Matt minus Jamie and Keitho, in an environment oozing with romance—AND in someplace other than South London or the immediate area around the office. Matt had taken me to a gorgeous little Italian restaurant on Edgware Road.

"They do really nice pizza here. You know, in those huge ovens," he said, immediately ogling the menu. No compliments. He'd hardly even looked at me.

"You look great," I said, admiring his crisp white shirt unbuttoned sexily at the neck, a wisp of hair just noticeable in between a button. In contrast, his face was freshly shaven and just so cute.

He looked up. "Thanks."

The waiter appeared. "Any drinks, sir, madam?"

Admittedly Matt's lack of compliments was far from thrilling; even I was prepared to stretch to "You look lovely!" whenever Abbi paraded round in her pink tutu.

I felt like an ass as I scanned the menu. For a soon-to-be homeowner and astute(ish) businesswoman, a goldfish had more experience when it came to dating, and it showed. My database of witty tales was now seemingly infected with a virus. Okay, enough with the IT talk.

In between mouthfuls of pizza we did manage to cover an array of interesting subjects—like, whether Bob in Accounts was shagging Dee in Personnel. At first the familiarity was comforting, but I soon began to think this was just another after-work gathering, minus the others.

"I'd really like to go into maintaining networks. That's where the money is," said Matt, placing the last of his pizza into his mouth.

"I have heard that."

"What do you think's the next big IT explosion? I mean, after the Internet—that will be hard to beat," he asked.

I sipped at my Coke and wondered what Corey was

doing, thousands of miles away in Paris. Was he, too, out dining with a girl? In some fashionable little café overlooking—

"Lois?"

"Sorry. What did you say?"

"The next big thing?"

"Erm . . . well . . . it's got to be wireless internet . . . for homes, cafés, even restaurants," I said.

"No way. It will be free internet calls over the phone. Everyone will be doing it in a couple of years. Sooner, in fact."

My mind drifted to Corey again. Wondered what it would be like, here, with him. We'd probably be discussing the Top Ten of Lo Bag's Embarrassing Moments: starting with the time I fell down that ditch, exposing my daisy-print underwear as Carla and her dad stifled guffaws. Like Matt, he would have ordered the meat supreme pizza, but instead of red wine, a beer.

"You're miles away. What are you thinking about?"

"Nothing important. Believe me. Now, where were we?"

At the end of the night Matt dropped me off without wading in for a kiss. A true gentleman, I suppose. Besides, I felt the date had gone quite well (although I hardly had a list of dates to compare it with). I hesitated on whether to call Carla for a post-date analysis, but decided to keep this one to myself. At least until I could report on something a bit more exciting.

I hoped that would be soon.

Monday and Matt was fine. Perhaps distant. But I understood his need for privacy, wary of becoming Monday-morning office gossip.

"Lois, I'm not sure what's going on with you, but you'd

better snap out of it," said Keitho in that New Zealand drawl the following day as I returned from lunch.

I made a confused face as he led me out of the office, away from the others.

"You were assigned a really important job last night, but you chose to go home—"

"Excuse me? I was assigned four jobs after four p.m. last night, the last one around a quarter to six. So I completed them all before I went home. Two log-on problems, slow email connections and a broken mouse. I did those."

"Well, I had a complaint from the director's PA saying she called the helpdesk way before five p.m."

"I didn't get any notification from Jamie or Matt . . . Not even an email."

"You sort that out with them, Lois. But just for the record, I'm not happy about this. Anyone but the director's office!"

I wasn't keen on Keitho's tone, but decided to let it go.

"I'm sorry, it won't happen again, okay?"

"Make sure it doesn't. Sloppy stuff like this reflects on all of us."

do we ever really grow up?

Kevin Trivia: ***I now realize it's best not to buy a new car unless you're mega minted—they lose hundreds as soon as you drive it out of the showroom!***

"There you go, Ms. Bates, it's all yours!" said the handsome salesman with a touch too much oil in his hair, as he handed me the keys to the sporty gray MG. It drove like a dream and, passing the busy streets of New Kent Road, through to Deptford and then home, I imagined Dad beside me with a huge grin on his face, ticking me off for my bad driving habits and wanting to swap seats, just to show me how to really handle "this machine."

I was desperate to show off my new car, and as Carla was away with Rob the City Banker, I headed to Mom's.

"Wow, it's a great little car!" enthused the Bingo Caller.

Mom joined us outside, Abbi trying—without success—to zap free from her grip.

"I hope it doesn't go too fast!" moaned Mom, with a sharp squint of her eyes.

"Faster the better!" enthused the Bingo Caller as I ruffled Abbi's soft hair. As always, her hand remained glued to that almost decomposed donkey, which, thankfully, wasn't stuck up her nostril this time.

"It's fine, Mom," I said, determined she wasn't about to dampen my mood.

Abbi sprang free from her captor and I clasped her hand.

"Can I have a go?" she asked in that sweet tone reserved for confectionery requests or when asked if she'd done a bad thing.

"No!" said Mom.

"Why?" she asked.

"I said no."

But like a dog determined to hold on to a particularly juicy bone, Abbi persisted. "Pleeease, Mommy! Please."

"Don't worry, Mom. We'll just go and get some gas then we'll stop off at Mr. Tally's and I'll have her back in about twenty minutes. Twenty-five at the most." It felt necessary to list my plans for Abbi. Ever since she'd wandered off, Mom's paranoia had, quite understandably, amplified.

"Well . . . Oh go on then!"

"I'll look after her, Mom. Promise."

"I know you will."

My little sister jumped up and ran around in a small circle like a dog chasing its tail.

"She's just happy to spend time with you," said Mom.

I checked Abbi's hands for any sticky substances and attempted to ban the donkey.

"Noooo, Lois!" she protested as I strapped her and, reluctantly, the smelly donkey into the seat.

"You are potty trained, right?"

"Lois, I'm four!"

"Just checking."

Offending half the driving population of Charlton with my ultra-slow pace, I pulled into the gas station.

"Out!" I ordered playfully.

"Me and donkey can wait for you."

My mind flashed back again to two years ago. Abbi missing. The panic. The sorrow.

"I don't think so. Let's go and pay together. There's a toy in it for you."

"Purple dinosaur on TV?"

"Maybe."

"And a chocolate?"

"Done."

I took Abbi's hand, helping her skip up to the paying booth, and then I heard my name.

"Lois?" a voice from behind me asked.

I turned, taking in the woman with a double buggy, shopping bags swinging from the handles. Short, unkempt hair, overlong gold chain, cleavage in need of plastic surgery, and dressed in a tatty tracksuit.

"It is you! It's me . . . don't you remember? We went to school together!"

The woman would have been a few years older than me, and as far as I remembered the older girls never really mixed with us.

"You're Lois, right? Lois Bates?"

"Yes."

"It's me!" She smiled, revealing smoke-stained yellow

teeth, yet still I couldn't place her. Abbi wriggled about in my hands.

"I'm sorry . . ."

"Sharlene Rockingham."

I located my shock. "Sharlene?"

"That's me!" She bent down to attend to one of the children, who'd begun to sob deeply. "It's me all right—SHUT UP YOU LITTLE BRAT!" she screamed at the child, which of course Abbi found totally hilarious, but for me it induced a barrage of unhappy memories. Memories I had long escaped from and had no intention of revisiting.

"These are my two, Robbie and Raven. Say hello to Auntie Lois!" she squealed.

"Hello!" I said with a short wave. The children's sobs subsided quickly, replaced with blank looks.

"I've got two more at school, Ricarde and Reeka. How old's your one, then?"

"She's my little sister."

"No kids then?"

"Say hi, Abbs," I said, ignoring her question, needing time to think.

Abbi refused to oblige of course, perhaps feeling cheated at the absence of the purple prehistoric teddy currently sitting on the gas station shelf or perhaps she was sensing what an evil, manipulative, horrible cow this girl had been and probably still was.

Sharlene's face drooped. "So, no kids then?"

"No."

"Oh . . . That's a shame," she enthused.

"You think so?' I replied sarcastically.

"We live up on the Hankle Estate. Ricarde is seven and he lives with his dad. Reeka is five, and then I've got these two. One and two. Just waiting to get re-housed at the moment."

"I really have to go, but it was nice seeing you again," I said quickly, heading for the car, pretending I'd left something, hoping she'd see what a success I'd made of MY life. I opened the door feeling the burn of her eyes upon me. And instead of the fear such a look would have invoked in the past, I felt nothing.

On hindsight, seeing Sharlene Rockingham again had been good for me. A kind of therapy I suppose. Because I realized she just didn't affect me any more. I'd moved on. I lived in a decent apartment and had a job I was good at. Well, at least, I *thought* I was good at it—because soon, mistakes began to appear. Small ones, like my call logs not being kept up-to-date, even though I was meticulous when it came to paperwork. I knew it wasn't paranoia. Someone was clearly out to get me, that much was obvious—and there were only three suspects.

Miscellaneous: Girls versus girls
I'm not saying women don't or can't get on, I just feel there's a difference in the way you are with one another and the way we boys are. The head doctors might say it has something to do with competing for us guys (and yes, your dad has had the ladies fighting over his affections in the distant past).

But just look around you, Lois. At how differently guys seem to interact with one another. Even when a guy's mad jealous of a man, at the same time, we still have a respect for him. An example? I saw this guy pull up at the gas station in a lovely red Jaguar XJ–S. Now, by the time you read this, you'll probably be using cars as mini airplanes, but let me tell you, my love, that was a beautiful machine. High-efficiency engine and the fastest automatic-transmission car in the whole wide world at 155 mph. Anyway, erm . . . getting a bit carried away there. What I'm trying to say is this: I looked at the bloke, and even though he drove a great car and had a rather fit young woman in the front seat, I also felt this surge of respect for him—even as I trekked back to my little old Ford Fiesta. And I mean that.

But this type of camaraderie I don't see with girls. Okay, you may say I only have Philomena and Ina and their constant sniping as terms of reference, but I've also seen it at MY workplace: "You wearing THAT today?" the constant competition for the best hairstyles, shoes, that kind of thing.

You are, of course, welcome to argue this point with me, but that would be a bit hard considering I'm dead!

"Well done. You found me out."

I pushed the soap dispenser button.

"It was me. Always has been," my previously silent enemy, admitted.

My suspicions had focused on Matt right from the start, so I decided to watch his actions around me. His tone of voice. How he looked at me. We'd never really spoken much about our "date" so when I decided to bring it up one afternoon, just to gage how he felt about the whole disaster, he just laughed and told me to "get over myself." As brief and as embarrassing as that exchange was, it convinced me that Matt wasn't involved. That just left Keitho, who seemed more concerned with the latest software and an online

New Zealand dating agency he'd just discovered. This just left Jamie and if I'd even bothered to suspect her in the first place, the following conversation would have taken place about a week before.

'It was me,' she said, rubbing the firm's frothy soap onto her palms, as if in glee. "I did wonder how long I could get away with messing up your call logs and—"

"Forgetting to tell me a user had rung through with an urgent problem, or telling me it's a software problem when it's actually a very urgent hardware problem."

Jamie rinsed her hands in the swanky glass basin and turned to leave.

"Which just happened to be on the director's computer. Again," she smiled, turning to face me.

"And that's it? That's all you're going to say to me, Jamie?"

She tilted her head. "What else is there? It's not as if you have any proof. I've been really careful."

"I just thought you'd made a mistake at first . . . I really wanted to believe that."

"No mistake. And if you want to think about reporting me—Keitho will back *me* up. Every time."

"Why did you sabotage all those jobs, making it look like I was slacking off? Why did you do that to me? I thought we were friends?"

"One shopping trip hardly qualifies us as that. And apart from anything else, you have to be the coldest person I have ever met, Lois Bates. I'm into fun, me, wouldn't usually be seen dead outside of after-work drinks with someone like you."

Jamie pressed the button on the hand-dryer, the sound effectively drowning out my next question. But she'd heard me. "The shopping, I only did for my own means. I knew that if I got you kitted out for a date with Matt looking all tarted up, he'd go off you in all that bad make-up. And it was bad. I just wanted you to look as ridiculous as possible, and you did. And he saw that too. You see, I know what he likes: what is it he once said . . . ? "Less is more." That's it "less is more." We talk, you see. A lot. I know that his favorite color is cobalt blue. That he loves basketball. That he once watched the ballet version of *Romeo and Juliet* and really enjoyed it, something he'd never tell Keitho. I know everything there is to know about him!" She was shouting now, her voice fierce but passionate.

"Jamie. What did I ever do to you?" I whispered. "This still doesn't make any sense."

"That's one thing we agree on then. First you walk into this firm with no real experience and take the position I've been after for ages . . . Then you just lean over to Matt and take him from me, too. Now, that wasn't fair." Her voice broke and suddenly she crumpled before my eyes. The transition so quick, so spectacular, my words failed to come out in the way I'd hoped, if at all.

"You took him away from me, Lois!" she sobbed.

"I didn't . . . ! I mean, I had no idea you were ever together. I thought you were in love with that secret—" Crush, who of course, happened to be Matt.

And with this new information, part of me wanted to console Jamie while another part wanted to get well away.

"I'm s . . . sorry," I stuttered.

"So am I!" she choked in between crying.

It suddenly hit me that the friendships I'd carved out for myself for more than two years had all been an illusion. I thought I'd been part of a team, a working team that included me in everything it did and experienced—but now it would seem nothing was left. Again.

So, I decided it was time to move on in my career. Perhaps Jamie had prompted this decision, but beyond that I needed to make my dad proud of me by becoming the success he knew I could be—and that was less possible with all the Jamie/Matt madness around me.

So, that evening, I emailed an employment agency before meeting Carla for a drink.

"I can't believe you're letting this bitch hound you out of your job," she enthused. She'd just been telling me about her and Rob's "wicked" time at a country retreat.

"I'm getting a bit bored anyway. A change of scenery wouldn't go amiss. Plus, the money's a lot better."

Carla raised her eyebrow at the mention of money. I'd always been wary of discussing paychecks and promotions with her because, together, that wasn't what we were about. Carla had never kept a job for more than two months, and ever since I'd known her welfare and a well-off boyfriend kept her in shoes. But I remembered how easy it had been to drift apart before, and this couldn't happen again. She was my only true girlfriend and the situation with Jamie had reinforced that resolve.

I changed the subject to one of common ground. "Guess who I saw the other day?"

"Who?"

"Sharlene Rockingham."

"Noooo!"

"Oh yes!" I replied, sounding not unlike that kid Sharlene used to threaten every moment she could.

"That little bitch! What she put you through . . ."

I felt my stomach muscles constrict at the memory.

"Did she see you?"

"Surrounded by about a hundred kids, yes."

"Is she a schoolteacher?"

"She has four children."

"But she's only—"

"Our age, I know!"

"Actually, I remember now. She got knocked up straight after school by that thug Ricky Wotshisface who's in prison now. Corey ran into her brother once."

My stomach flipped at the mention of Corey's name. "That must have been dad number two, because number one lives with her eldest."

"Oh yeah, that's right, and then she got knocked up by two blokes within a year. Brothers, apparently! What. A. Slut."

"How do you know all this?"

"I remember Daisy from our year telling me when I ran into her in Lee Green."

"You never told me."

"I didn't think you'd want to know! You've left all that behind you."

This disclosure shocked but secretly thrilled me. "You think so?"

"Of course. You own your home, have a job with prospects, drive a fancy car. You're sorted!"

Even though I was touched to hear this from Carla, I knew that all I'd achieved still wasn't enough. Dad wanted more for me. He'd died before he could fulfill his dreams so wasn't it natural he'd want me to do more with my life? Reach higher than I could ever have imagined, fulfill his wildest expectations? Be respected, strive for financial security, work hard? Luckily, I was now part of the world's fastest growing industry, so I was in a good place to achieve this.

I wasn't about to let my dad down.

Some of the IT employment agencies had promised to find me work within days. Days turned into two weeks before they finally shoved the address of a suitable interview into my inbox. I almost leaped onto my desk with excitement while I studied the brief: five grand more AND a company car. This was the big-time and I told myself I'd get this job.

And I did.

The day I received confirmation, I couldn't help almost skipping into work, awash with the glow of happiness—and freedom.

"I heard about the job. Congratulations," said Matt by the office cooler.

"Thank you," I replied sincerely as I switched on my computer. Just four more weeks of this to go, I thought.

"Sorry things didn't work out," he said.

"Me too, but I think the new job's going to be great. Might even get to build networks, which would be something different."

"I meant me and you."

I stared at my computer screen, not knowing what to say.

"Maybe you should look closer to home for a date," I said, as my eyes darted to Jamie's empty desk.

Matt's eyes followed then shot straight back to me. I wasn't sure if I saw regret or sadness, but all that didn't matter any more. I'd be leaving in a month—and I couldn't wait!

* * *

My last day finally came and was mostly spent saying goodbyes and pretending to "love" the limp bunch of flowers and sterling-silver bracelet from H. Samuel presented to me by Keitho. I cleared my desk for the last time, uttering an even limper excuse about having to catch a train and thus not being able to make my own leaving drinks. I doubted anyone gave a damn, especially as the foursome had quickly become a comfortable threesome over the weeks that I worked my notice, with Jamie not speaking to me except when absolutely necessary. But I couldn't have cared less, as it was time to move on to bigger and better things. Relationships with people weren't supposed to last anyway.

"Take care," said Matt with a chaste peck. Keitho offered a salute while Jamie muttered "Good riddance" as I removed the flowers from their makeshift vase.

Something inside me threatened to explode. You see, I'd been fair, kind even, by not embarrassing Jamie and revealing all to Matt. But her time had just run out.

"Jamie, if YOU are to blame for me leaving then thanks a bundle," I said calmly.

"What are you talking about?"

"Because of your helpfulness, I'll now be earning over twenty-seven grand, have a company car and, oh . . . an expense account!"

Stunned silence.

I continued. "Oh, I've made a mistake . . . because I already have a car, I get to have a car "allowance," which means an extra four grand on my basic, which means . . ." my eyes rolled as I pretended to count, "almost thirty-two grand a year—at MY age. See ya! And thanks again!"

The look forming on Jamie's face was worth it. And just to twist it up a little more, I decided to dispose of the vase of water quickly and economically. In her face.

"You cow!" she roared, rubbing furiously at her smudged eyes as the boys looked on (Keitho ringing his hands at the possibility of a catfight). I gathered my things and made for the door, shaking at my impromptu act. I wasn't even sure what had possessed me—years of bullying at school or the need to see her make-up run—all I knew was it felt good.

> *Most negative emotions take a lot of energy. Energy that could be used more positively and someplace else. So don't let anyone have that much power over you. I could have done with this advice just before kicking Tommy Arden's head in during games, but that's another story.*
>
> *Just let it go.*

Being part of a multinational construction firm meant having to blend into a large team in a busy IT department, a faceless number traveling round various building sites to set up and maintain computer networks. A lot of the time I'd be the only female on a site full of randy builders quick to offer a wolf whistle before realizing I was part of the team.

Luckily, traveling to different sites meant "friendships" could be kept brisk and light, just the way I preferred things. I was also the only girl among a team of nerds—like Keitho nerd but worse—men with bad hair days and a questionable taste in ties.

* * *

Of course Mom insisted I was overworking and she was probably right. So Carla and Rob inviting me round for dinner was a welcome diversion. Also, it would be my first sighting of this Rob guy since their romance had begun.

I should have known Carla was up to something, though, the minute she suggested I "put on a frock," which I did after a quick shopping expedition. Ever since the Matt incident I'd decided to actually experiment more with my look, but had yet to trust myself in a dress, until now.

"Hello, Lois, I've heard so much about you!" enthused Rob, planting a smarmy kiss on each cheek.

He was skinnier than I'd imagined, with a large nose and huge hands (but, as Carla once disclosed, he confidently upheld the famous stereotype). Placing a bottle of wine into his arm, I followed him into an open-plan lounge, tastefully decorated with a huge painting of red splotches as the centerpiece of the room. The man was obviously minted and I'd just given him a three-dollar bottle of wine. Oh well.

"Take a seat. Can I get you anything?" he asked, taking my coat.

"I'm okay for now. Thanks. Where's Carla?"

"She's in the kitchen . . ."

"Babe!" Carla called out as she walked toward me, a dot of flour on her nose and dressed in an apron.

"Where's my friend Carla? What have you done with her?" I joked as we hugged. I'd obviously failed to notice just how much she was changing. Carla—cooking! The Carla I knew and loved would never slave over a stove and a cookbook or put on an apron to please a man.

Men were usually trying to please *her!*

"You can talk. You look wicked!"

"No I don't," I said shyly.

"That dress is a little tight. I approve," she joked, nudging me a little too hard and pulling at the jersey fabric.

"It isn't tight!" I protested.

"What I mean is, I can actually see a hint of curve! Oh and, shock horror, you've actually changed your hairstyle! Go Lois!"

"I just straightened it a little. Nothing major. It'll be back to major frizz in the morning!"

I sat down on a tall bar stool that had the magic of making your bum look twice as huge as it really was, as Carla chopped onions like a pro.

"Isn't he great?"

"Yeah, he seems nice. What's for dinner?"

"Paella, what else?"

Paella was the *only* dish she'd ever mastered—ever since fourth-year Home Economics after Mr. Greenwood had commended her so highly at our Spanish Foodfest day. Although over the years she'd experiment with sausage meat instead of prawns or noodles instead of rice, it was always paella and I was delighted that some things hadn't changed.

I sat on the huge sofa, which resembled a blob of chewing gum, while Rob joined Carla on the other one, slobbering over her like a St. Bernard on Viagra, planting her with kiss upon kiss. Carla seemed happy enough, if the beaming glow of happiness spreading across her face like a fresh sunset was anything to go by. My mind began to race over—wondering how anyone could afford to live in such an apartment.

"Guess what?" whispered Carla as I followed her into the kitchen.

"Rob's invited one of his friends." Before I could question her a bit more, the doorbell sounded. Rob's "friend" Oliver slid out of his coat and I realized he too was very skinny and too old—he must have been at least a hundred years old. Well, thirty-seven apparently, but way too old for me.

"One of my oldest friends," announced Rob as Oliver smiled in my direction.

Oliver was pleasant enough company for an older man—we even had stuff in common, like a love of RnB, *Coronation Street* and a fondness for overripe bananas.

As we ate, I found myself mindful of my table manners and hoping a rice grain wasn't stuck between my teeth.

"They seem really in love, don't they?" whispered Oliver as Carla fed Rob a forkful of chocolate cake.

"It's sweet . . ." I lied.

"Makes you sick!"

We both giggled wildly as a self-satisfied smile appeared on Carla's face.

So, throughout the course of the evening, it was easy enough to warm to Oliver. And when he walked me to my car and asked for my phone number and whether he could pick me up the following weekend for blackened bananas and cake, I thought, Why not?

Oliver was great. A real gentleman who even opened doors for me and stood up at the table when I excused myself. Not the best-looking man I had ever seen, but what I found most attractive was his confidence. He was just so self assured and I liked it.

Oliver and I slept together six weeks after meeting and I felt okay about that. It didn't set the world on fire, but I enjoyed the affection and how he took time to kiss me, look at me and totally drink me in, whether we were in a restaurant or sitting in a traffic hold up. But when he told me he loved me just over two months after meeting, I could only answer with a swift "Me too," merely because it felt better than saying "Why, thank you . . ." I did try and search within and ask myself if I felt the same, but I knew I didn't. But I wanted to make this work, I really did, so when he asked if he could move in with me a month after that, I said yes. He was just so kind, so caring, it almost felt rude to say no. Even though, deep down, it felt a tad suffocating.

I managed to get work to send me up north a week before the move, just so I could escape the madness of it all and breathe. No matter how much I tried, at twenty-four, I just wasn't ready for Oliver, or a serious relationship

Miscellaneous: To move or not to move?
You may have heard the term, "Why buy a car when you can hop on and off a bus for free?" Or maybe not. When a guy asks you to move in with him, it may seem like one of the most fantastic things in the world, but think carefully about WHY you're doing it. Is it the lure of cheaper bills or do you really, really love him? Also think (and talk to him) about why HE'S doing it. Again, is it finance, or that he can't be bothered to make a proper commitment to you? Again, Lowey, I'm not saying a man's got to marry you (me and your mom lived together happily for two months before we wed), I just don't want some guy taking my precious little girl for granted. If you are satisfied for all the right reasons, then you know what you have to do—only you can make that decision.

Dad's miscellaneous entry did nothing to quell a deep feeling of dread in me at the thought of moving in with Oliver. So, instead, I decided to ignore it as I opened the door to his suitcases, pet fish and a saxophone that he admitted he'd no idea how to play.

"Our own place. This is going to be great."

"I know," I said unconvincingly.

"Just think, waking up to each other EVERY morning . . ."

I tried not to think about it and instead became transfixed with finding a place for the damn saxophone.

Before the end of our first week together, I knew I'd made a huge mistake.

Actually, the minute he moved his massive size tens into my territory, things began to change. Gone, the dashing older man who'd introduced me to a sophisticated type of male, and hello to someone I began to recognize as a lazy asshole who only occasionally made the effort to wash.

Oliver was kind enough to put in a good word for me with Rob and within days I got a call from him, tipping me off about an IT role at his firm.

Finding out I'd got a new job with the investment bank was the best news I'd received in ages, yet it was eclipsed by a wave of dread as I walked through the door of my apartment to witness an unkempt Oliver sporting a rapidly expanding waistline and using my Catalonian handkerchief to dust his saxophone!

"Hi, honey," he said in that fake American accent I'd once found soooo cute.

"Hiya," I responded as he placed the saxophone to one side and leaned over to dab at the now weakened remote-control buttons.

"What's for din—" he began, before possibly remembering I didn't do domesticity on request.

"I thought we'd get a takeaway," I replied in between yawns.

"Okay," he said, one eye on the TV and a program about racing robots. The man was almost thirty-eight.

I know you don't want to hear this, but we never grow up.

I kicked off my heels and tried to snap out of the mood I now found myself in.

"How was your day?" I asked Oliver.

"Good," he replied, staring toward the television.

"Anything you want to talk about?" I tried to remain calm.

"YES! SIR KILLALOTT."

"Oliver?"

"Sorry. Work was fine. You know how it is . . ." He made a number of hand gestures directed toward the television, then, as if suddenly remembering my physical existence, stood up, planted a wet kiss on my cheek—with one eye on the TV—before placing his bum right back down again.

"You know the job that Rob told me about?"

"Yep. Rob."

"I got it."

Pause.

"That's . . . That's marvelous," he managed in a monotone voice, eyes fixated on the TV (my new rival for Oliver's affection). Even things in the bedroom had changed; a quick fumble if his favorite soccer team won that Saturday—or if he had nothing better to do.

I stormed out of the lounge and phoned Carla.

"Give Rob a huge thank you from me. A bottle of his favorite wine is on its way."

"You don't have to do that! Besides, d'you know how much that stuff costs?"

"Well, if it wasn't for his recommendation—"

"You'd STILL have got that job, Lois."

"Thanks for that," I said with surprise. It was hard for me to see the part *I* actually played in getting the job and it was unexpected of Carla to be the one to show me.

Soon the conversation shifted.

"Rob and I are having such a good time. I just love being with him. Waking up with him. It's like we're married. Do you get that feeling with Oliver?"

I heard a triumphant roar coming from the lounge.

"Lois?"

My stomach tightened. Carla was the type of girl who'd dreamed about her wedding from the year dot, while I tried never to let it enter my head—especially when I looked at the hassle and misery it so obviously caused: Carla's mom and dad; Mom and the Bingo Caller; the majority of soap-opera marriages. To find that "special someone" Carla often spoke about was rare. My mother had found that in my dad—he was perfect—and . . . well, he died. No. I couldn't see how marriage could be for me, or cohabitation for that matter. So, that night I decided enough was enough.

Miscellaneous: How to dump him

So, when you started out he was the best thing since ra–ra skirts. Holding hands in the park, gazing into each other's eyes as everyone and everything carried on around you. Cloudless skies hovering above, everywhere you went, that song by the Carpenters constantly playing in your head . . .

*Now he irritates the c**p out of you and you've probably fantasized on constant occasions about placing a pillow over his dozing face. Perhaps it's time to end things, baby. Only you will know if it's time, though, but the fact you're reading this entry probably means you're seriously thinking about it.*

There's no law on how to do it and sometimes there's just no need for a long, drawn–out explanation. It could be simply because he forgets to rinse his mouth in Minty Fresh now and again and telling him would be cruel (or kind if you think about it).

He actually might want to know why he's getting dumped, though, which perhaps means he's a masochist (i.e. a bit weird). If he does, this is a good line: "Babe, things just really aren't working out. I'm sorry." Then sigh. Then, "Perhaps I'll see you around some time?" Then sigh again.

If he doesn't accept that then maybe you'll need to be a bit more direct. But try your best not to get in any deeper, it just gets ugly.

My relationship with Oliver came to an end a few weeks before Carla's mom's wedding to Calvin. It wasn't the best thing I had ever done, telling him it was over, but he took it quite well. No drama. No silliness. The only strange moment was watching him through my window, loading the saxophone into the cab. The way his shoulders slumped forward. The sadness etched onto his face. I really hoped I hadn't caused him so much pain, he would hate me. I really hoped I had done us *both* a much-needed favor.

But I had to move on. In a few weeks time I would be seeing Corey again.

As Carla fixed her mother's hair in a bedroom strewn with all things white and pink, I decided to get some air outside, where I found Mom and Abbi sitting on the steps to their house, Mom looking done in.

"Lois!" sang Abbi, her yellow ballerina style dress flapping around her as she jumped up.

I sat beside Mom as Abbi squeezed herself between us. I checked Abbi's hand for anything sticky before holding it.

"Hi, Mom."

"Hello. You look nice."

I looked down at my silk and organza skirt, which Abbi had begun to stroke. "What are you doing, Abbs?"

"I think she likes the feel of the fabric," said Mom slowly.

"My little sister has a fetish!" I laughed.

Mom stared blankly toward nothing in particular.

"Lois, what's a fatash?" asked Abbi curiously.

"Never mind." I looked down at those beautiful bright eyes staring up at me. I hated to admit it, but for a kid (one from my family at that) she was quite beautiful. So innocent and fresh-faced, I doubted anyone could ever refuse her anything.

"Do you want to come with me and Carla to the wedding?"

"Your car's a two-seater," said Mom.

"I have a new company car . . . I've just started that new job. Last Monday."

"Oh, you didn't say."

"I did. Told you a few weeks back."

"Sorry. I've had a lot on my mind. What's it like? Who's it with?"

"An investment bank in the city."

"With the computers, like before?"

"Sort of. Only this time I'll be in charge of the IT systems of the bank's Asia and Middle East operations."

"That's lovely. Sounds really important. I could have done a small tea for you and invited next door."

"I didn't want any fuss, Mom."

"It's not every day my girl gets a fancy job in the city. I am so proud of you."

"Thanks Mom," I said, not knowing what else to say, yet feeling a little emotional.

I looked at Mom's face. "Mom, are *you* okay?"

"Don't worry about me. Just a bit busy, what with this one! So, you've got the car already? Let's have a look."

"I don't actually get it until next week. We'll be taking Rob's car today."

"Can I go with Lois, Mommy?"

"Of course you can."

Abbi's smile resumed its rightful position as she got up and began a skip with an invisible rope, her soft curls bouncing up and down with excitement.

"I haven't seen much of you," said Mom inevitably. It was as if seeing me would always force out a moan, whine or criticism of some sort—which obviously partly explained my absences.

"I'm just saying. Abbi's always asking for yo—"

Luckily, I was spared another ear bashing as Carla appeared, informing us the bride was on her way out.

I tried not to giggle as Carla's mom teetered down the tiny aisle of the registry office to the tones of "I Will Always Love You," heels clinking and dressed in a pink miniskirt and matching stiletto heels. But the sight of Calvin dressed as a pimp in a purple suit, complete with a diamanté-decorated cane and silver hat slipped to the side was ridiculous in the extreme. Luckily any comments were masked by the song, leaving Abbi the pleasure of announcing in a loud and excitable voice, as soon as the song finished, "He looks like my dolly!"

The ceremony was about to begin, the door opened, and in walked Corey. More confident than the last time I'd seen him, smiling proudly, showing off his beautiful dimples. Beside him was Blonde (extensions) Bombshell Mark Two in tow, a skinny little thing, clutching a neatly wrapped gift with a huge silver bow.

"Sorry!" he whispered to no one in particular. He was now sporting a goatee and shorter hair, looking more handsome than ever. I tried not to think about our last and very sensual encounter, concluding I was right to have run out the following morning. He'd obviously moved on, just like I knew he would.

The ceremony was quick. The reception took place in a small community hall in Greenwich where the newlyweds fed one another cake. Not as bad as my last experience of a wedding, but still as boring.

It would seem the music etiquette of weddings hadn't changed much since Mom's, and yet again we were forced to listen to the cheesy rants of yesteryear. Luckily, Calvin's influence ensured a steady medley of classic soul hits, which, although still ancient, did score higher than "The Birdie Song" in my book. The couple's first dance, to Marvin Gaye's "Let's Get It On," raised a few eyebrows, but looking at the newlyweds it was clear they just didn't give a damn.

"Hi stranger," said Corey's voice.

"How are you!" I enthused, genuinely glad to see him, a lone butterfly flitting around my stomach. As we hugged, I enjoyed the sensation of his body heat against me.

"I've been better, Lo Bag," he replied.

"I thought you liked Calvin, at least you told me that the last time . . . we, er, saw each other."

The uncomfortable silence lasted too long.

"Oh, I do like Calvin, he's great. I just don't need a song reminding me what they'll be getting up to later. Too much information."

"He seems to really love her."

We both shot a look at the couple on the dance floor. Eyes only for one another. Had we been like that once?

"How's *The Manual*?"

"The Manual?" It felt so strange hearing somebody else refer to something so precious to me. The fact that Corey remembered its existence moved me somewhere deep within, allowing the lone butterfly in my tummy to acquire a friend. Then a whole group of friends. I just wanted to thank Corey for remembering. I wanted to replace the previous "polite" hug with a huge humdinger of a squeezefest. But instead I shrugged slightly and said, *"The Manual*'s okay thanks. Going along nicely." Just as Blonde Bombshell Mark Two bundled along, holding hands with MY little sister.

"Hi there. Isn't she cute?" said the Blonde Bombshell.

"Yes," I replied, wanting to shove my finger in her eye while reminding her Abbi was MY sister and I knew how bloody cute she was.

"This is one of my oldest friends—Lois," Corey announced to her.

"Nice to meet you," she remarked, letting go of Abbi, who quickly scarpered.

I went through all the pleasantries and finally escaped when Carla (an absolute vision in a tight red skirt and corset combo) dragged me away with boring tales of Rob.

"He keeps saying he has something to tell me," she said.

"Really? Where is he?"

"He's coming back later. He had to go back for the present, which he forgot! What if he wants to propose?"

"Huh..?" I replied absently.

"What are you thinking about?" questioned Carla, planting a glass of champagne into my hand.

"Corey . . . he looks good—" I began, just as she squealed in delight, catching sight of Rob striding across the hall and carrying a huge pink and white box.

"Baby!" she squealed as he placed the present to one side and scooped Carla into his arms. I found myself with Mom as Abbi rounded up various bored children of a similar age to disappear into the land of mischief.

I wondered, not for the first time, the real reason for the Bingo Caller's absence. I suspected another row, although Mom vehemently insisted he'd been unwell since Friday with a tummy bug.

"Hello ladies!" said Calvin as he approached our table, smiling widely with happiness and I suspect one too many glasses of champagne. Carla had disappeared and Corey was trailing coolly behind him. "Would you like a dance?" he asked Mom, who attempted to feign embarrassment but managed to pull herself up off the chair in record speed.

"Oh, have you seen Abbi?" she asked quickly.

"Over there!" replied Corey, pointing to a bunch of girls led by Abbi and engaged in something involving wedding cake and some poor woman's handbag.

"Still a bit paranoid since she went missing . . ."

"No need to explain. Now come on, it's Earth, Wind and Fire! A brilliant rare groove!" roared Calvin as Mom stifled a giggle. I wondered if she'd ever fantasized about Calvin in any way or whether the dance would start that all off. I stifled a giggle.

"What's making you smile, Lo Bag?"

"Oh, nothing. Just a joke."

"I mean what's making you smile these days? Or *who*, shall we say?" He offered his hand, which I took without hesitation.

"Oh, no one. Just a brilliant new job, which I know I'm going to enjoy . . ." I said a little too enthusiastically.

"You don't have to explain yourself. If that's what's making you happy then that's good. Now tell me more about what's been happening in your life, while we show the oldies how to really get down!"

"To this ancient song?"

"A classic."

"Yeah, right!"

"Oh come on, Lo Bag . . . !" he whined.

"What about your girlfriend?"

"She had to leave. She'd only planned on staying for a bit anyway."

As we reached a quieter spot on the dance floor, the DJ decided to lose his mind and slow things down again.

The Bangles' "Eternal Flame" began to play, immediately transporting me back to my childhood.

"Remember this?" Corey whispered. Before I could protest my inability to slow dance without looking like a demented moron, Corey tightened his grip around my waist until I was able to relax. I'm not sure if it was the words, the familiar smell of soap or the memories of him and me together that suddenly came rushing back, but when he pulled me even closer into him, I responded. And when I felt his breath on my ear, my body began to weaken. I rubbed his back, softly first, as if feeling him for the first time, and then with so much firmness I thought I'd leave a mark. I was ready to melt into him as my head bent softly onto his hard shoulders, as Corey pulled me in closer.

He said something, but the music and the intensity of the moment allowed me to miss the words. But he spoke again. And this time I heard.

"Let's get out of here."

"We can't just go," I said as we hovered by the door.

"Why not?" He took my hand and dragged a more than willing me through the back, into a sort of garden and out the gate. It all felt dangerous and exciting to be jumping into his rental car, heading off without really knowing where we were going.

We finally found ourselves approaching Mount Road and pulled up right at the top of Tree Top hill a few yards from Treetop Towers in Charlton, where we just stared at one another, drinking each other in. Brazenly, I traced his newly shaven goatee on fresh spotless skin, my fingertips warm with every stroke.

"So here we are," I said, a slight huskiness to my voice.

"Yep. Here we are."

An unrecognizable heady feeling escaped from inside me. And I felt tingly as Corey's finger brushed across the outline of my uneven eyebrow to the curve of my crooked nose, to the top of my lip. Beneath my silk suit, I felt a little clammy, especially as he moved closer to me.

I closed my eyes in anticipation.

"Oh!" he said.

My eyes sprang open. "What is it?"

"These stupid cufflinks have linked onto your silky fabric!"

"Are you serious?"

"Don't move, I don't want to tear your outfit!"

I giggled. "Silk and cufflinks. Not something you'd usually associate with us, right?"

"Nope. Lo Bag the tomboy in her jeans and puffy coat and me in my baggy rolled-up cords, thinking I looked *so cool*!" he said, attempting to free me from the cufflink.

"Freedom!" I sang as Corey finally managed to unhook them.

"Not quite," he replied with a hoarse voice. That "thing" between us was back, his beautiful face edging closer, and again my eyes snapped shut. Waiting. I felt his hot breath waft over my face as my lips fought the urge to break into a smile, puckering instead, ready for Corey. When I didn't feel anything, my eyes opened just as Corey's butterfly kiss met with my forehead.

He forced a pained smile. "You don't know how much I want to kiss you," he whispered.

"Then . . ."

"But, I can't, Lo Bag. It . . . This isn't right . . ."

"It's just a kiss . . ."

"It's never 'just a kiss' with us, Lo Bag. It's always so much more than that. To me, anyway."

I looked down.

"I'm with someone and it just wouldn't be right to do this to her."

"I know." I brushed my lips against his forehead, now furrowed with anxiety, and opened my mouth to speak. Then shut it again. There was no need for more words because nothing needed to be said. And as we sat in the car overlooking the streets of our youth, remembering scenes of kiss-chase and childish dreams (I was going to be a scientist, Corey a pilot), I realized we were both edging toward paths that did not involve one another. And probably never would.

We'd truly become adults.

our song

Kevin Trivia: *With a wife and the birth of my beautiful baby girl, I became . . . complete.*

With each birthday I'd taken the actual day off work—a sort of build-up to the reading of Dad's entry. A ritual that had never and would never involve someone else. But the night before my twenty-fifth I found myself in the unenviable position of unplanned babysitter to Abbi, Mom literally dumping her at the apartment before rushing off to "do something urgent." Twenty-five, to me, was a milestone and I was confident my dad thought so too, so his entry would be special, poignant and I didn't want my little sister smearing sticky fingers all over it.

"I like your apartment!" announced Abbi, precariously handling the Bang & Olufsen remote control as I placed *The Manual* onto the highest shelf I could find.

"Come on, eat up!" I encouraged an hour later.

"I hate spaghetti!" spat Abbi as she twirled long swirls of spaghetti plus sauce in and around the bowl with one hand, clutching her very lifelike dolly (named Doll) in the other. Thankfully smelly donkey days were long gone.

"It's yummy!" I replied. I'd read somewhere that pasta was an excellent sleep aid. "Look, Doll loves it!" I said, dragging the doll off the table and almost dipping its head into the spaghetti bowl.

Abbi found this funny. "You're so silly!"

"Eat up . . . and there's ice cream for afters!"

I tucked little Abbi into the spare bed by about eight thirty, and reached for *The Manual*, unable to wait until the allotted time of midnight. I still felt excitement whenever I opened the dulling green cover, unmatched by anything or anyone in my life. Even opening my first huge paycheck after starting my new job hadn't induced the same feeling. Never would. This was it for me. Hearing from my dad.

Twenty-five! Twenty-five!

I don't know about you, but twenty-five was a strange one for me. It felt . . .

I heard a scream, then ran into my room to find Abbi perched on the bed, with tears tumbling from her eyelids.

"What is it, Abbs?" Without a thought, I placed an arm onto her tiny shoulders and pulled an errant curl away with my hand.

"I want my donkey."

"I thought he'd . . . gone."

"I want him back."

I distinctly remembered offering to set fire to it after Mom had successfully prized it away.

"How about a story, instead?"

Abbi swiped at her nose, nodding her head furiously.

"Let me get you a tissue!" I said quickly.

"No, okay, please read me a story then, Lois." She said this so sweetly, the little minx. So much so that I was willing to temporarily forget the current threat of a snot invasion.

"I'll have to make one up."

"Okay!" She snuggled in closer as I recited the tale of an ex pop princess marrying a footballer and riding off together on their great big bling-covered motorbike. The End.

"More!"

"No way!" I said, tickling her just under her chin, which led to a bubbling outburst of giggles. Then, for no reason at all, I brought Abbi into my chest, placing my nose into her soft curls, feeling this strange but overpowering swell of protection toward her.

I finally got her down in the early hours of the morning and, with my feet resting on the coffee table, continued with *The Manual.*

. . . grown-up. I suppose it's that realization that you're on the wrong side of twenty-five—I don't know, but it means different things for different people. Or it may not mean much at all to you, just another number.

What's clear is the fact you're not my little girl any more. No, forget that last bit—YOU'LL ALWAYS BE MY LITTLE GIRL. Remember, the last time I saw you, you were only five . . . And every day I wonder what you look like now. Long hair? Short hair? A bright pink Mohican? All I can visualize is you dressed in a yellow dress with a white lace hem, tiny bunches of hair and looking up at me with those huge innocent eyes and a smile that could melt three ice fountains in a split second . . .

I thought about Abbi upstairs—Lots more havoc to wreak and a barrage of hearts to break. Her life just beginning, as mine was when Dad left. I continued.

. . . your mom telling you off and you running to me for the sympathy vote—and almost always getting it. The games we used to play. The songs we'd sing. Oh and the boogying. Your old man could dance, but you could really move! I remember you used to love this song that came on the TV. To me the worst song in the world, but as soon as you heard it, you were off. Tiny little legs, getting all excited and manic. You'd actually shed a tear as it finished! So, of course I had to buy it for you (just one of the things you my child, made me do against my will). The song's called "With Stars On." And at one point it was all you ever wanted to hear. You'd beg me to play it, then wrinkle your nose in delight as you heard the chorus. That was "our song," Lowey.

I found it again, a few days after the diagnosis, and the words, well, they just hit me as it summed up everything I wanted to say to you (well, almost everything if we put The Manual *into the equation). I waited till now to remind you about it, because I figured you'd be mature enough to listen to it without wrinkling your nose and sniggering at the two guys in flares and thinking, "Could things get any cheesier? What is my dad liiiike?"*

As I said, by now you'll be mature (and strong enough) to know what I'm trying to say to you. Again, the song's called "With Stars On" by Jimmy K. Jones and Sister. I don't need to say any more. Just listen to the words.

I was intrigued. Dad had set me a challenge. Little did he know that with the Internet I could just about find anything, and locating an old record from the Seventies couldn't be *that* hard?

Okay, it was. The obvious place to start was in Mom's store cupboard, but of course all of dad's things were gone.

A week later, I realized it would be easier to find a crappy gold bullion triangle than Jimmy K. Jones and Sister's hit record. During my rare lunch breaks I phoned practically every record shop listed in the phone book and scoured the Internet, but to no avail.

But I had my dad's camera, his manual, and I was determined to find the record.

Post break-up with Rob, Carla needed a place to live.

"I just can't bloody cope with Mom and Calvin acting all lovey-dovey around me," she cried. Her eyes were red, mascara-smeared, but her hair remained pristinely silky and soft as it tumbled down her back.

"I still can't believe he did that to you."

"After all his promises as well. Let's not forget about those. Being together forever, and all that stuff!" She shook her head mournfully and began to sob again. I hated seeing her like this, but perhaps I was the last person who should offer advice, because I had never loved a boyfriend the way she'd loved Rob. I had always shied away from that type of thing, and watching my best friend crumple right in front of me reinforced one of the reasons why.

"And can you believe he dumped ME and blamed ME? What, did I force him to have text sex with lots of women, including his PA?"

Of course, after just a few days I began to remember what it really meant to be "roomies" with Carla. An experience long consigned to the "trauma, keep out" part of my head. Carla had managed to remain almost as lazy as she had been when we first lived together and was probably worse than Oliver. Only, instead of socks on the floor, there were bras and lace panties draped all over the place.

"You really should think about getting out and about again," I said gently, returning late from another day at the office, shattered and totally ready for bed.

"I will. It's not as if I have a job, though, is it? Rob paid for everything. And, talking of which, do I owe you any rent?"

"Don't be silly," I said sincerely, although surely, I thought to myself, it wouldn't have broken a nail if she'd cooked the odd meal. I pulled a coaster under her steaming mug of tea. "You'll need to face the world at some point, you know."

"I know. I just thought . . . I just thought he was 'The One.' You know?" Her voice broke and I noticed the tears begin to well.

But, no, I didn't know. I'd never, ever thought of anyone as "The One," and frankly found the whole notion quite silly. Wasn't meeting someone just about timing anyway?

Corey had proved that if the timing was right, we'd have gotten further than we had done.

I placed my hand on her arm. "I'm here, all right?"

"Yeah, I know. And thanks for letting me stay in your posh pad. Wasn't like this when I was here."

"You mean it wasn't this clean, madam!"

A smile. "Point taken."

We both laughed.

"Lois, can you do me another favor?"

"Yes . . ." I replied wearily.

"Open that bottle of tequila me and Rob bought you from holiday."

That night Carla was able to temporarily forget her heartache by falling asleep with a half empty bottle of tequila by her side. If only it was that easy to find Dad's record. Much to my colleagues utter shock, I took an unplanned day off to spend time scanning an array of speciality record shops in the West End yet to succumb to the lure of CDs. I finally located a dusty copy of "With Stars On," and got it home before realizing that a three compact disc player with treble base system wasn't actually suitable for a twelve-inch record.

I rushed over to Mom's, as I'd promised to go for Sunday lunch, but made my excuses to leave straight after dessert, heading next door to see if Corey's record player might still be about somewhere. No one was home except Calvin and I reluctantly explained my dilemma.

He adopted an exaggerated thinking pose. "As far as I know, Corey took all his stuff with him to France, including the record player. It's almost a vintage piece now."

I let out a puff of exasperated air.

"But I used to be a DJ and I still have my Technic decks!"

"Really?"

"Yes, really! Follow me!" he smiled warmly, leading me to Corey's room, which was now used as part spare room, part storage space. Calvin's decks were set up in one corner of the room. I slipped the record out of the sleeve and attempted to switch the record player on.

"Let me," he offered.

"S . . . sorry . . ." I stuttered, feeling a little nervous because I was about to absorb something new from my dad.

The needle swung into action, and suddenly this ultra-dodgy piece of music began to fill the air. Calvin tried to keep a straight face as if hoping it would get better.

I will never forget
The very first time that we met
You looked at me with those big doey eyes
You're my girl
You're my girl, all the while
And I knew from afar
That you would be my star
With stars on
With stars on
A very special love
With stars on
With stars on
A special, special love

Suddenly Dad was in the room. Holding me. Listening to me. Breathing the same air as me. Letting me know he still loved me. His daughter. His love. Something in me wanted to crack open a rush of emotion, but I couldn't. I had to keep it together.

With stars on
With stars on
A very special love
With stars on
With stars on
The only one that comes with stars!

The record stopped too quickly, so I played it again. And again. And again.

I hadn't even noticed Calvin leave the room until he returned with a bowl of chips and a drink, to find me kneeling on the floor with warm tears racing down my face.

I'd never planned it this way. And it definitely would have been to a different person. But opening up to Calvin—the only person within a two-second radius—felt surprisingly good, and I felt purged afterward, plus he was a good listener. This only made me appreciate Corey more, seeing as he was the only one I'd ever really opened up to about Dad before.

"Thanks, Calvin."

"Any time. He sounds like a great guy, your dad. But the song . . ."

"A bit cheesy, I know."

"I was going to say, he obviously loved you very, very much."

I heard the front door open.

"Hi, you two!" sang Carla's mom, immediately grabbing her husband and planting an array of kisses onto his lips.

"I'd better go," I said, placing the record in its sleeve.

"No, stay. I have the best news!" she said, clutching Calvin's hand. "Corey's only gone and done it!"

"Done what? Won that art prize he was going for?" I asked.

"Oh, darlin" . . . I'm not sure if I should say . . ." she said, biting her lip.

"You can tell me!" I said with a smile.

"All right then, only because I know you'll be okay about it all. Well . . . he's only gone and proposed! He's engaged! My little boy's engaged!"

Miscellaneous: Getting dumped as a teenager and getting dumped as an adult
I've lumped these together because getting dumped is hard at ANY age. The only clear difference being, as an adult you'll have lots to keep you occupied, but as a kid . . . we're talking drag, drag, drag.

Yes, getting dumped feels really hard and can seem like someone has just cracked and broken a giant raw egg onto your world. I mean, who's ready to sit and listen to a row of sentences that basically form the same message, however cleverly put together? It all means the same thing: rejection. I won't mince my words: IT HURTS. A LOT.

You might hear the old analogy "there's plenty more fish in the sea" quite a bit and want to thump one of the many mouths it comes out of, so I won't say that, or any of the mass of other clichés so freely used. I will say, just because this particular idiotic, silly, deluded, unwise guy wouldn't know a good thing if it hit him in the face, does in no way mean a smarter, better (and great at soccer) guy isn't out there waiting just for you.

Good, eh?

I so wish I could make you feel better right now. Hold you in my arms until the tears stop . . . Oh, I admit it, I'm welling up myself here and I haven't even been dumped (not since Ella Jones, anyway). But here's the good news: the hurt does leave the building, decreasing little by little each day. You go from thinking about this guy every waking moment, to thinking about him one hundred and fifty times a day, then one hundred and forty–nine, then one hundred and forty–eight. A little less each day until it whittles down to nothing. I promise you, it will get better. You'll learn to get on with things. You'd better too! It's the only life you've got, so please don't spend it thinking and hurting about someone who isn't actually worth the hassle.

Since the announcement of Corey's engagement, I'd been locked in a world of nothingness. I tried not to think about it all as I got on with my day-to-day life of working, sleeping and eating. But not even work could excite me, or the letter that arrived informing me of a pay raise. I suppose Corey's news allowed me to feel as if I'd lost a friend. No, it wasn't that. Corey had lived in France for years. I'd lost a lot more than a friend. Perhaps I'd lost hope. But hope for what? I knew we'd never have pursued a full-time, all-consuming relationship, so I wasn't sure why I was feeling so . . . so empty.

Instead of thinking too much about the Corey situation, it became easier to plow myself into my job, and for the next six months I regularly worked twelve-hour days and some weekends until I could almost see the promotion in the near distance. Carla did a good job of cheering me up a little when she said that Corey just wasn't the "marrying type" and had probably been coerced into it by The Blonde Bombshell Mark Two. Of course, I knew Carla was still smarting over Rob's betrayal and remained committed to the ridicule of anyone in a remotely happy relationship, but still, it hadn't hurt to hear it.

When I received an email from the Big Boss summoning me to her office, as always I felt fearless and ready to take on whatever she had in store for me.

"Lois. I know you are a very busy lady, so I'll keep it brief," she said.

I shuffled about in the chair and watched a rare smile appear on her face.

"How would you like to become Senior Market Data Analyst for the firm?"

The way she looked at me suggested she'd just asked if I'd be interested in fancy chocolate and not a job that would see me with a salary increase of almost eighty percent!!!!

"Yes, that would be fine . . . Thank you."

the best

Kevin Trivia: ***What have I learned? You can do anything you put your mind to? You need to believe in yourself, though.***

Lois, you live in a world occupied by zillions of people. Different countries, cultures, all walks of life and with many different experiences. Within that, there's bound to be someone better at sports, richer, quicker with numbers, more popular at staff do's, prettier (no, we'll scrap that one, obviously), funnier; in short, a tad better at something than you are.

That's life.

It matters not, my dear daughter, how good you are because some sly bastard will always be lurking around the corner to show you up, let the rest of the world know just how much better they are than you.

A lot of us (me included) aren't that supersonic at anything much. Don't get me wrong, I'm GOOD at soccer, but hey, I was never going to be the next Kevin Keegan. I eventually (and after multiple head-pattings by my dad) accepted this and begin to appreciate little bits of success I ***had*** *achieved. The positives as opposed to the negatives. For example, I'd never played for England, but I had won three trophies for my fancy footwork AND been responsible for one of the best headers this side of Southeast London. I'd also always wanted a huge brood of kids, but instead ended up with THE most fantastic little girl I'd ever had the good fortune to experience time with. You.*

Not bad.

Don't get me wrong, Lowey, competition in life is great and there is a healthy place for it—but I guarantee you it will feel a lot better when you're competing solely with—wait for it . . . drum roll— ***Miss Lois Bates.***

I think my dad would be proud of me if he knew that I could actually afford to move to a bigger place if I so wanted. But my apartment had come to represent so much to me. The first place to ever feel like a home. And I was staying. Besides, it was almost unrecognizable with a newly decked-out kitchen, a huge Smeg fridge and a washing machine delivered sparkling new from John Lewis. The lounge was cozy but modern and minimal, and best of all was my company car—a Jaguar XJ-S. I knew it was mega-flash and at first felt a bit of a twit, driving to work the first morning, but it handled like a dream and I knew that Dad would have been thrilled, what with the earlier model being his favorite car of all time!

So, working a seventy-hour week was fine.

Being woken up in the middle of the night to take an overseas call for work was also tolerable.

As were the accompanying headaches, due to lack of sleep. And the bags lurking under my eyes.

I was hardly seeing Mom and Abbi. Although I tried to make it up to Abbi with a trip to Hamleys for her fifth birthday, spending close to a hundred dollars on her, when admittedly she would have been content with a trip to McDonald's. That's guilt for you.

But work had to come first, right? Being successful was what fueled me; nourished me like food and was everything I needed to function. Craving the next task, the next mountain to scale. Yearning for work like Carla yearned for a man. And if anything, work had proved more reliable than men. So what if I was alone, with only a handful of friends? I was okay. I'd be all right. I still had Dad.

It seemed to take Carla about five minutes and fifteen dates with ten different men for her to finally land "the real love of her life." Markus, a freelance thingamajig (which basically meant he spent oodles of time at home), who came complete with Raymond, the live-in brother. It wasn't long until she'd shipped out of mine and into their typical bachelor pad—because, in her own words, it needed a shot of femininity.

My invitation to dinner soon followed.

"Hi," said Markus as he opened the front door to me. Curving large lips—an attribute Carla boasted had made her fall in love with him, oh and how he used them—smiled warmly toward me. I greeted him, shrugging off my coat just as the brother breezed into the room dressed in a trendy pair of jeans and controversial white FCUK T-shirt over a nicely gym-toned chest. As well as natural good looks, Raymond seemed to hold good conversation as Carla and Markus caressed each other with doe-eyed gazes over my best friend's speciality paella.

"Carla never told me she had such a pretty friend," he said.

"Thank you," I replied, before taking a bit of wine. The way he was looking at me made me nervous—in a good way.

"This isn't great, honey," commented Markus, poking at the food with his fork.

"Sorry, babe. What is it this time? Too much pepper?" asked Carla in a little girl's voice, which for a second I mistook for sarcasm.

"Not enough actually," he said mid-mouthful as Carla leaped from her chair, returning with the pepper shaker. I struggled not to make a comment.

Apparently Raymond worked for an insurance firm where he did "exciting" things with forms. Although he described his job wittily, my eyes were almost glazing over by dessert. I was absolutely exhausted.

"Am I boring you?" he asked self-consciously, suddenly appearing younger than his years. Carla and Markus had disappeared into the kitchen.

"No, I've just been working late. Sorry."

"That's okay. Carla said you were a workaholic."

"Charming. Nice to know how others see you."

"But she didn't say how pretty you were, remember . . . ? I'd get a new friend if I were you . . ." He smiled and I noticed a perfect row of very white teeth.

Raymond was twenty-two and happy to do all the things a lot of twenty-two–year-olds cherished. "Killing" his brother at the latest Playstation game, apartment-sharing and sporting a serious aversion to being tied down. So at first glance and perhaps to the outside world, Raymond and I were total opposites. But his refusal to be pinned down made him a *very* attractive proposition for me, because with him I could bury the fear of someone wanting more than I was willing or able to give. And without a man around I was content with my toys—and we're not just talking about my new Nikon digital camera.

So being with Ray on a Sunday and Thursday evening each week also felt right. Just as laughing with him on the phone and in between meetings did. Everything was moving just the way I liked it and *always* to my schedule.

But the day I had to tell two senior members of staff that we needed to let them go—that felt so, so wrong and was one of the hardest days I'd ever had to face at work. Having no miscellaneous entry to refer to on this, I was clueless as to how to deal with such a situation. But I found the strength—or nerve—to inform the first person and then the second (just before slipping them the website address of my employment agency). Still, the whole process left me feeling like shit and wanting to talk to someone. Anyone.

I was exhausted by the time I reached home.

The answer-phone beeped through with a message from Ray. I dialed his number on my cellphone.

"Hi, Ray." I undid my jacket and placed it on the side of the sofa. The lounge, in fact the whole house, still smelled of fresh paint after having it redecorated only three days before.

"You sound down. Are you okay?" he asked.

"I'm fine. Just a hard day at work." I hit Play on the stereo remote control and the tones of Amy Winehouse burst into the room like silk and honey and my muscles began to relax.

"Do you want to talk about it?"

I thought for a moment. "No."

"Are you sure? I'm a good listener!"

"No!" I snapped, feeling my hackles rise. Wondering what a twenty-two-year-old in a dead-end job could possibly know about the mechanics of firing good people. A decent man, with two teenagers and a wife to support. A young woman with a mortgage, just like me.

"I'll come round, shall I? Can I come round?"

"When?"

"Tonight?"

"Instead of Thursday?" I asked, kicking off my shoes and slipping aching feet into a pair of yellow fluffy slippers—Abbi's Christmas present last year. My time with Ray was strictly Thursdays and Sundays and he knew that—then again, I could do with some company after the day I'd had.

"I'll be truthful . . . with Carla and my bro always getting it on . . . it's a bit much. Then there are the rows. I could do with the peace, to be honest. Plus you can tell me what's on your mind . . ."

Knowing what it was like to perch in the shadow of Carla's exploits, I agreed for Ray to invade my space for one extra night.

And I had to admit, it did help me to forget about the firings temporarily and I was able to sleep soundly for the first time in weeks.

The following morning, I awoke to find him fiddling with my new camera.

"We should take a picture together. This has a timer, right?"

"Yes, it does . . ." I replied suspiciously

"I bet they'll come out all professional. Digital technology is supposed to be better than the old stuff. Talking of which, why is that old camera in your cabinet? Why don't you just chuck it or give it to a charity shop."

Now I was angry. I padded into the kitchen as he followed like an irritating little lapdog. My plate of oats began to warm in the microwave, and he continued. "We haven't got any pictures together, Lois. Perhaps we'll take some when you get back?"

"Sure, but not right now, okay?" I replied, knowing deep down that I was not interested in taking any pictures of the two of us.

I canceled Thursday.

"Corey will be here next week!" gushed Carla's mom as "With Stars On" came to an end. I decided there and then to purchase the retro-style record player I'd found on the Internet, skipping any chance of bumping into Corey and his Blushing Blonde Bombshell Mark Two Bride to Be.

"I'm sure he'd love to see you, Lois. Just think how great it will be to have him close by when they get married!"

"I don't understand," I said, slipping the vinyl into its sleeve.

"He and his wife will be moving to Greenwich." As soon as she said it, she realized. "You are okay with this, darlin'?"

The vinyl almost slipped from my hand as the ramifications of such a move became clear. "Of course I am!"

"I knew you would be. You and Corey were years ago. Childhood sweethearts. Over with now, right?"

"Right." And that was true. I had no real feelings for Corey, I just didn't need the reminder of a one-night stand constantly biting me on the ass every time I ventured out of my house. And when I thought nothing else could add to this magical moment, she added, "AND they're both coming to England to discuss wedding plans. Next week!"

The following week I pushed forward a planned business trip to Dubai. By day, heading up the new team in tall, plush offices, a backdrop of clear skies and a searing sun. By night, lying on a four-poster hotel bed, listening to cable, working from a laptop, trying and succeeding to place all thoughts of Corey securely where they belonged—out of my head.

Upon my return, the happy couple were safely back in France.

"I can't believe you went to Dubai without telling me!" moaned Ray after an exhilarating bout of lovemaking. While Oliver had been a tender, sweet lover in the beginning, Ray took to the task with gusto, desperate in his quest to please me and doing quite a good job. If only he wouldn't whine so much.

"Oh Ray, it was just a spur-of-the-moment thing. When the company says jump, I have to!" My hands behind my head, I sighed deeply, my lower body snug under the duvet.

"Doesn't seem fair."

"Ray . . ." I said, with just a tinge of exasperation.

His bottom lip shot out out like Abbi's. "Just let me know next time, that's all. Perhaps I could come with you. We've never been abroad together."

"Okay!" I sighed, knowing that would never happen.

"Talking of going out . . . I was wondering, instead of me coming here on Sunday, why don't we . . ." And on he went. The whining, the chatter, the questions. The only two words I did manage to identify were possibly the most important. Sister and park.

"The park?"

"Or we could take her to the zoo—whichever. Take some pictures—you never use that top-of-the-range camera of yours!"

The whole concept seemed alien to me, this idea of some warped "family" outing, complete with snapshots. My eyebrows scrunched in confusion as I searched for a get-out clause and found one in Carla—who was scheduled at my place for dinner with Markus this Saturday. Only, she didn't know it yet.

Luckily, Carla did manage to persuade Markus to come over on Saturday, and while we left the brothers catching up in my lounge, Carla frogmarched me into the kitchen.

"So, what's this all about then?" asked Carla, one eyebrow raised.

"Thought it right to return the favor."

"Liar. I know you'd rather boil your own toe than spend time with Markus."

"Don't say that!"

"I know you don't like him," she spat quietly, just as Markus appeared.

"Darling, have you seen my phone?"

Carla placed a hand over her mouth. "Oh, babe, I think I left it on the sofa at home!"

Markus's nose flared and his eyebrows arched. "But I told you to go and fetch it when I was looking for the car keys!"

"I know, and I'm sorry," she replied, truly apologetic.

I left the ensuing row to see what Ray was up to. After five minutes I headed back toward the kitchen, stopping just outside the door, hearing obviously raised voices.

"I said I was sorry!"

"Why do you have to be such a dumb bitch, huh?"

I waited for my best friend to slap this man's face—at least verbally—because no one had ever spoken to her like that. Not since Tommy Wannamaker called her Tuls ("slut" backward) in the third year.

So I waited.

"I'm really sorry, Markus," I heard her mumble apologetically.

Was this for real?

"I hope this doesn't happen again," he said, footsteps heading toward the door as I made a quick backward retreat into the toilet.

Two days before my twenty-sixth birthday, Carla slipped me some Ann Summers coupons just as I was about to broach my concerns over Markus. Mom, armed with Abbi in tow, dropped by for the first time in history to hand over a DVD of some sloppy movie. And I had to admit, it was a nice surprise having them over and I even took some beautiful pictures of Abbi before they left, just as Ray phoned claiming his surprise would wait until a few days AFTER my birthday, because of work constraints. This was okay with me, considering the only thing I really wanted to do was read another birthday entry from Dad.

The day before my birthday, I bounded into the office, anticipating a pyramid of work requiring a clean-up before my day off. I waved to the security/door man as usual, retrieved a fresh mug of coffee from the kitchen and switched on my computer to catch up on the million or so emails. One, purposefully highlighted in blue, immediately caught my eye. An email from the boss. She wanted to see me.

Her office was larger than mine, more plush, two pictures of each of her children gracing a rectangular mahogany desk.

"Sit down, Lois."

"Good morning," I began, before noticing the blank but almost sympathetic look on her face. No change there. The boss was hardly a barrel of laughs at the best of times.

"I have some news for you."

"What is it, Joan?"

"I'm afraid . . . I'm afraid there are going to be further job losses and I wanted to tell you about them."

My circulation seemed to stop as I wondered who I had to sack next. Hating—no, make that despising—this side of the job.

"I'm afraid . . . I'm afraid we are going to have to make you redundant, Lois."

Her words made a fist of my intestines. "Sorry? I don't

understand? Are you saying . . . ? Are you saying I don't have a job?"

"I'm afraid so, Lois."

I bet you feel really old now. Wrong side of twenty-five. Closer to thirty.

Yes, I know, because I felt worse on my birthday, so Charlie and Philomena accompanied me to the pub for a slight . . . erm . . . session of drinking.

I'd be fibbing if I told you twenty-six wasn't meaningful, because it is. So if there are any loose ends that need tying up or if things need changing, this is the year to do it.

I love you, with stars on. Dad.

I banned any celebration and even told Raymond not to bother me for a while. I needed to find a new job and immediately began an Internet search, trying to ignore the recruitment agency's spiel: *"The IT industry is not as lucrative as it once was. Jobs are really thin on the ground, Ms. Bates."* Of course, the redundancy package and savings would allow me a certain amount of breathing space, but could only be temporary. I needed my dad to tell me what to do, how to get out of a hole I never thought I'd find myself in. Besides, he'd never actually thought his precious daughter would ever get made redundant, because the company needed to make savings and I just happened to be one of the "last in." I had to give up my job and everything that went with it, including the car. *Dad's favorite car.*

Because of unused leave, I was able to leave within weeks as one of the agencies quickly came up with a temporary post paying less than thirty percent of what I was used to—but it was work, and as my recruitment consultant said, it "would only be temporary."

Against my wishes, Ray had my very belated birthday card, along with a huge bunch of flowers, delivered to my new workplace. I immediately called him up with a thank you and we decided to meet up at a little restaurant half a mile from the office in High Street Kensington, right near the subway station.

"I've missed you," he said.

"I just needed to sort my life out. I'm sorry."

"I know you are. You're so thoughtful," he said, sipping on a glass of wine he'd insisted on ordering.

"Why d'you say that?" I tucked into my usual prawn tempura starter and for the first time noticed a strange glint in Ray's eye.

"Saying you wanted a Thai restaurant, when you know it's my favorite food."

"It was near the subway station."

"Oh."

One prickle of guilt. "But Thai being your favorite is a bonus."

"No, you're my favorite, Lois."

His handsome, boyish face seemed to beam.

"I know I haven't been the best lately . . . not seeing you and that—" I began.

"That's okay. I know things have been stressful, what with the job situation. But I want you to know, I'll be there for you."

"Thanks."

The beautifully dressed waitress placed the sticky rice in front of me.

"We're sharing that," I said. She ignored me and I looked to Ray, who was smiling like a horny tomcat.

"Have I missed something?"

"Look in the rice," he commanded quite uncharacteristically.

I peered into it but I couldn't see anything but rice. Then I noticed it—a slight sparkle from inside the bowl.

"Take it out," he instructed excitedly. The waitress was on apparent standby beside me.

I picked up the cheap piece of jewelry that had been embedded within the bowl of sticky rice and just stared at it, feeling a little numb.

"It's an engagement ring," he said anxiously, his hands tapping nervously on the table.

Bile rose up in my throat.

"That's . . . er . . ." The words wouldn't come. I felt a little hot and then an urge to leave as I placed the ring on the table and looked at it. Then I took a sip of water, wishing it was alcohol. Ironically, a bottle of house champagne appeared out of nowhere from a second waitress.

"I love you, Lois. So, so much, and I want to spend the rest of my life with you." He took my hand. "You're the one."

"I didn't . . . I didn't think you were into all that." I shook my hand away. "Plus you've only just turned twenty-three. Aren't twenty-three-year-olds supposed to be out partying?"

"Not this one. I'm ready."

A movie reel of pros flashed in my mind for a total of six seconds, followed by a rush of cons:

- The L word (and never actually having said it to him).
- My total inability to give up space in my apartment.
- My lack of faith in long-term relationships.
- My total inability to give up any part of my life for a man (Oliver, case in point).

Especially a man who, without warning, suddenly dropped to his knees in a begging pose, right there in the restaurant.

"Marry me, please. I love you, Lois." His eyes were wide open and I thought I could see tears. I looked down at the ring and then around the restaurant in total amazement-cum-embarrassment, unable to match the looks of complete excitement etched on the faces of people who clearly needed to get a life.

I looked back at the man who had just asked me to marry him. And I closed my eyes, not wanting him to see my thoughts.

"Well?" asked Ray, with the look of Oliver Twist pleading for a bowl of porridge. I opened my eyes to yet another beautifully dressed waitress standing beaming behind him, ready to attack with full applause. I felt as if I was suffocating. My blouse began to stick to me like glue; the air around me felt tight.

"I need the loo," I said, jumping out of my seat, much to the thorough disappointment of three beaming waitresses.

I hunched over the freestanding sink in a vomit pose, but knowing I hadn't reached that stage yet. This was all too much, though. I mean, in normal circumstances it would be too much, but in the current climate it just about made my bad day/week/month/life seem that bit worse. Ray was a good man, but I didn't want this. I didn't want *him.* The only man I wanted was dead. Staring at my reflection, mascara halfway down my cheeks, suitcase-sized bags under my eyes, I knew I was in a giant, humungous mess.

Of course, I turned down Ray's proposal, which he took a tad better than when I told him we were over.

For good.

I reeled off a mass of "It's not you, it's me" clichés borrowed from the TV, but it seemed I'd underestimated Ray once more. The calls, texts and emails were at first relentless, slowly petering away in time.

Of course there were the expected recriminations from Carla, painting me as the wicked witch from the south. Even Mom wanted to know why I'd dumped a perfect man. But I simply told them all to mind their own business. Especially Markus, who one evening had the audacity to confront me, just as Carla disappeared into the bathroom of the bar where we were having drinks.

"I don't like the way you treated my brother," he said with obvious venom.

"And I don't like the way you talk to Carla," I responded defiantly.

"Lois, you don't know what you're talking about."

"It's like you don't have any respect for her. It's sick. Just . . . just tone it down, okay? She doesn't deserve this . . . or you."

The huge lips my best friend found so irresistible curved into a crude, creepy smile.

"Want me for yourself, do you?" he said quietly.

I felt waves of revulsion. "Are you mad?"

"Is that why you dumped my little brother? Wanted me all to yourself?"

I uttered some obscenity and he retaliated with firm, confident words.

"At the end of the day, who will she believe when I tell her? You, or me? Want to take the risk? After the way you've behaved lately, I doubt she'll believe anything you say anyway."

When Carla returned, I was all smiles. I decided Markus would keep.

I didn't miss Ray as much as Carla insisted I would. And that was a plus.

The temporary contract ended and I waited for the next job. It gave me the space to think about what I was going to do with the rest of my life, but each time I drew a blank. Computers were all I knew.

As usual, the employment agency offered me the world and delivered nothing more than a crumbling town center in the form of a one-month contract at a steel firm along with constant negative references about the IT sector. This just made it easier to plunge into a dark, dark place I didn't recognize.

After the job ended, I spent most of my days lounging about, ingesting bad daytime television, my hand buried within huge packets of chips. The phone hardly rang, except for Mom inquiring about my health or Carla, as usual occupying her own little world, which didn't include my current plight. I was jobless and, worst of all, felt really hopeless, sometimes without enough will to step out of my sagging jogging bottoms or to tidy myself up. I just couldn't give a damn. And, after paying the bills I often couldn't afford to get my hair fixed at the usual plush salon, so made do with hair bands—tying it up and forgetting about it, just like the IT world had done with me.

It was time to face facts: at twenty-six, I was on the scrapheap. Without a job, with paltry severance pay and with a mortgage I could only just about afford thanks to my savings and help from the DSS. My life had sunk to such depths and I didn't even have the strength to begin to pull myself up and out of it.

you never get used to being the lamppost

Kevin Trivia: ***England, at last, qualified for the World Cup . . . and I had to miss the first match against Belgium because the TV couldn't be bothered to work!***

After the diagnosis, I began to look at nature a bit more—trees, flowers and girly things like poetry (yep!). There's one poem I can't remember the name of, or what it said word for word. But it's stayed with me. Now, how did it go . . . ?

Lowey, look in your garden. If you don't have one, look in someone else's, and if you see a flower, a weed even, any one of these, look closely at the color, smell the scent (if there is one).

I looked out of my window, but all I saw was the gray of the sky and spots of sleet falling heavily from it.

That flower or weed will definitely need sunshine to grow (you should have learned this in school, it's called photosynthesis), but if it gets too much, it can burn, then wither away, the dried remnants sinking into the compost. The plant will basically need rain too, so it can drink and then grow into the wild, colorful and beautiful living thing it's destined to become. A bit of sunshine here, a bit of rain there, both working in some type of natural harmony. What I'm trying to say is, what I think that poem was trying to say was this: there will be times when you get rained on, when the weather's bleak and perhaps seems never-ending. But it simply can't always be about the sunshine. It can't. I'd be fibbing if I said it could be.

Do you understand me?

Of course, I don't want my daughter to ever go through any sort of pain. I don't. And I wish I could tell you that life is . . . well, a bed of sweet-smelling roses . . .

But I can't.

I wish you could, Dad. Why aren't you here? With me? Protecting me from all this stuff? Shielding me from the disappointment? The hurt?

I asked these questions the minute I opened my eyes each morning to drawn curtains and the rancid smell of hopelessness, until that last moment at night as I chased sleep. I'm ashamed to say this next bit—even think it—but waking up sometimes equaled instant disappointment.

I'd wish I'd just forgotten to wake up that morning. I craved my dad more than ever. Needed, wanted to see that beautiful smile, freeze-frame it in my mind and refer back to it whenever I needed to. I'd close my eyes, imagine his face. The mole. Did he snort when he laughed at something funny? Did he have smelly feet after a hard day of soccer? Did he hate raw onions like I did? Where are you, Dad? Where are you?

I opened up *The Manual,* hugging it close to me in desperation. I fell to my knees, my chest heaving, needing to feel him. But it was like the most fragile part of me could not connect with him any more. He was only available to me when I was happy and following *The Manual.* When everything was on track. Now I'd deviated from that neat route and I couldn't feel my dad's presence any more.

Two months into unemployment and the night after a bad dream (involving me as a homeless woman scouring the streets of Barcelona) a shiny prospectus for the local college was delivered to my door instead of a neighbor's, finding its way onto my mat underneath the mountain of bills that had quadrupled over the last few weeks.

I scanned the courses on offer: Spanish, cookery, Japanese, singing, photography, then glanced toward the expensive camera purchased at the height of my career, a lasting memory of my one stab at frivolity.

The smarmy jerk behind the computer screen at the dole office smirked as he "assessed" my claim with the enthusiasm of a tortoise.

"So you're a computer person, are you?"

"I've been working with computers for years. So, yes."

He couldn't have been more than twelve. "We have loads of jobs working with computers. Have you looked at the five on offer? They're on the display board." His voice was loaded with sarcasm.

"I thought I'd seen all the jobs . . ." I said, responding to this new ray of hope, suddenly awakened.

"Here, I'll bring one up . . ." he said, tapping wildly at the keys. "This one." He turned the screen to face me.

"Data inputter?" I said.

"Why not?"

"Well, the wages are a—"

"Works out to just over the five pounds and five pence minimum wage. What more do you want? Unless you are prepared to go back to college . . ."

"I was thinking about starting a photography course."

"Why?"

"I . . . I like pictures . . ."

He snorted at that and urged me to look closer at his screen; to the long hours and wages that would barely cover the mortgage, let alone basic food portions. The little weed went on to explain that my refusal to go for jobs could result in any benefit being stopped, and while his voice droned on and on, all I could hear was *blah, blah, blah* as the clutches of despair actually tightened its grip on me.

I spent most of my time refusing to answer the phone to anyone and leaving the house merely to visit the dole office and sign on, a move I was forced to take for fear of losing the apartment. But I just couldn't find anything permanent job-wise, while my savings had begun to dwindle down to meager portions.

I decided to enroll at the local college to study photography. At first it was to get me out of the house, but the twice-weekly class preserved what little sanity I had left as it allowed me to pretend, at least to the outside world, a reason for my existence.

And I soon began to enjoy it. Learning about angles, lighting and how Photoshop could transform pictures. Speaking to people who shared a passion—one that soon began to surface in me. Conversing and laughing with those who had no idea of what a failure I had become. Biyi, one of my classmates, and I seemed to bond quickly after pairing up for a class exercise. About my age, tall, gangly and with the girliest eyelashes I'd ever seen, he was quiet but at the same time had this ability to pull me into a conversation, allowing me to warm to him instantly. In no time I'd learned the basics of digital photography, and unlike many in the class I had a top-of-the-range camera, housing just a few pictures of Abbi, gathering dust at home.

Biyi liked to walk me home from college most nights, and one evening decided to plant me with a wet smacker of a kiss. He also said I was beautiful, which (judging by my current lack of care and hygiene) was probably a lie but sounded like the most natural comment in the whole world. Admittedly, hearing this felt good, just like kissing him felt good. And just like waking up in his arms did, the following morning.

Because photography was the one thing we had in common, this dominated our times together outside the classroom. Reading photography books in the library; aiming the camera at anything that moved in the park; or drinking coffee in the bookshop as we scoured the shelves for new publications.

Biyi was so sweet, and as well as *The Manual*, I suppose, he kept me going. Though he never asked me for anything, content to see me whenever he could. I never disclosed much about myself—I guess old habits are hard to break. Although once I did tell him about my dire financial affairs, which merely left him impressed that I'd amassed so much at an early age. Yet his admiration of me still seemed misplaced. Hadn't I screwed up on a huge level by losing my job? Hadn't I let myself and, worst of all, my dad down? To Biyi, the answer would be no. He called me his whiz kid, his jetsetter, when all I saw staring back at me in the mirror was a failure.

Biyi and I hardly went anywhere, happy to stay at my apartment, taking endless pictures of one another. Biyi, lounging in bed on a late sunny morning as the light through the blind captured his smile; me, arched over the sink brushing my teeth, pretending to be angry as he snapped away. Loving the thought of capturing a moment in time that could never be repeated, but could be kept forever. Like I had done clumsily with my last picture of my dad. And just like Dad had done with *The Manual*.

Gradually, I slithered out of self-imposed purgatory, ready to face the world again. I sold the MG and noted my savings had now dwindled to just under fifty pounds. The course was also nearing the end, and I felt enough had been soaked up to take things to that all-important next level: starting up my own photography business.

"Are you sure this is the right thing to do?" said Mom right on cue as I succumbed to a rare visit to my childhood home, this time with my camera, ready to snap every moment. It had been Biyi's idea to take it with me wherever I went.

"Yes, it is, Mom. It's what I want to do," I said, a picture of Corey flickering through my mind. He'd found his creative calling and now I'd found mine. I pinched a piece of cold toast as Abbi ran into the kitchen faster than the speed of light.

"Hey, Abbs!" I said as she planted a soft kiss onto my cheek—spontaneously, unasked for, but absolutely and without doubt very welcome.

"We've missed you!" she said.

"I've been a bit busy."

"I just hope you've really thought about this. Starting your own business isn't easy. And how will you find the money?"

"That's the best bit. I've sold the car and all I had to find out of that is a month's rent and money for paint."

"Paint?"

"For the shop."

"You still need the customers, though. You would have been better off staying in computers . . ."

"Perhaps," I said, through gritted teeth and pursed lips. Of course, Mom had no idea of my life over the past few months. And her reaction now proved I was right not to mention it.

"If it's what you want . . . then it's worth a try. But you know you won't be earning like you did in the city," said Mom, who I think had enjoyed telling the neighbors about her high-flying daughter.

A petite Abbi jumped on my knee and wriggled about, beady eyes suddenly locating my camera beside us.

"Leave it!" I ordered just as she jumped off my lap and, yes, headed straight for the camera.

"I just wanna look. Take one of me!" whined Abbi. I rescued the camera from Abbi's reach and stuck my tongue out in glee. But, of course, I began to snap a delighted Abbi in various rugratty poses around the house as Mom busied herself elsewhere. The kid was vain, insisting I photograph her in every party outfit she owned. Ballerina, princess, Harry Potter. Kissing Doll, posing on the pink bike with yellow tassels she couldn't actually ride without wobbling like a mound of blancmange. Kicking her legs in the air with chocolate (quite disgustingly) smeared over her cheeks. Her curt insistence on proofing every shot (once she'd found out my "magic" camera could do such things) didn't help. The last set I took was with Mom beside Abbi on the sofa. Mom, staring back at Abbi as if she were the most precious thing in her world. I found myself overwhelmingly moved by this and also filled with sadness. It was time to leave.

As I headed toward the door, the Bingo Caller walked in.

"Hello girls," he beamed, his face beaded with sweat. He looked slightly out of breath as he carefully attempted to pick his daughter off the floor.

"Get down, you're too old for all that!" insisted Mom as Abbi crumpled to the floor with full melodramatic/spoiled-brat gusto.

"That's not fair!" she wailed.

"You okay?" Mom asked the Bingo Caller.

"Yes. Don't fuss . . . ! How are you, Lois?"

"Good," I replied, trying my best to stay polite. I gathered my things.

"See you soon?" sang Mom, as I kissed her and Abbi on their cheeks and rushed out the door.

I inched toward the bus stop, glad I'd done my twice-monthly duty AND gotten some great snaps in the process. But ten minutes later, the bus was officially late. Bad. Then I heard my name being called. Very bad. Because the voice belonged to Corey.

Got any advice for this sort of situation, Dad? No? Thought so. Great.

"Hi, Corey!"

"Lo Bag!"

I wished he wouldn't call me that.

"I am now twenty-seven years old, Corey!"

"Oh yeah, happy belated birthday!"

"Didn't feel like celebrating this year." Even Dad's message had been brief; A quick *"Have a happy birthday Lowey! And don't forget to enjoy it!"*

Corey kissed each of my cheeks and his lips felt really soft, like warm caramel. He was also clean-shaven and smelled of fresh soap.

"Now that's a shame. Feeling a bit old are we?"

"You could say that."

"Why?"

"Too old to start modeling if I had the looks. Too old to hold on to a young person's railcard—if I wanted one. And too old to be called Lo Bag."

His smile straightened. "You definitely have the looks."

"Anyway . . . it's . . . it's nice to see you again," I stuttered, unsure as to where my embarrassment had sprung from. "I knocked on your door earlier, to say hi to Calvin and your mom, but no one was home."

"They've gone to some dodgy fetish exhibition—don't ask—and won't be back till much later."

"So how long are you in town for?" I asked, not quite sure where the word "town" had sprung from.

"Funny you should ask that, but I'm going to be here indefinitely. I'm moving to Greenwich, didn't Mom tell you?"

The insides of my tummy began to swirl without permission. "She did say you and your fiancée were coming." The word fiancée just didn't sound right coming out of my mouth.

"Here's your bus."

The bus! I shook my head brazenly, determined to wait for the next one.

"You sure?" he asked.

I nodded my head as the bus shot past, beckoning for him to sit on a graffitied bench, noticing "Carla, Lois and Corey was 'ere '91" carved onto the armrest. Faded so much it was barely legible. The swishing in my tummy was immediately replaced by a feeling of warmth and familiarity.

"You look fabulous," said Corey.

"I look the same as always!"

"Yeah, right! The last time I saw you, you were all businesslike."

My head turned away in shyness. "And now?"

"Beautiful."

No one had ever called me that before. Except Dad. "You should have seen me a few weeks ago, Corey."

"Well, you look great. A lot more relaxed. Carla tells me you're studying photography."

"She has a big mouth."

"For once, my little sis isn't to blame. I'm always asking her about you. Even in France when I'd call home, I was always asking about my Lo Bag." This disclosure shocked me. "Especially when you ignored my postcards . . ."

"They were just postcards, Corey. You're not supposed to reply to postcards . . ." I began to feel uncomfortable at the stupidity of my words.

"Carla tells me you're thinking of starting a business?"

I waited for the criticisms. "Yep."

"I think it's great. It couldn't have been easy for you, going back to college."

"It was awful at first. But I think I'm going to be okay now."

"Of course you will. Lo Bag's a fighter. I have no doubt you'll get there."

At that moment I wanted to thank him for believing in me, for saying things I daren't think myself lately.

"Corey!" someone shrieked from a distance. "Corey!" came the yell again, this time closer. He stood up and the next scene I witnessed disturbed me a little bit. Well, a lot actually.

"I've been looking for you everywhere, Corey baby! Missed you!" said the Blonde Bombshell Mark Two, dressed in the season's gypsy skirt complete with tassels and beads at the hem. A demented hippy. She grabbed him and smacked her lips onto his, Corey's eyes locking with mine for a brief moment as he came up for air.

"I was talking to one of my oldest friends; you remember Lois from next door, right?"

"From the wedding? With the beautiful little sister? Yes, of course. How are you, Lois?"

"I'm good."

"Come back to the house with us and you and Corey can catch up properly!"

Mercifully, the bus arrived. "Sorry, I have to be going!" I said, waving a weak goodbye. The bus pulled away with me on it and I turned for one last look at Corey's beautiful face, before he disappeared with his bride-to-be.

I sat back from the laptop and couldn't help but admire my work. Abbi. Beautiful smile, full of youth and innocence, sitting on her bike with the yellow tassels, owning the picture. And for the first time in ages, I realized I too had something to smile about. Being creative, taking snaps, and adjusting them to perfection on the computer—that's what made me happy! Witnessing the change in one image, whether it be a slightly smaller tummy (Carla's mom) or bigger boobs (Carla), I just couldn't remember ever feeling this useful or creative in the world of IT. Corey had been right, perhaps I was better suited to creativity.

Biyi popped round that evening, overly impressed with Abbi's photos. It was nice explaining how the process of saturation worked on the yellow tassels, allowing them to stand out. I even showed him before and after shots, feeling a mounting pleasure when he congratulated me on a job well done. And, slowly, my confidence grew and I felt sure enough to show him other shots I'd accumulated on my hard drive. Like one of a homeless man sitting on a bench down at the rec. A woman holding a pug dog to her face as he licked the tip of her nose (while I found this act quite gross, the love she carried for that pet oozed from her eyes, screaming out of the shot like a mask of blinding sunshine).

"These are fantastic. I can't believe you've been hiding them!"

"I didn't think they were *that* great. Plus, I didn't want to get sued or accused of being a Peeping Tom!"

"They're great. You're great."

I was aware of the way Biyi was looking at me. I'd seen the look before—in Greg, Oliver, Ray—but I wasn't about to internalize any of it.

My agency called with definite work for the next three months. Further proof that things were indeed looking up. Working the occasional nine-to-five would leave weekends and evenings free to pursue my photography while providing a much-needed income.

I paused at the doorway to the solicitor's, patting down my striped jacket, noticing a slight crease in my matching trousers. Looking meticulous for work had always been a minimum standard for me—whether I was project-managing a team of seven or temping in a solicitor's for a quarter of the pay, I still had pride. So, even though it wasn't the job of the century, it was still a job, and I felt very strongly about making the right impression.

"I'm here to see a lady named Marjorie," I said to a woman in her early fifties.

"Oh, that's me! And you would be Lois Bates, from the agency?"

I smiled warmly. "Yes."

We headed toward what would be my office for the next three months or so, passing a large space with the look and feel of an old black and white Fifties movie. We seemed to be walking for ages until we reached a tiny room. I removed my blazer.

"Oh, you do look rather grand. Wait here," she said.

She returned, clutching a gray carrier bag. "Silly, silly girl."

"Who is?" I asked defensively.

"The girl at the agency. I told her to tell you not to dress so . . . expensively."

"This old thing?" I looked at Marjorie's smartly dressed appearance and wondered what she meant.

"Not to worry. Our last girl—so silly—left without taking her things. About your size. Oh, and if you could wear a pair of old jeans and a T-shirt tomorrow, that would be much advised. You can get dressed in the toilet. Be back in, say . . . five minutes? Or ten? I know how you young girls like to take your time."

I peered into the bag and pulled out a pair of jogging pants and a T-shirt with a huge hole in the front, remaining silent as I stepped into another person's clothes, hoping they'd at least worn underwear at the time.

Some minutes later, I stood in a windowless room surrounded by piles of old, decaying boxes dripping with the dust and secrets of yesteryear. Apparently my job today and for the next twelve weeks would be to sift old client files and file them in alphabetical order. And there were thousands.

I wanted to cry, but knew I'd never quit anything in my life. Hadn't Dad said something about working hard, and doing the best you could? I wasn't about to let my dad or myself down again.

So I got to work.

After the first week I bought an old transistor radio into the boxroom, before realizing it couldn't work because I was so far below ground. The silence and loneliness was stifling and I quickly ran out of ingenious ways to stem the total boredom of my day. I was reduced to singing and talking to myself, thinking of Biyi in various sexual positions and imagining the time when my life would be good again.

Sometimes, Lowey, things have to get really bad before they can get better.

Accept that some days you'll be the puppy . . . other days, the lamppost.

Every evening, I'd arrive home exhausted. Even more so than when I used to work twelve-hour days. At first Biyi waiting for me on my doorstep with a thoughtful gift of scented bubble bath or a favorite chocolate bar was a welcome joy. Or when he insisted on making me dinner with unlimited foot massages for dessert. However, when he asked the impossible—"Why don't you let me have a key?"—I felt that old feeling of fear make its appearance.

"To my apartment?" I swallowed hard.

"Why not? We've been going out for ages. I could have things ready for you when you get home—even help out with the bills . . ."

"Er . . . No, I don't think so, Biyi," I replied softly.

"No? Just like that? No discussion, nothing?" he said, obviously irritated.

"Yes. I'm sorry . . . really, I am . . ."

"Aren't you even going to think about it?"

"There's nothing really to think about."

"I just don't get you, Lois Bates."

"That makes two of us," I whispered, turning my head away solemnly.

"What?"

"Nothing," I said, when what I really wanted to do was explain. Explain why I wasn't ready—would never be ready—to fully give myself to him. It just didn't feel right. It had never really felt right . . . with anyone.

"All I ever want is the best for you. I'm not here to make things hard for you, Lois." And at times, I had seen that. Appreciated it, even. I just couldn't allow myself to believe in any of it.

"I don't want to talk about this any more," I said.

"I think we should talk about this. About us," he said, reaching for my hand.

"No, I can't, Biyi . . . Please . . . let me—I mean *it*—go . . ."

He tried to change my mind with soft words and promises, but I was fixed on my own reality and, finally, he respected my wishes—but only after a stream of sad words and tears that coated his lovely girly eyelashes like a slippery silk coat.

I just had to let him go.

Temping work began to dry up with some agencies not even bothering with a courtesy call. Even the words of *The Manual* again failed to make much of an impact on my general sense of unwell-being.

And things got worse.

Following yet another pointless interview, I began the short walk from the bus stop as rain pelted onto me. Having forgotten my umbrella, a pair of suede boots that had cost a fortune a year and a half ago gratefully soaked up excess water. Outside my apartment, I rummaged around my oversized bag for my keys as the downpour increased with new vigor and my hair stuck to my face. Inside, I felt something was amiss and my instincts led me into the lounge where chaos was everywhere. Water, seeping from the bathroom and into the corridor had swept through to the living room.

A flood.

My heart traded places with my stomach. I began to perspire, my mind was blank, my body catatonic until a thought hit me.

The Manual.

I raced to the bedroom, tearing at my clothes in the wardrobe—jeans, belts, blouses, all bought at the height of mini-wealth and now discarded onto the floor like garbage, because the only thing of any real value to me was *The Manual.* And when I located it, still in its usual place—the top section of the wardrobe—I held it close, eyes squeezed shut, releasing a heavy sigh.

It was safe.

My dad was safe.

I stayed at Mom's while the apartment got sorted.

"There are clean towels in the basket . . . well, you know where everything is," said Mom as Abbi looked on with intense curiosity. I unpacked my hastily put-together suitcase. Getting rid of the water, cleaning up the house, negotiating with insurance companies and plumbers had all taken its toll, but Mom looked more worn out than I did. I'd never seen her this way before, having always taken pride in looking "well turned out," as she liked to put it—if only to put Carla's mom's nose out of joint. Now, her hair was in need of a brush, her clothes crying out for an iron. The Bingo Caller had said a muffled hello earlier then disappeared off to bed at the rather early time of seven thirty.

I finished unpacking in my old room, now a spare, and gave out an exaggerated yawn. "Thanks, Mom."

"What for?"

"For letting me stay."

She placed untidy strands of hair behind her ear. "You don't need to thank me, Lois. You're my daughter."

"Are you okay . . . ? I mean, you look tired, Mom."

She sat on the edge of the bed and seemed to have aged ten years. "Just a bit of sleeplessness. Nothing to worry about."

"Why aren't you sleeping?"

"Don't fuss, Lois. It will pass."

Abbi joined Mom on the bed, complete with a distorted drawing of a puffin bird that she felt needed our full attention, and I decided to lay off Mom. But I was worried.

I needed to assess how much the flood would cost me if the insurance didn't pay up. A few items had been damaged—luxuries I'd surrounded myself with over the years, like my DVD recorder. I remember being filled with elitist joy upon realizing I was probably one of the first people in the country to own one—its $500 price tag a mere glitch in my ocean of high earnings. The Bang & Olufsen wall stereo system had survived, though, but this hardly mattered, since I hadn't used it in weeks.

"Why are you sad?" asked Abbi.

"I'm okay," I shrugged, bending down to retrieve my toiletry bag, suddenly eager to be alone.

"Was it because of all the water?" pressed Abbi. I wanted her out of my room. I wanted to be alone, to fully grasp what had happened, what had been happening ever since I'd been made redundant. Being kicked in the ass by everyone and everything. I was so fed up. I was so tired. I was so sick.

"Abbi! Bed!" called Mom from the corridor.

Abbi obeyed. I opened *The Manual,* hoping it would make me feel better.

It didn't.

mistakes are okay

Kevin Trivia: *After peeling off some of the colors, I finally managed to master the Rubik's Cube one fine Sunday afternoon as my daughter snoozed on my lap.*

Considering the kicking I'd had lately, I was actually surprised when the insurance check arrived, pushing away the last of the murky clouds that had been hanging over me. Life back at Mom's had started off fine. Taking Abbi to school, her little friends staring up at me with wonderful childhood fascination as none of them had ever seen "Abbi's big sister" before. Unlike my own time at school, Abbi was popular among both sexes and this didn't surprise me in the least, what with her vivacious charm and a face that grew more beautiful each day. After the school run I'd sit in an overpriced coffee shop with my iced chocolate froth, trying to formulate some type of plan, armed with a notebook, camera, my laptop and *The Manual*, sometimes all four.

Miscellaneous: Mistakes

Yes, you'll make a few. You're human, imperfect and basically set up to make mistakes from the moment of birth.

I've definitely made a few. I suppose my biggest mistake involved my sisters Philomena and Ina. They had a big row once—I won't go into the details because this manual is for and remains about YOU—but I took sides and I shouldn't have. However, that falling out has had consequences for our relationships today. But I have learned from that mistake. And I really hope that Ina comes round. Especially now.

Anyway.

Guaranteed, you'll probably make a few mistakes in your life too. Hey, what did you expect me to say? The trick is to learn from these mistakes, grow from them. If you don't, then it's all been a balls-up for absolutely no reason.

The night before the check arrived, I walked in to find Mom and the Bingo Caller with Abbi nestled between them, dozing in front of the television. I stood and watched for the longest time as something unfamiliar, unexplainable, grabbed me from within. A sort of loneliness. A sadness that stayed with me as I headed back to the bedroom feeling like an intruder.

Thankfully, the check arrived in the morning and by the start of *EastEnders* I was back at my apartment, albeit in the middle of a building site.

I chose to spend the first day of my twenty-seventh year on this earth hidden under the duvet, hoping that everyone might have forgotten. But as I padded into the corridor I noticed a stack of envelopes underneath the letterbox. A soppy card from Biyi, an x-rated one from Carla and a cutesy contribution from Mom, Abbi and the Bingo Caller. I had to admit, a little part of me was glad they'd all remembered.

You're twenty-eight! Hurrah!

My little girl is growing up.

I know something will have changed for you by now. Perhaps you feel more at ease with yourself? I'm asking this because post twenty-five is when I really came into my own as a man. Something inside changes—and yes, I suppose I can only talk from my own experiences (plus I'm aware that men take a tiny bit longer to grow up than women, so forgive me if none of this applies to you and you are a fully fledged, fully rounded adult and have felt your age from day one!) . . .

Thankfully the smell of damp had subsided soon after the workmen had left. And after paying for repairs and replacing items with much cheaper versions, I felt I was on my way up again. Biyi was thrilled when I called to thank him for the card, insisting he come over, which I agreed to. I told myself I needed him, allowed him to make love to me while I lay there trying not to connect my heart with the moment. Especially when he whispered my name and told me he loved me.

"Are you okay, Lois?" he asked as we nestled against one another.

"I think so."

"Then I'm happy."

I wanted to smile. But I didn't. I couldn't. "You do know . . . that this . . . this is a one-off . . . I don't . . ."

He placed a finger onto my lips and nodded his head. "I know."

*. . . Of course, I don't want to put pressure on you. Perhaps things aren't great. But however bad they seem, remember this,—**where there is life there is hope.** You're alive. Embrace this, Lowey, because you can do ANYTHING while there is breath in your body. If only I'd remembered that when I was alive.*

I love you, with stars on. Dad

Dad's words seemed to slowly pump the air back into my body. Breathing out slowly, I read the paragraph again. And again. And again. And again, until I'd learned it word for word. Until I'd allowed it to seep into the very depths of me.

I was alive.

People were dying every day.

But I was alive.

Alive.

. . . because you can do ANYTHING while there is breath in your body. If only I'd remembered that . . .

As my body refilled with air, specks of new hope followed. I stood up, experiencing a heady rush as I realized Dad was right. I was still healthy. I was alive.

*There will be times when some a****** or a situation gets one over on you, leads you to the brink. And there will be times when it seems like the world is just taking a P.I.S.S. I'm sorry to say, it's highly unlikely you'll pass through life without experiencing such stuff (remember the lamppost analogy?). So, all I'm going to use to wrap this bit up is a mega cliché that I've always liked; and that's to see these various slaps in the face as a stage you will eventually get through, with hard graft, help, whatever. And I hope that when you do, you'll be able to take stock of what's happened, learn from it, and **DON'T LET IT BEAT YOU.***

It wouldn't be easy, I knew that. But for the first time in months I could glimpse a view over that familiar horizon of doom.

The rent was well over the odds for Deptford and passing trade would be minimal, but two weeks after my birthday I placed a hefty deposit and two months' advance rent on a small business unit. So what if it was the last of my insurance money and a cash advance from my credit card was the only way I could pay for the super-duper laptop and printer needed to complete this new project? I had to start believing in myself again, that I could make a go of this photography business. K Pics (K for Kevin, of course!) would be about "making over" the customer and producing shots that could pass for edgy, unique and current, unlike the corny pictures currently on display in some photographic shop windows.

Carla was a star, helping me clean and decorate the shop,

while Mom backed out at the last minute because of the Bingo Caller being unable to look after Abbi.

Regardless of some minor setbacks, K Pics was supposed to be opening in three weeks. Admittedly, it was touch and go considering the amount of talking (instead of painting) Carla and I got through. Particularly when we got onto the subject of her big brother.

"Who would have thought Slut of the Year Corey would have settled down!"

I stopped painting.

"A different girl every week, that one. Don't you remember when we were at school?" She thought for a moment. "Oh, sorry . . ." She looked guilty.

"Forget about it. I have," I said quietly.

"Really? Or are you just saying that?"

"A mind-reader now, are we?" I snapped.

"I just want you to be happy too, like me and Markus . . . That's all."

Carla droned on about how incredible it was to be in love as I drifted off, uninterested in her wistful tales.

What was love anyway? I asked myself.

Miscellaneous: Love

Love can be anything.

There's probably a whole load of theories on being in love. A chemical reaction, a state of mind, blah, blah, blah. And there is a definite sense of division among the egg heads on this thing called love.

I'd say it's relative to who's actually feeling it. When you're still a kid, getting your hair pulled by some other kid could be a way of him letting you know he fancies you. A few years later, you might find yourself dreaming about some spotty boy with massive feet who sits behind you in Science. Your mind's racing, your palms are getting all clammy. That's what we call lust, my darling. Just early lust. Love—real love—comes with so much more, Lowey, and must not be confused with lust.

So what is love?

Love is . . . loving someone even when they look like they've been dragged through a muddy hedge sideways and then doused in manure for good measure.

That's a good place to start.

But loving someone can be . . . one minute this unexplainable connection as you both sit in silence watching the TV, knowing you'd never want to be apart from that person; the next day trying to decide the quickest, cleanest way to finish them off. A bit of a contradiction, but it's usually the good stuff, like the tummy flips, the longing and constant reel of thoughts about that special someone that are great. Thankfully, these don't last, as something a lot more important slips into place. Just trust me when I tell you this: when you feel it, you'll know. Just like I knew with your mother, you'll just know. You may find this aged eighteen or eighty-five. I was lucky to find it the day I met your mom.

And then again with you.

With stars on, Dad

By midnight we'd finished all the painting and clearing up, and despite her protests Carla stayed behind to help with the finishing touches—strategically placing huge plants to cover the odd fracture in the wall and arguing over where to place the tripod.

"Why didn't you ask Biyi to help? I thought you were at least friends now?"

Miscellaneous: Male friends 2
Can men and women be just good friends?

Yes.

But make no mistake, he's dreaming about and living for the day you'll be desperate enough to, well, you know . . .

Again, look up the section on hormones and teabags—that never really goes away. So even if you've been friends for a long time (he's seen you with snot dripping from your nose, or covered in sick after a particularly bad case of food poisoning) he still wouldn't be knocking over chairs trying to get away if you asked him to take your friendship beyond the boundaries, if only for one night.

Okay, maybe I'm being a bit unfair. Mature men and women CAN be friends. But only if the friendship has never, and I mean NEVER, been contaminated with that old thing called . . . lust. A kiss . . . the other stuff . . . even unclean thoughts. Because then a line has been crossed and it's hard to get back to that wholesome platonic friendship level you had before.

Hadn't Corey proved this theory?

I held up images of Abbi and Carla to the wall.

"I'm bored of talking about men!" I said, deciding the one of Abbi on her bike would be the centerpiece of the shop. The kid was just too cute. "Carla, what picture do you think should go here when the wall's dry? You in the red dress or the blue?" I knew her vanity would win, and predictably all thoughts of Biyi disappeared as she concentrated meticulously on selecting her "sexiest" photograph.

I called a cab for us both as Carla was on her phone to Markus.

"Sorry, Markus, we got a bit carried away here, but Lois has just called a cab and I'm on my way."

Carla's smile crumpled and she turned away from me. Her voice was low, but in the still of an empty shop after midnight I could hear the conversation clearly.

"I'm sorry, Markus. She needed my help. You know I'm never usually out this late . . . no . . . I . . . Sorry."

I pretended to busy myself, but my ears remained transfixed.

"Yes, bu— No, I am not talking back, Markus. I will be home very soon—yes, I . . . Markus? Markus? Are you there?"

She closed the phone and turned to me. "He's a bit peeved with me."

My friend, the ballsy chick who took no crap from anyone at school, suddenly looked lost, if not a little frightened.

"Carla, are you okay?"

"He's so angry with me, Lois . . ." She sat on a stool still wrapped in plastic, head bowed.

"Is . . . is he going to have a go at you when you get in?"

"A bit. He just loves me so much. Doesn't like being away from me."

"He's a control freak, Carla!"

The cab beeped its horn outside.

"Don't start all that again. I've gotta go. Now," she said with sudden urgency.

As the cab pulled up to their apartment, I sensed her

body stiffen. We said a hurried goodbye and she shot out. I asked the cabby to wait. The lounge light flicked on. Two shadows came together. Body language strained, at one point a little too aggressive from his point of view. I waited—more than ready to barge in if I had to.

The two shadows embraced. I told the cabby to move on.

On the day of the opening I was filled with shreds of anxiety. Would anyone actually like my pictures? Apart from the praise of a proud mom cooing over pictures of her little girl, a vain best friend, a seven-year-old and the man who'd been sleeping with me, I'd yet to show my work to anyone else. Having placed advertisements in the local press and shop windows, I hoped the promise of free wine would encourage customers through the doors.

Within the first half-hour, though, only two people came in.

"Wow, that's lovely!" said a toothy woman who admitted she hadn't seen any of the advertisements, merely dropping in out of curiosity.

"Thank you," I replied as her eyes roamed slowly around my new shop.

"How much do you charge for a full session?"

"Twenty pounds per shot," I said. Although I'd already agreed a price in my head, after careful negotiations with my calculator, hearing it said out loud induced a little trepidation within me. A fear of rejection. A belief that the customer would soon realize what a fraud I was, before storming out to find a "real" photographer.

"Okay."

"Okay?"

She sat on one of the stools. "Do I bring my own make-up?"

I turned to the side, Abbi's adorable grin staring back at me.

"Yes, if you could. Plus two changes of clothes and . . ."

And as I continued, the lady with an abundance of teeth had no idea that she was my first paying customer. That any mistake made with her booking would be a learning curve. That I would work doubly hard to give her the very best service I could.

Two days later, she returned for the shoot. The test shots were awful, as were the ten after that, but slowly I began to develop my own rhythm. Learned her best angles and the right things to say to make her smile. And hours later we sat at the laptop picking the best shots. Far from being a fussy customer, she just had one stipulation: "Can you do something about my teeth?"

By the end of my third day in business, I had five orders pending.

Carla had an idea to put a small placard outside the indoor market, displaying my work, which seemed to entice passing trade, and within one week my orders doubled. My three star models (Abbi, Carla and the lady with the now airbrushed teeth) took pride of place in the studio. Abbi in a pink fluffy dress munching on an ice lolly, all doe-eyed and innocent, and the earlier shot of her riding the bike with the yellow tassels. On the far side, Carla looking rather sexual, mouth slightly open, her gorgeous face slightly shrouded by shadows. It was an absolutely stunning shot that hadn't needed much of a touch up anyway.

And then the toothy lady with her foot on a stool, smiling at the camera. I hadn't felt this good, this alive and full of purpose in ages.

I put together a makeshift website, displaying a show-reel of my photos, and even though I had yet to receive any inquiries via email, a presence in cyberspace somehow legitimized the business for me. Deep down I still couldn't believe I HAD a business, let alone believe I was actually any *good* at photography. I'd never once questioned my ability in IT, but something as creative as this uncovered new sets of insecurities that had been lurking deep within. Yet despite all of this, I felt alive.

My camera was now a part of me, and I was unable (or unwilling) to go anywhere without the black case and strap swinging from my shoulders. It wasn't easy without a car, but it was manageable.

I arrived at Carla's mom's feeling slightly nervous and uncertain if I'd bump into Corey. I was going to take some shots of Calvin with Carla's mom to add to my portfolio of couple photographs. So while strangely excited about depicting the love and passion they still shared for one another despite their difference in age, I was relieved to know that Corey was out house-hunting in Greenwich with his bride-to-be.

I took various shots of the happy couple in a variety of poses around the house. Still astounded as to how much Carla's mom and Calvin were so obviously very much in love, when contrasted to the staleness of Mom and the Bingo Caller's relationship next door.

"You look great!" enthused Calvin as Carla's mom reappeared in her fourth outfit of the day—a red off-the-shoulder dress so short I could probably wear it as a bikini top.

"Thanks, babe!" she trilled, draping long, shapely legs around her husband and perhaps totally forgetting my existence as she proceeded to stick her tongue down his throat.

I cleared my own throat loudly, before reluctantly shooting them in near pornographic poses, relieved to hear the front door open and the couple relax their positions somewhat.

Corey, minus the Blonde Bombshell Mark Two, appeared.

"Hi," he said solemnly, eyes facing the laminated floor.

My heart stopped.

"What's wrong, Corey?" asked Carla's mom, pulling the hem of her dress downward.

"Nothing, Mom," he replied, throwing himself onto the armchair. Something was wrong and I suddenly felt like an intruder.

"Let's go and make something to drink, Lois!" said Calvin, ushering me out of the lounge and into the kitchen. It seemed clear that mother and son needed to be alone.

"Do you think Corey's okay?" I asked as Calvin fixed himself a straight rum on the rocks and mine with coke.

"I suppose we'll find out sooner or later. Probably that girlfriend of his."

"Oh?" I sipped at the drink, the sharpness of the rum gripping my taste buds.

"I really shouldn't say this but they've been arguing a lot lately, you know . . ."

I didn't know. Carla hadn't mentioned it. Not that I'd asked.

Calvin took a large slurp of his drink and flinched a little. "It's not until you live with someone that you know what they are really like. That's why I'm so lucky with my wife. We're just meant to be together. You know what I mean?"

I didn't, but I nodded regardless.

"You should have brought your record round to play."

" 'With Stars On'?"

"Yeah, that corny one. I'd like to hear it again"

I playfully pinched him on the arm. "It's not corny! Besides, carrying my camera equipment AND an old vinyl record on the bus? Too much.

"Why don't we download it!"

"Can you believe, I just never got round to doing that?"

"You've had a lot on your mind. No problem, we can do it right now. Might take a bit of time to find it on the Net and downloading it will take at least half an hour," he said.

"You mean you haven't got broadband?"

"Nope."

"Sorry, I forgot to mention that this creative photographer thing is merely a disguise, there's always going to be a nerd fighting to get out!"

Half an hour later, Calvin had located Dad's song and sent the MP3 file to my email box ready to download. A bloodshot-eyed Corey and his mom soon appeared.

"Can we finish this another time?" asked Carla's mom.

"Sure," I replied as Calvin handed his stepson a straight rum. Corey finally acknowledged my existence with a nod just as I was leaving.

"Good to see you, Lo Bag."

"You too," I said.

He followed me to the door and I faced him.

"What?" he asked in an ironic tone. I wanted to hold him, smooth over whatever was making him so sad.

"What is it?" I asked.

A pained expression followed and for a second there I

thought he would fall into my arms, rest his head and just *be*.

Instead, with his hand on the doorknob, he said, "It's nothing. I'll be fine."

Carla never really did fill me in on what had happened, only that Corey and the Blonde Bombshell Mark Two parted soon after the very day I'd seen him, with Corey immediately taking a flight out to Barcelona, to his dad. Something that I totally understood he had to do. I ran a finger over *The Manual*, hoping to feel my own dad's presence, but after reading a few past entries, I realized something: *The Manual* was almost coming to an end. Bookmarking where I had now reached meant the amount of pages on the right were so much less than those on the left-hand side. I gave out a sigh. No one, Corey included, would ever truly understand what *The Manual* meant to me—especially when all he had to do was take a two-hour plane trip to see his dad. I'd never see mine again.

I invested in a colorful portable MP3 player and the first song I loaded onto it was Dad's song. So now it was as if I could hear his voice as I traveled on the bus into work or during the less busy moments in the shop. And that was nice.

I was soon able to break even with the bills and pay myself a tiny wage that would keep me in hot food. It was tough, but I found myself smiling more and more with each new day.

The cloud had lifted.

Thanks, Dad.

do something silly

Kevin Trivia: ***I slept through half of* ET*—but don't tell your mom!***

Miscellaneous: Advice—some rules

You'll get to an age where you probably think you've seen a lot, done a lot, heard a lot. So it's easy to want to pass these experiences onto others, especially those you care so deeply about (just look at me!).

But try not to impart words of wisdom that border "advice" territory—not unless someone literally begs you (while dangling dangerously on the edge of Big Ben's long hand).

*Yes, I'm contradicting myself, considering this manual is all about me advising you on every facet of your life without actually being asked, but . . . erm . . . oh, b****r it, I'm a dying man, give me a break.*

* * *

My best friend and I sat opposite one another, tucking into a selection of oriental starters at our favorite Chinese restaurant, just off Deptford High Street.

"It's like I've just told you the worst news in the world, and not that I'm marrying Markus, the man I love. Sorry for thinking you'd be happy for me," she said, crunching into a mini pancake roll.

"I want to be . . . but it's him. He isn't good enough for you," I said fervently.

"And that's your expert advice?"

"It's not advice as such . . . just my opinion . . ."

"Just what have you got against him?"

"You have to ask? I don't like the way he treats you, for a start."

"He doesn't hit me!" she said a bit too quickly.

My tummy muscles tensed as I watched her shift bits of pancake roll around her plate.

"I know you don't agree with marriage and that but don't try to ram it down my throat . . ."

"You know that isn't it."

"Then what is it then?"

"I have just told you."

"Tell me again."

"His jealousy . . . the way he talks down to you, Carla. I've seen it and he doesn't care who he does it in front of." Against the paper tablecloth, our fingers met, her engagement ring tinkling against the artificial lighting.

"Please, just think about it before you tie yourself down to this man."

She drew her hand away and we ate in silence as I thought about just how much none of this made any sense. I'd dumped boyfriends nowhere near as bad as Markus. And yet Carla was willing to forgo any feeling of self-worth to settle for a moron who lacked basic respect.

I was confused.

Saturday was the busiest day at the shop, which meant I was unfortunately only able to spend an hour at Abbi's birthday party.

"I don't know why you can't stay longer. Abbi loves seeing you!" complained Mom, transporting a fresh tray of jellies onto the kitchen table. Funny, the Bingo Caller—her own father—had hardly made an appearance and I was tempted to point this out.

"Mom, I'd love to stay among fifteen screaming little girls all day, but I have a shop to run and bills that won't pay themselves!"

Abbi ran in looking cute in a pair of bell-bottomed jeans with pink stitching, hair up in a bun and curly tendrils on each side of her head. She was definitely growing up.

"Lois, can you come and take some pictures of me and my girls?"

"Your girls?" I said, surprised at how much of a teenager she was sounding.

"Yeah."

"Are you eight or eighteen?"

"Lois, are we going to do this or not?" she replied haughtily, as I followed her to the lounge where I was instantly reminded of my own birthday parties. Of the last one, especially. Corey handing over that LL Cool J tape; which along with *The Manual* and Dad's camera, has to be one of the best presents I had ever been given.

Abbi and her assortment of "girls" posed like mini Gwen Stefanis.

"Erm, you in the red . . ."

"My name's Michaela!" snapped the girl.

"Could you move in a bit, I want to get you all in the shot!"

Michaela and the girl with large pigtails and a bit too much strawberry lip balm continuously giggled as I snapped away. The session took longer than an hour, of course, due to the incessant questions ("Have you really taken a picture of Kate Moss?) and the insistence they view (and argue over) every single shot.

"Thanks for that, Lois," said the Bingo Caller, appearing at the doorway. He looked tired.

"That's okay."

"Kids can wear you out, right?" he said, perhaps reading my thoughts. I smiled a goodbye and as soon as I was out of the front door, found myself in the path of Corey.

"You look as bad as I feel, Lo Bag."

"Cheers! Blame Abbi and her 'girls' demanding I take photos of them in every corner of the house!"

"Say no more."

We walked together and the nerves appeared.

"How are things, Corey?"

"Could be better. It was good being at the old man's. Spain was great, basically because I wasn't here. No reminders, you know. Hey, let me carry that big ol' thing," he said, placing the strap of my heavy camera case over his own shoulder. "Where was I? Oh yeah. Space. Space to think about what I really want."

We stood by the bus stop.

"And did you manage to figure that out, Corey?"

"You *are* kidding? What with Dad's mad girlfriend Soli and all those sangrias? No way, Lo Bag."

I smiled.

"Seriously, though, I did manage to think through a few things. And I even came to a couple of conclusions . . ."

"Two, huh? Clever boy!" I said, staying with the joviality, while Corey's look became more serious.

"Care to know what one of those conclusions was?"

The familiar red blob came into view. "That's my bus. You'd better tell me quickly!"

"Maybe another time," he said, handing back the camera.

I stepped onto the bus, loaded with ambivalence. Wanting to go, but also wanting to stick around to listen to whatever Corey had to stay.

"See ya, Lo Bag!"

I turned back, but Corey was gone.

Twenty minutes later, I hopped off the bus in time to find a young woman peering through the window of K Pics while muttering on her cellphone. A paying customer, I hoped.

Some weeks were slow, on others I had too many pictures to take and not enough hours. It was never as simple as just taking a few snaps; they had to be airbrushed, at times with special effects (one lady wanted her eyes to literally sparkle, complete with mini stars floating from the eyelids!). Aware of how work obsessed I could become again, I was keen to adopt a sort of work/life balance, so agreed to a cinema trip with Carla.

However, she stood me up.

"I'm so sorry, babe. As I was about to leave, Markus came down with something. He's quite sick. Sorry, babe, will make it up to you. Promise!" she said when she finally called three hours after we were supposed to meet. "He's waking up, Lois. Got to go!"

If you find you're always hearing "sorry" from the same person or perhaps YOU always seem to be the one saying "sorry," perhaps the friendship needs to go back to the drawing board. Wipe it clean and start again—or place it carefully in the bin. Some things need to be looked over from time to time. Reanalyzed, if you like (something I can say that as a man I have never had to do. Okay, maybe once when Charlie kept running to the toilet every time a round was due).

It would be a lie to say I'd never thought of life without Carla. She had a selfish streak that grew with each new boyfriend. We wanted different things; we were so different. But somehow I'd gotten used to her ways, and that in itself was comforting. Plus, I hardly had a mass of best friends vying for my expert make-up tips.

True to form, when we met up again Carla asked if I'd photograph her wedding without mentioning her "no show" the other night.

And I agreed because she was my best friend.

Twenty-nine; two nine; twenty add nine. Whichever way you pronounced the words, they still allowed me to imagine the sight of a great big bulldozer swiftly heading my way. Yes, I was officially twenty-nine years old, and while it stunk like fresh shite I still wasn't as devastated as

Carla, who as always got there a few months before me, refusing to answer her phone for a week, surrounding herself with brochures about "face decreasers" and basically undergoing intense hibernation.

The last year of your twenties. Don't waste it, babe. Do something silly. Not too silly, mind, but something you've wanted to do but thought might offend! You're still young! But I know me writing it down probably won't make you believe it. Anyway, you've still got twelve whole months to get away with whatever you decide, so get going!

Shall I tell you what I did?

Of course I'm going to have to give a toned-down version. Oh, but wait a minute . . . you're twenty-nine now, so I suppose you can handle it.

Okay.

It was 1982 and Charlie wasn't bothered about hitting the big three-oh (as he liked to call it) while I groaned about it being my first ticket to granddad-dom: slippers, pipe, that kind of stuff. So after work one day, instead of the pub, we decided on a club over in Wandsworth. Now you have to understand, Charlie had a wife and two kids, I had you and your mom—we hadn't been clubbing in years and so much had obviously changed. The music . . . Ultravox? Clothes. I mean, flares were cool (sorry) but some of the lads were now wearing tight trousers with long shirts and . . . ruffles. I mean, ruffles! This is almost too painful to write about. Anyway, needless to say, we felt like a right couple of "uncles" floating into the club that night, the young kids gazing at us with pity and wonderment. Perhaps won-

dering why we weren't at home snoring in the armchair. Looking back it probably wasn't the right club to go to (I'm more into Barry White than Visage), but we didn't exactly have a pool of reference to choose from and we were looking for the seemingly impossible—a club that catered for the not too young, but not too old either. The confusion! Anyway, there was (clearing of throat) a certain young lady giving Charlie the eye. He got all flustered and, being the alpha male that he is, thought he'd try out his chatting-up skills—you know, just to see if he still "had it." I stood by with my pint and watched the scene unfold.

Charlie: *"I saw you watching me from across the room, babeeee."*
Girl: *"Really? I thought you did!"*
Charlie: *"Fancy a drink, then?"*
Girl: *"Great!"*
Charlie: *"So do you come here often?"*
Girl: *"Yes, me and my friends."*
Charlie: *"Far out!"*
Girl: *"So, are you Monica's dad then?"*
Charlie: *"Who's Monica?"*
Girl: *"A friend of my sister's. Was hoping you were, so we could all get a lift" she said, pointing to a mixed posse of guys in frilly tops.*

Needless to say, we left sharpish (with Charlie vowing to keep his stud days a fond memory and spoil the wife for at least a month).

And you know what? I wish we had stayed. I wish

we'd borrowed some ruffled shirts, painted our eyelids black, and laughed and bopped the night away to that new romantic music, sliding home in time to hear the birds singing. Really, as I write this manual, I so wish I had, Lois.

So, believe me when I say something happens when you get to thirty, and I'm not telling you what as it's a little unique to everyone.

For now, ***just do something silly.***

With stars on, Dad

I managed to drag Carla away from Markus and her duvet long enough to jump onto a bus to the West End.

"So, you've taken me out of my home, away from my fiancé, to do . . . what, exactly?"

"Get stupid!" I roared in the middle of Trafalgar Square like an unhinged woman. Scarily, no one gave me a second look. "I want to do all the things I missed out on when I was younger!"

Carla rolled her eyes. "Oh, like having sex, you mean?"

"No! I dunno, when's the last time I got drunk?"

"Never. Even when we went to Spain you only drank about two cocktails."

"There you go then. Let's get drunk! It's my birthday and I only have twelve months until I'm thirty! Come on!"

As I said it, I realized that in essence I did have a whole year to "get stupid" but I figured I should start now. Besides, I'd be expanding the business soon.

"Oh big deal. I've got drunk loads of times!"

"In a strip club?"

"Excuse me?" Carla stopped in her tracks like a car coming to an abrupt halt. "Did I hear correctly?"

"You did!"

"Ohmigosh, let's go now, quick, before you change your mind!" She grabbed my hand excitedly. And all I knew at that silly, frivolous moment was that I had to live silly—if only for one night.

Tincurbelle's opened the doors to women every last Thursday of the month according to their Internet site.

"I can't believe we're doing this!" I giggled as Carla explained to the macho bouncer why she wouldn't be presenting him with her cellphone number any time soon. A huge neon light flashing the word "Tincurbelle's" glowed before us.

"What are you waiting for then?" asked Carla as the rejected bouncer reluctantly opened the door for us. I knew that after reading Dad's entry I had to do something out of the ordinary because I had never really let go of my inhibitions before.

Ladies' night at Tincurbelle's had a "no male customers before ten" rule that ensured any inhibitions regarding male strip joints were left behind, as women were free to scream, chuck (panties) and desire without fear of reprisals from hubbies and boyfriends riddled with low self-esteem (Markus, case in point). The venue remained dedicated to female pleasure and the odd hen night judging by the small group currently surrounding an overweight blonde dressed in a curtain veil and L plates. My mind drifted to Corey and his failed wedding and Carla's impending one. Time for a drink, I decided.

"Are you listening?" snapped Carla, bundling me into another room. "The main event's about to start!"

I bought another drink and was yet to feel the effects, something I wished would hurry along if only to block out the effects of the so-called male stripper who suddenly appeared on stage, a rather average looking, if not beer-bellied man dressed in tight fitting James Bond attire. The familiar theme tune pulsated through the room as the crowd roared its approval.

The women jostled wildly as, piece by piece, "Jamie" Bond clumsily removed every item of clothing to reveal a generous girth and a bum in need of Clearasil. Of course, my expectations had clung on to the hung-like-a-horse six-packed type currently gyrating on the company's website.

"Hello everyone!" he shouted. The crowd squealed and roared as he began a descent into the world of hip-thrusting and swirling his body out of tune to the music (not blessed with the dancing skills of Justin Timberlake, clearly). But as soon as he requested his very own Pussy Galore, a bevy of eager volunteers sprang forward in apparent hunger for this man's generous amount of flesh. Carla, absorbing every moment, squealed with delight as I merely shook my head in bewilderment. Dad's words were popping into my head as I decided to make the best of this night and really let my hair down, so to speak. So I grabbed her hand and began the arduous journey to the front, pushing, shoving and almost kicking our way through the crowd of screaming, swaying women, quickly gaining entry to the most envied position in the club.

The front row.

Where I, despite my initial embarrassment and not knowing where to aim my eyes, enjoyed the remainder of the show.

"That was brilliant!"

"He was awful, Carla!"

"Yeah, I know that, but that's the point I s'pose!"

"We must do something next week. Or next month? Or maybe in a few months as I'm going to be flat out with K Pics, hopefully."

"Wow, I knew it wouldn't last! Anyhow, I've had a lovely night. Thanks for this, I really needed it."

"Things tough at home?"

"I didn't say that," she said awkwardly with a wave of a perfectly manicured finger. "Don't spoil a brilliant night."

The next morning I awoke to the feeling of fifty woodpeckers pecking at my head, a mouth reeking of rotting chicken and the doorbell ringing incessantly.

"All right!" I groaned as, across me, on the left-hand side of the bed, a body stirred. My mind wandered back to the night before. The strip club. The stripper. The taxi home. The body in my bed didn't move, merely grunted its disapproval as I leaped over it to answer the door.

"Who is this?" I asked through the intercom.

"Markus."

I buzzed him in.

"Where is she?" he asked, no "hello," nothing.

"Carla's upstairs."

"She'd better be," he said, pushing past me and into my room.

"Hey, you can't just barge in there!" I called out.

"Carla!" he said harshly, shaking her awake, a little too roughly for my liking.

"Don't you touch her!" I protested. Markus merely ignored me as Carla slowly opened her eyes, at first unable to make out the emerging scene.

"Markus?" she asked mid-yawn.

"I've been up all night waiting for you! Why didn't you come home?"

Carla rubbed her eyes, the remnants of mascara smeared across her cheek. "I told you I was staying at Lois's."

"No, you didn't! You said you were coming home!"

"I didn't!"

"Are you calling me a liar, Carla?"

"No . . . I . . ." she backtracked.

"No. Now get your things and come home NOW!" He grabbed her arm, still displaying the green ticket stamp from the night before.

"Ow, you're hurting me!" she protested.

Watching him hurl her out of my bed—T-shirt tucked into her thong and still within the realms of sleep, made me very, very angry.

"Oh that is it! Get the heck out of my house!" I screamed.

"Lois, don't . . ." said Carla, who once again transformed into a wimp right before my very eyes. As if she was another person in front of Markus.

And I didn't like it. Didn't like what he was doing to her.

He shoved her arm away as she scrambled for clothes. "Listen to her, Lois. Don't get involved in things that don't concern you."

"This does concern me! I don't like the way you treat her and I'm not going to let you do it in my house!" I screamed.

"Not a problem, we're going home now. Come on!" he roared, grabbing her by the arm again. Just then, I saw a red flash and then it happened.

Miscellaneous: How to make a man temporarily helpless? Aim for the balls

This can work both ways.

I will not tell you about the first way, because you are

my daughter. But I'm sure, as you get older, your friends will be able to erm . . . confirm the following gossip: that grabbing a bloke's balls in **any** *situation will always render him temporarily helpless . . . Enough said there. Thank you.*

The other way, I'll explain.

If you ever (and I pray you never do) find yourself in a dangerous situation with a guy, just aim for the balls. The pain is unimaginable, will bring actual tears to his eyes, and whatever he was trying to do before (and in my case, just kick a soccer toward goal) will now seem a distant and painful memory. Nutshell (yes, I know), just aim and strike. But only in extreme circumstances, and not if the boy next door nicks your Milky Bar.

Thankfully, Carla forgave me for kicking Markus in the nuts, and in a beautiful twist told him their relationship was over. I wasn't sure she meant it until two days later when she appeared on my doorstep complete with suitcase and a dominatrix teddy bear tucked under her arm.

With Carla settled in her old room, I kissed *The Manual*, convinced that if my dad was looking down at me, he'd be smiling, make no mistake.

By the middle of 2007, Carla had moved back in with her mom, Calvin and now Corey. And at last able to trust my new part-time assistant to run the studio on her own, I knocked on Carla's door after a visit with Mom and Abbi.

"Can Carla come out to play?" I asked in a fake child's voice.

"Oh, F off!" replied Carla sweetly. I followed her into the

lounge to find Calvin and Corey fiddling with the CD player.

"What are you two up to?" I said as Corey winked in my direction. Of course I ignored that.

"Trying to fix the portable MP3 onto the CD player speakers," replied Calvin.

"I'll have a try," I offered as Carla's mom appeared.

"Lois, how's your mom?"

"She's fine, why?"

"Nothing. You staying for dinner?"

"Go on, Lo Bag," said Corey. Thankfully, he was looking a lot happier than when we'd last spoken at the bus stop.

"What's for dinner?"

"Chicken and fries. Here, they got you fixing stuff?" said Carla's mom.

"She's a man in women's clothing!" said Carla as I slapped her playfully on her arm.

With the MP3 player hooked up to the speakers, and a full belly, Carla suggested the three of us take a walk down to the rec.

"To walk off Mom's fattening dinner for a start. Come on, it'll be like old times!" she said.

"Which worries me," I mumbled to myself.

We headed to the rec, arriving at our favorite little wall.

"Sit down then, girls."

"It's dirty!" I complained. Corey pulled himself onto the wall, swinging his legs effortlessly in front of him.

"Too old to get up, more like."

"Shut up, big bro, you're already thirty. We're spring chickens compared to you!"

"Here, take my hand, Lo Bag."

As soon as my hand brushed Corey's, I felt a surge of

electricity pass between us. Corey smiled. I pulled away, and with great difficulty I made the quick hop onto the wall. Sure enough, our graffiti had long since succumbed to time and the council's new cleaning system, but the memories—they remained.

"I can't believe I'm back living with my mom AND she's married to a man cooler than me!" said Corey.

"I can't believe I'm single for the first time in like . . . ever! And I'm holding down a job!"

"I can't believe Abbi's growing up so fast. AND that Carla's been working at Selfridges for more than three months!"

We laughed in unison, pausing as a group of teenagers fled past in the midst of tomfoolery.

"That was us once," said Corey, perhaps articulating what we all felt. One of the boys playfully ruffled the hair of his sweetheart, who smiled coyly in return. Hang on . . .

"That's Abbi! Hey, Abbs, where are you off to?" I ran over to my sister, dressed in a tight pink top, skinny jeans, a slither of eye-shadow across each eyelid!

"I'm going to one of my friends' houses!"

"On your own?"

"I'm almost nine and it's only three o'clock in the afternoon!" she said, circling her head like a snake ready to pounce.

"Does Mom know you're out?"

Her eyes betrayed her.

"Who does she think you're with?"

"Michaela."

"And where's Michaela?"

"Over there." She sighed in exasperation and pointed to a girl and a boy about the same age, in deep conversation.

"Can you go home please? Now!" I said firmly.

"You're worse than Mom! Just because I went missing when I was a kid, she's all paranoid!"

"I'll be ringing Mom in about ten minutes to check you're at home. By the way, who's the boy?"

"My friend."

"How old is he?"

"Eleven."

"A friend? Nothing else?"

"He's not even buff, I wouldn't look at him twice!!! Duh!"

"Kids, eh?" said Carla, as we slowly headed back.

"I feel about a thousand years old now! When did my little sister grow into a teenager?"

"Trust me, we were never that grown up at her age. It's all different now, what with the Internet. I bet Abbi even has her own email address," said Corey.

"Stop sounding like our parents! We're still young!"

"Oh behave. We're lucky to be alive, aren't we? Some people don't live up to or past thirty. Remember that."

They both fell silent, realizing the significance of my words. And the silence remained until we arrived at Mr. Tally's, overexcited at the sight of an elusive bag of cola cubes.

Carla spent her thirtieth birthday getting drunk and puking all over Calvin's sneakers outside a Greenwich pub. She soon concluded that the build-up had been worse than the actual day because once she actually got there (well, the day after anyway) she began to feel really good about it all. Better than she had thought possible.

As *my* twenty-ninth year on this earth continued, so did

the days, weeks and months—until four weeks remained until the "big day." Of course, Carla and Mom put my violent refusal to discuss any birthday plans down to the clichéd fear of aging, when deep down I knew the real reason: only one more chapter remained of *The Manual*.

your longest chapter my shortest

The tiny love heart slowly grew into a quick flash of stars, ending with a tinny version of the familiar "Happy Birthday" ditty, "love Abbi" appearing at the bottom of my cellphone screen.

So, I'd almost got there.

Thirty.

More than just a milestone for me, this was undoubtedly the last chapter of *The Manual.*

The last ever chapter.

Of course, I'd thought about the various locations I wanted to be when I read Dad's last entry, but the only place that felt right was back in my room at Mom's, one-eyed teddy beside me just as it had been eighteen years ago.

But my room was now a spare bedroom, populated by Abbi's old bed, cardboard boxes, the one-eyed teddy long binned. Yet still, I needed to be there again. Where it had all begun. So it felt fitting and not at all unusual for me to be alone in my childhood house as Abbi, Mom and the Bingo Caller spent the weekend in Cornwall. I snuck in with my key, into my old room, *The Manual* tucked under my arm in a plastic bag.

Well it's here. You're thirty. Feel different yet? It may not happen today but somewhere along the way you will have grown into the woman you're probably going to end up being until you die aged one hundred and nine. I'm not saying you won't continue to grow—experiences, the people you meet will all contribute into shaping you, molding you into Lois Bates. You never actually stop growing. Isn't that great?

By now, though, I hope you'll have become confident and unconcerned about what people think of you (unless they're your boss). I hope you will have acquired this inner confidence that others can see and you can feel every waking moment of your life.

Yes, there'll be knocks, but by now you'll have figured out ways to get yourself back up again and so on. If not, go right back to the beginning of this manual and start again, or you can just chuck it in the dustbin because you feel it to be all a load of old nonsense.

Because, you see, I don't claim to have all the answers. I can only work from what I've been given up to the age of thirty. Like parenting, life is about continually learning (hey, there should be a manual given out to all parents in the maternity ward, now that would be something) and you probably still have a bit to learn, as do I.

You may or may not have kids, a good job, a boyfriend, hubby. Lois, I can sit here and second guess all day, but as you know, I haven't got much time left (boom, boom!) so I can only really hope that by now you'll have learned a few things, like:

- *Don't ever imagine you can really change a male—unless he uses a pacifier and sits in a baby carriage.*
- *Learn how to accept changes.*
- *You are beautiful.*
- *The toast will ALWAYS fall on the buttered side.*
- *Even though you may want to reach the top, score the winning goal at the World Cup, happiness, joy, fun, games, LIFE is still going on while you are busy strategizing.*

Hours had passed. I just lay on the bed, not daring to complete another sentence. Wanting to absorb every last word, thought, inscription.

The doorbell rang.

I didn't care.

Just a few pages remained. Including one headed:

So, what do I think the future holds in terms of technology?

Video laser disks will take over vinyl records, for sure.

I shut *The Manual* and stamped my eyes shut. This felt so hard. So very, very hard.

Robots will be cooking dinner.

I moved over to the window. It was getting dark, but I could see Corey striding confidently across the road to his front door, my tummy undergoing that familiar spin just as he looked up and our eyes connected through the glass.

"Lo Bag!" he mouthed. I went down and let him in. I led him upstairs.

"I thought I saw you come in. I rang the bell earlier."

"I'm not supposed to be in here," I whispered. Although the house was technically my home, I'd still felt a bit weird sneaking in like this.

"Are you going to tell me what you're up to?" he asked. But with a quick glance at *The Manual,* his expression changed. He knew. He'd remembered. I suspected he was the only person in this world apart from me and Auntie Philomena who'd ever remembered.

"Hey, I can give you some privacy if you like."

I suddenly felt cold, a little scared. Not wanting him to leave.

"Lo Bag, are you all right?"

Without warning, I found myself entrenched in his grip, as if he was holding me up.

"I'm sorry, I don't know what . . ." I said, still a little unsteady on my feet. He moved me to the bed and then it happened.

> ***And along with the pocket television, state-of-the-art pocket radios that also open car doors will be common.***

A surprised Corey moved away just as our lips touched for the second time, looking exactly as I remembered pre-kiss, except I now saw him with fresher, newer eyes. He opened his mouth and out shot a sound. Words. But I wasn't listening. Instead, I placed my lips onto his again, our hands combining, merging into one. The years were ebbing away and once again we were teenagers. And as his hands cupped my face, I began to understand with stunning clarity that my feelings for him were deeper than I'd ever thought possible.

And I suddenly wanted to stay like that forever.

"Lois . . . I . . ." he said huskily. I soothed him with another kiss, this time deeper, and with a longing I had rarely felt in thirty years. Corey was peeling away the layers I'd built up over the years to guard my emotions. And as the sound of *The Manual* hitting the floor startled me, I knew it wasn't time to psychoanalyze those feelings, but time for once to bask in them. Enjoy being with this man, a man I had known almost all my life. Enjoy the feel of him as we connected, every part of me wanting him to take me further and further away from reality.

"I love you," he whispered, and I didn't care if it was the lust talking or if he actually meant it.

I just wanted to stay. Like this. Forever.

I just wanted to trust and, for once, I really wanted to *believe*. I even tried to look away, but he gently pulled my face to him, forcing me to look into my own reflection through the beauty of his eyes.

"I love you so much, Lois. Always have."

"I love you too," I said finally as our lips met again—meaning it for the very first time. Saying it because I felt it and not because of obligation or an offshoot of lust; but because I had loved this boy since we were children, lusted after him when we were teenagers, and finally fallen in love with him as an adult.

It had always been Corey.

It would always be Corey.

My mind remained focused on the moment.

Tomorrow was another day.

But I wanted to stay like this forever.

. . . I don't really see portable telephones taking off. There just isn't the technology to see that through. From what I've read, those prototypes are way too heavy for a start . . .

For once, I didn't fight a strong urge to leave, feeling strangely content to just lie in Corey's arms and not think about anything more taxing than how I felt at that precise moment.

I just wanted to *be.*

So it was easy to fall into a peaceful sleep, only to wake the next day to an empty bed and a prickle of hurt.

Corey was gone.

I called his cellphone.

"Where are you?"

"Downstairs. Come down."

Wrapped in a sheet, I found him in Mom's kitchen, his luscious body draped in a tiny towel.

"Morning, darling, and happy birthday!"

It felt strange to hear him call me such an intimate term, making a welcome change from "Lo Bag." But too shy to reply accordingly, I perched on a breakfast stool and watched.

"We have burned sausages, over-crispy charred bacon and orange juice freshly squeezed about a year ago and laden with preservatives and E numbers."

"It smells lovely!"

"I'm a crap cook and I'm not sure where your mom keeps the ketchup," he said, placing the food on the table before me.

"What happened last night?" I blurted out.

Corey slid a piece of bacon into his mouth as I watched, remembering his mouth on mine. Stop. Focus.

"Come on, Lo Bag, it's not as if it was the first time!"

Something inside me threatened to explode.

"Eat up!" he said.

"No . . . hang on . . . Is that all last night was for you? For old times' sake?"

I stood up.

"That's not what I said."

"So, what did you say . . . ?" A mound of insecurities threatened to pop up and pierce this perfect moment.

"I'm saying, even though it was some time ago, coming out of a serious relationship was intense and I'm not sure—"

I didn't need to hear another word and, armed with a heavy feeling, raced from the kitchen to begin the search for my clothes, all spread around in strategic points in the spare room upstairs. Shoes under the bed. Skinny jeans on top of the boxes. Blouse hanging from a loose nail sticking out of the door.

I dressed in record time, but still felt naked. Vulnerable. And I didn't like this feeling.

"Where are you going?" he asked. I remained silent, knowing my reply would be followed by a barrage of hot tears I'd no intention of offering. Carla was right, Corey was in slut mode and I'd fallen for it a second time.

Mumbling something stupid and forgettable, I left the house and raced to the bus stop, tears running down my face. Weeping for all of Corey's silent, broken promises and for opening myself up to him emotionally only to be shown the door. I wept for telling him I loved him and meaning it. And I wept for Dad—the only man who'd ever *really* love me. With my head in my hands, it was easy to sob some more, berating myself for looking back, just in case . . . just in case he'd run after me.

But, of course, he hadn't.

Space travel by now should be as common as a trip to Spain.

After thirty minutes, the bus hadn't appeared, so I faced the indignity of walking back to Mom's to retrieve my cellphone, last seen upstairs, and call a cab. Just as I was about to turn the key in the lock, I heard Corey's voice.

"I was hoping you'd come back."

"Only for my phone."

"Come inside."

So I did, and I wasted no time in emptying the contents of my mind. "I don't like being used, Corey."

"I'd never do that to you. You didn't give me a chance to explain things before you rushed out. If you'd let me, I would have said, 'ever since splitting up with my fiancée, yes, it's been hard.' "

I scoffed.

He smiled. "Very funny. Anyway I've been on a few dates, seen a few people, but they've never lasted because every time the same thing would happen . . . they just weren't good enough. I probably called off my wedding for the same reason."

"She wasn't *good enough*?"

"Will you just listen? She/they weren't good enough because they weren't YOU. They weren't you, Lo Bag!"

I took a huge breath.

"I love YOU, Lo Bag. Have always loved you."

"Corey . . ." I exhaled.

"Remember when I gave you that LL Cool J tape at your party? I loved you even then, although I may have been more in love with your ever-expanding chest. Hey, I admit it! But after last night, I finally knew you felt the same way, and you know it felt so great knowing that you . . . that you . . . that you feel the same way."

"But why didn't you follow me?"

"What, dressed in a towel? You are joking, right?"

"You could have gotten dressed when I did. Anyway, it doesn't matter now. It would never work between us."

"And you've already decided that?"

"Yes."

"Based on me not wanting to run after you in a cold street dressed in a towel? Now why doesn't that surprise me."

"I'd better call that cab."

"You'd already made your mind up before it happened, hadn't you? Admit it?

"I'd better . . . go . . ."

"I'm no therapist, but it's my guess you do that to all the guys you meet. Make sure you never get too close. I'm right, aren't I?"

"I'm sorry." I turned to leave.

"Wait!" He gripped my arm softly. "I look at you and all I see is one of the most beautiful women I have ever met. Inside and out. And yet. And yet . . . I know that every relationship you've been in has left you . . . I dunno . . . it's like you want to be this 'alone' person . . ."

"Can you blame me? So I'm right . . . Yes?"

"Oh, so when did you decide this, Lo Bag? Aged five?"

I scratched my nose.

"I've nothing to lose by being frank with you, you've already shredded any possible relationship between us anyway, so I'll go for gold. Is that okay?"

"Go ahead," I spat, willing the moment to be over so I could run next door, grab my phone and get as far away from this place as possible. And more importantly read the last few remaining pages of my manual.

"No matter who you've met in the past, they will NEVER and I repeat NEVER live up to the wonderful superman of a dad that was Kevin Bates."

I moved into the lounge, just to get away. "Don't speak about him like that."

Corey followed. "Why not? It's the truth. You've built him up so much in your mind that no bloke could ever compete with him, least of all ME. Plus he died, all young and perfect. What poor bastard could live up to that?"

"Shut up!"

"You've always hid behind your dad, and *The Manual*, ever since, and you KNOW IT!" Corey was shouting and my body was closer than ever to producing a bucket of tears I hadn't even ordered.

"Look, I'm sorry, Lo Bag, but it had to be said."

"What you're saying isn't true, none of it! They never stuck around! No one ever sticks around, Corey!"

"That can't be true."

"It is!"

"Think about it, Lois. Every single person?"

I thought of Dad's sister Ina, never getting in touch. Charlie, his best friend had also disappeared. Then there was Greg and Erin, who'd soon faded away. Then again, I also hadn't bent over backward to get in touch with *them*, by not replying to their initial letters. Okay, that's a point . . . Then there was Oliver, Raymond, Biyi; all relatively good men and yet I'd found it easy to push them away because . . .

"You never allowed any of them to get close to you in the first place. You made damn sure of that! I'm surprised you're even friends with my kid sister, considering how difficult she can be. But she's your only close friend, though, Lois, everyone else is just an acquaintance, right?"

I felt a tear.

His expression faltered. "You're just scared, that's all—of them all leaving you, just like Kevin." I scratched my nose and swiped at the tear, confused at all this psychobabble. "I've always been there, though."

"Except when you were in France," I rebutted him.

"I have always been there. Always loving you . . ."

I wanted to scream and tell him he was wrong. Laugh it off as a product of a wild imagination and too much *Oprah*. Instead I said, "I've got to go into Mom's. My cellphone."

Because he was wrong. Dad *was* perfect. *My* very own Superman.

I ran away from Corey and back into Mom's house, where I found the Bingo Caller slumped by the stairs and barely breathing.

Oh, and England will win the World Cup again, again and again.

"You saved his life," said Mom, mascara running down her cheeks. We were both in a hospital room.

"I'm just glad I got there when I did."

Mom rested a weary head on her husband's thighs as he lay hooked up to a hospital machine. Wires, drips and a cocktail of technical sounds complemented her weeping.

"I thought you were in Cornwall."

"We were, but he wasn't feeling too good so we came back early. Thank God you were home. What were you doing there cooking breakfast? Not that it matters now. The point is you were."

"Yes."

"I know it looks bad and he's unconscious, but the doctors say it's looking good for him. Thanks to you."

"What happened, Mom?"

"He's had hypothyroidism for a while now. Not enough thyroid hormones, apparently. It's got worse as he got older. Then he got an infection and that's how he ended up like this. I'll explain more later, I just haven't got the strength right now."

I stayed and Mom talked as she effectively explained the physical changes over the years. Why he was always tired being one. Of course, if I'd ever given him the time of day, I'd have noticed the weight gain, his tendency to get a cold quite easily, I'd have noticed all that. Perhaps if I'd been a better daughter, Mom would have come to me when he was diagnosed and not just gone to Carla's mom.

Although Mom looked tired, something in her eyes simmered expectantly.

"How's Abbs? I should go and see her," I asked.

"No need. Abbi's fine, she's with Calvin. You don't think I'd leave her on her own?"

"No, I don't."

My eyebrows scrunched as Mom plunged into her bag

robotically and retrieved a tissue. "She loves you so much, running after you—telling all her little friends about you. You're her heroine. And yet sometimes . . . sometimes it seems like you can't get away fast enough! It actually makes sense that you'd want to come home while we were away, now I come to think about it."

"Mom, don't. Not now."

"Why not now?" Mom was talking to me but looking at her husband as he slept, hopefully miles away from the frost radiating from my mother's mouth and into the room.

"Okay, well, how can you say that?"

"Very easily. Because it's true. You've never really loved her."

"I do love Abbi," I protested with a touch of guilt.

"If you say so."

Because of where we were, we whispered, but the words remained sharp and so very painful. A pain I felt with every syllable. It was as if Corey had opened up this well of emotion inside me.

"You've always been like it, Lois."

"Can you blame me?" In hindsight, this wasn't my best moment and I probably sounded twenty years younger than my age, but at that time I responded to the urge to get things out into the open.

"Go on, please don't stop," she urged. Bloodshot eyes ready for battle.

"You've never been bothered about me.'

"Is that so?"

"I even remember you not bothering to attend my thirteenth birthday. Carla's mom had to put something together for me. I could go on, Mom, but as I said, this isn't the time or the place."

She stared toward the hospital bed again and sighed. "The day of your thirteenth birthday party, I had a miscarriage."

My mind attempted a rewind job back to that time, but all I could recall was Corey handing over that LL Cool J cassette.

"I told everyone it was flu, but it was a miscarriage, Lois!"

I thought for a moment and whispered, "I'm so sorry." Quite rightly, I felt truly and utterly pathetic. Poor Mom.

"So if it seems like I loved Abbi too much, then maybe I do. I'd already lost a baby. And then when she went missing that afternoon . . . I thought . . . I thought . . ." Her body convulsed with emotion.

I stood. "I know, Mom. It was awful . . ."

Before my eyes, my mother became small, fragile, and I wanted to touch her, embrace her and bury my head in her chest.

"But to accuse me of loving one more than the other . . . that's just . . . WRONG. So very wrong." She slowly took another tissue from her bag, swiped at her eyes and sniffed. "Anyway, Carla's mom will be coming soon so you can go on your merry little way like you always do."

I could have put down her anger to her husband's condition, but there was something else.

"Talk to me, Mom?"

"Oh, just go! Never mind your sister, you've always hated him, her dad, my husband! I bet you're even sorry you found him. Because even now you can't look at him. The man who put food on our table. Tried with you when all you could do was spit it back in his face. AND NOT EVEN NOW CAN YOU LOOK AT HIM!"

I tried to look at him. I really did. But all I saw was a sheet leading up to closed eyelids and an expressionless face. He looked dead, just like my dad would have done all those years ago. "I can't, Mom."

"Why?" she pleaded, among more tears.

"It's not what you think, Mom."

"So you're telling me you gave him a chance, is that it?"

"No, I didn't . . ." I was all jumbled up and confused now. A mass of emotions percolating in that hospital room. "I was . . . I was angry with you for marrying him."

"And why? Didn't I have the right to move on? Did you see Carla and Corey playing up when their mother remarried? No."

"They were much older."

"So?"

"Their dad was still alive!"

I'd raised my voice and felt certain a Sister or someone would come in and chuck us out.

"Oh, so that means I have to be on my own forever, is that it? You don't realize how this man—" she pointed toward her husband—"this man allowed me to love again, be as happy as I had ever been in my entire life!"

That stung. "You were happy with Dad."

"Is that what you think?"

"What are you saying?"

"We were having problems."

"That's not true. Are you saying he didn't love you?" That when Dad wrote about loving her and marrying her and she being one of the best things he'd ever done—that was all rubbish? Was she trying to tell me he lied? My anger simmered just below bursting point.

"No, he did love me. Once. But as the years went on, we just . . ."

"Just . . . ?"

"Fell out of love."

"You just fell out of love?" If I could have seen my face in the mirror it would be one of horror and total disbelief. "Fell out of love?"

Mom dabbed at her eyes. "It happens, Lois. We both felt the same way—wanting to stay together for you. But it got to the stage where that just couldn't happen." I thought I saw Mom's eyes glistening yet again, but within my own mounting rage I couldn't be sure. "So, just before he was diagnosed, we . . . we'd begun proceedings . . ."

My eyes widened.

Mom continued. "Divorce proceedings. It's what we both wanted, Lois, we were so unhappy. So very unhappy. He wanted custody of you and I said no way, but we vowed to remain friends and bring you up together. He'd even planned on living close by so he could see you every day."

My stomach began to contract.

"But after the diagnosis, I couldn't . . . I couldn't leave him. It just wasn't an option any more."

"You loved each other! You stayed together!" I said, trying to ignore the time bomb that wanted to explode from deep within me.

"The deterioration was so quick, Lois. It wasn't easy for him and it wasn't easy for me either. Especially when you began to pick up on things. Playing up. It wasn't easy to cope, but I did."

"So let me get this straight—you probably didn't help his illness by threatening divorce?"

"YOU'RE NOT LISTENING, LOIS. YOU'RE NOT A LITTLE GIRL ANY MORE, YOU'RE A GROWN WOMAN!"

My tummy contracted. Aagh.

"It's what we BOTH wanted!"

Silence ensued. I needed to digest this. I sat down, ignoring how uncomfortable the arms of the chair felt against my ribs.

A very deep breath. "Carry on."

"The . . . the deterioration was quick. So very quick. What little strength he had, he saved for your manual."

My eyes widened in disbelief. "You knew about my manual?"

A wry smile. "He was writing away most nights. He even said I could look at a few passages, but I thought it best not to. That was between the two of you—father and daughter."

"So you knew about it all the time?"

"Yes, I did, Lois. Philomena called the day before the wedding to tell me she'd be giving it to you. To be honest I was relieved she had it. I thought it was lost, or packed away somewhere."

"Why didn't you say something?"

"Perhaps the same reason you didn't. I don't know . . ." Mom placed her face in her hands and I thought she was going to cry. But just as I felt bad about reducing her to this, a flash of clarity took over.

"So *that's* why he didn't trust YOU enough to give me *The Manual* and he gave it to his sister instead! He obviously didn't trust you. You were hurting him so much by all that divorce talk . . ." I couldn't stop the hurtful words from escaping my mouth.

"Lois, don't." She stood and tenderly placed her palm on

my shoulder. "For whatever reason, your father thought it best to give it to his sister. I'll never know why. They were close and, yes, things were a bit strained between us at times. But that is not the issue here."

"What's the issue, Mom? I mean, why have you told me about all this divorce stuff? Do you want sympathy? Is that it?" I looked to her and I felt a single tear stray from beneath my eyelid.

"No. I just want you to know what happened. That things weren't always rosy. That he wasn't perfect. Wasn't perfect for *me*. That I had found the perfect man for me in Derek. And he's lying in front of us on a hospital bed and I'm wishing so hard that he isn't about to be taken from me."

"Are you saying Dad was a bad father?" I asked, the information still not seeping through.

"He was a *wonderful* father, just not a great husband as it happens."

Tears began shooting from my eyes and nose, like a never-ending river of frustration. The hurt; the grief. I even heard a shrill cry—and it took me a few seconds to realize the sound was coming from my own mouth.

Everything else after that was a blur. Mom pulling me into her arms. Holding me tight. My body shaking as she soothed me with words. Stroked my hair. Planted wet kisses on my furrowed forehead. Whispered that she loved me.

And then, peace.

Everyone will own one of those Kodak disc camera things. Ahhh, to capture those lovely family moments.

I lay on my own bed and stared up at the ceiling. In twenty-four hours so much had happened. Telling Corey I loved him, Derek's illness, and then finding out my dad and Mom had been about to divorce.

My phone rang and I wished it was Carla. It was Corey. I ignored it. It was time for me to read the very last page of *The Manual.*

Last words (yes, yes, I know . . . but I always have to have the last word!).

Lowey . . .

Well, this is hard for me.

It's the end of The Manual and I've run out of paper—can you believe it? What am I liiike?

Anyway, I really hope you've enjoyed our time together. I have, because I got to spend the most fantastic first five years of your life with you and the thought of not being around for the rest scared me so very, very much. Writing this manual has helped me to stamp out some of that fear.

So, I don't want you to be scared.

Of anything.

I'll always be there for you. Promise. But I have to go now. We both knew this day would come anyway: a) because it had to stop somewhere, and b) I can't advise you over the age of thirty because, well, I never got past that age!

But always know you can look back on The Manual, OUR manual, any time for my—at times useless—bits of advice to squirm at or to follow.

Any time.

So no grand gestures here, honey . . . just something I want to share with you. I wrote it some time ago when

I started drafting the letter I originally wanted to send to you (which ultimately turned into this manual). So, my beautiful, brave Lois Bates, here's a few last words from your dad:

There will be times when everything feels like a struggle, a chore, the ache in your heart just growing bigger and bigger as you experience the absence of a special someone or even **something** *in your life (this can be a person, a way of life, an object) that has stuck around you and been with you for eons. And suddenly, poof!—they're gone without warning. And what follows is every part of you screaming for them to just come back.*

But they don't. They can't. No matter how loud you scream, or how heartfelt your pleas—they just can't.

So then what?

You might sit back and let a kind of depression set in as you secretly wait for the day they'll miraculously float through the door and into your life again. Or you sit by the phone and wait for someone on the other end to confidently let you know it's all been some wind-up or a forgivable mistake. Anything to make the now seem unreal. But that just doesn't happen. And I'm sorry, but it's never, ever going to happen, is it?

What a lot to take in. Absorb. Come to terms with. To embrace.

But you know what? You can and will be able to clinch this reality. Because time's an inevitable twist to the plot, Lois. At first unwelcome, but soon one of the very things that keeps you going day to day, helping you to pump air into your chest and breathe again. And it's through time that you notice life having the cheek to carry on as normal all around you; spiky-haired kids still getting excited over a Number One, the mile-long traffic jam toward Blackheath Common still occurring every weekday between three thirty and six thirty. And what's more, it's all going on WITHOUT *that same thing or person you miss with every waking breath, every dream and with every muscle in your entire body.*

So now comes the best bit: remembering to live again. REALLY LIVE *again. Especially when you then begin to fathom that what was lost, taken from you, wasn't the whole sum of you. I mean, even now, as you read this, you're actually adding a new experience and feeling to the life, person, being that is* YOU. *Moving forward and treading a path that will lead you to where you need to be.*

It worked for me, Lowey.

Everything I tell you in this is from experience. Every feeling. Every knock. Every word. But now it must all become about you.

So the very end of **your** *life book, if you like, depends on who or what has been popping up in your chapters. You've probably met a few of them already, but maybe you haven't even set eyes on some yet. The ones you love; the ones who love you back. The ones you respect. The ones who influence you in some way, either large or small. Each will play their own important part.*

So, the very last thing I ask is that you allow yourself the chance to really feel and experience these people as they slowly or quickly (and sometimes without warning) become a part of who you are and are yet to become.

Now the clock is ticking clear
And our time is drawing near
My heart is aching for just one more smile
You're my girl
You're my girl
All the while
I knew that our love
Would never, ever die

With stars on
With stars on
A very special love
With stars on
With stars on
The only one that comes with stars!

The only good thing about losing someone at five years old is the strange luxury of not recalling the actual moment it happened. The moment the first man I have ever loved was ripped away from me like an errant chin hair by an angry pair of tweezers. The realization that the man who'd read me stories at night, kissed me goodnight, every night, was no longer breathing in the same air as me. Whatever I was doing the precise moment he took his last breath; thought his final thought; blinked for the very last time, can't be recalled. And all I can remember are flashes. Flashes that are quick to blur in my mind. Dad showing me how to kick a ball correctly into goal down the rec. Or had it been Carla's back garden? With Carla's dad, even? Chastising me for a minor indiscretion involving a pair of treasured clippers—or had that been Mom?

Yes, finishing *The Manual* was like losing Dad all over again. My deep feelings of dissatisfaction were fresh, raw and all too consuming. I would never again be reading a fresh piece of advice from Dad. Never again be able to laugh at his crummy jokes for the first time. No more brand-new entries to look forward to.

I could just get angry.

But I cried. A lot. And instead of sinking into a place I had been before, this time I was determined to move on.

Hope.

That's what pulled me up then and that's what's doing so now. To quote my dad: "where there is life there is hope." I would be forever sad about the end of *The Manual* but I'd only let this sorrow be a small part of me. It would not—*I* would not allow it to—stop me from living and loving. I was here with a fully functioning heart and for the first time in my entire life felt more than ready to share it with someone in sweet abundance.

Now I just had to hope he felt the same way.

I realized it would have been wise to ask the cab driver to stick around in case he wasn't home. In case the whole family except Corey *was* home. Then again, if this was meant to be, he'd be there, I told myself, with a temporary belief in kismet, serendipity et al.

Corey answered my knock.

"I've been trying to call you," he said.

"Here I am." I took a step closer. "And I need you."

His arms opened up to me and I molded myself into his chest and wept freely with abandon; for the last strenuous few days and for the last twenty-five years too.

epilogue

The sky was a dull shade of gray, cloudless with a promise of rain as my insides became gripped with the warmth of a fresh sunset. I moved from my window and back to the screen of the laptop just as it flipped into screensaver mode, effectively blanketing the latest cheesy family shot I'd been given until Thursday to edit. Clicking onto a fresh document, I waited, just staring at the blank screen and smiling gracefully as I placed a palm onto my tummy.

My phone sang an incoming text message from Corey. He was going to be late home and did I fancy another pizza, this time *without* the raspberry jam, gorgonzola and green chili topping? I smiled. So much had changed over the past twelve months. Life was something I actively took part in now, experiencing every second, minute, hour and day. And this included my family: Derek, Mom, Abbi, Calvin, Carla, her mom and Corey.

Although we weren't about to become the Waltons, I secretly looked forward to our new Sunday ritual involving a roast dinner at Mom's and drinks next door with the others. I was trying. Mom was trying. Everything was so new. Not least being with Corey in a real life, grown-up relationship. I was enjoying the intimacy, the closeness that existed between us, and I never, ever wanted it to end. That much I knew.

I typed the first word.

Hello.

I hit delete.

I located *The Manual* in the lounge cabinet—beside the Kodak Tele Ektra camera—in its new home and no longer part of a secret hiding place. I used the hem of my tunic to swipe at the film of dust that had gathered on top. Although I hardly ever referred to it any more, it remained an important, affectionate piece of my history and something I felt any child would very much love to have, if received in the proper way. Turning to the first page, I felt the words almost leap from the paper and into my consciousness.

And then I returned to the laptop.

Perhaps you have your daddy's eyes or your grandfather's wit or even your Auntie Abbi's cheek, who knows? But even though you haven't been born yet, I can still picture you. Yes, really. And I can't wait to hear how your voice will sound, or find out what your little habits are or what your favorite color is—mine's yellow by the way. Okay, now where was I? Oh yes. I'll start.

I think that every little boy or girl should have one of these. Something for the future. A reference to look back on when they are feeling sad, happy or just something to show THEIR children. So, this is my (Lois Bates's) manual to my son, Kevin junior. The Love of My Life (along with your dad). I hope this explains things. Maybe it won't. Perhaps I just have too much time on my hands.

But first, let's start with the rules of *The Manual* . . .

FROM

LOLA JAYE

AND

AVON A

Why not produce your very own manual . . . ?

There's really not much excuse not to these days as we are surrounded by so many ways of recording "the moment" as it happens. Kevin didn't have the choices that we enjoy today, like computers, DVDs, CDs, digital cameras and multiuse cellphones, so why not give it a try?

A good starting point.

Without getting morbid and thinking about what you'd like to leave when you're gone, how about approaching it as something to enjoy NOW?

What are your favorite things?
What makes you tick?
What is currently happening around you?

You could place a newspaper cutting of a historic moment alongside your prom corsage into a box and already, you have recorded moments in time that you have enjoyed, ready for someone else—whether it be your future children or godchildren—to enjoy.

If keepsakes aren't your thing, though, what about a picture diary in a scrapbook? For example: "Dana at fourteen months,"

"Dana graduating from high school," "Dana marrying Dave," "Dana holding Davey Junior for the very first time . . ."

Or what about a video diary, of special events all kept on one DVD for people to watch in the coming years? It could include a much cherished holiday abroad, or clips of a much loved pet chasing its tail—moments in time recorded forever. The good news is, films can be produced and compiled on home computers nowadays—all you have to do is get on with it or ask someone technologically minded to edit it for you.

We live in a fast-paced society and compiling your very own manual doesn't have to be time consuming, but should be handled with a lot of love, care, and attention.

But don't forget—a tried and tested formula is still available for you to take advantage of—pen and paper. It may seem as if they just aren't "fashionable" anymore, but I believe that nothing beats receiving a handwritten letter from someone you care about. Scruffy or neat, joined up or upright . . . as long as it's just from you.

Whichever method you decide to choose, the sentiments will be heartfelt and personal and the lucky recipient will hopefully appreciate the effort and love that you have put into it—as well as all those memories!

Why not give it a try?

Meet Lola

What inspired you to write *By the Time You Read This?*
I was sitting at home transfixed and utterly moved by an episode of *Oprah* that featured a dying mother who left a collection of keepsakes for her daughter. A whole host of "what if" questions started flooding my head:

- What if there were no computers, DVDs, MP3s, or video cameras?
- What if this was a father? What if he simply wrote a letter to his beloved daughter?
- What if I switch on a computer and see what happens?

I wrote 6000 words that very day.

Some reader might expect "The Manual" to be written from a mother to a daughter, why did you choose a father?
I suppose most people would instantly think of a mother writing for a daughter, so I felt very strongly about writing something from the point of view of a man. A man who thinks, feels, and loves. A strong, beautiful man who loves his child with everything he has, and is not afraid to cry or to tell his daughter that he loves her. But also, at the same time a man who is a man's man and loves soccer!

There has been a lot of press in the last few years about dying parents leaving memory boxes and video diaries for their children; do you think it's something every parent should do?
Who knows when it is your "time to go?" Okay, I don't want to get morbid here so it's probably best to approach it with the

thought of simply making a documentary of your life so far—something to show the next generation. I for one would love to have seen a clip of me being born. Okay maybe not! But times are changing all the time and it's nice to be able to show these developments in the future. Plus, there's really no excuse these days as we are surrounded by so many ways of recording "the moment" as it happens. Indeed, setting the end of Kevin's life in the 1980s allowed me to go back to a time that even I (gulp) could remember which now almost seems prehistoric in terms of technology and our current means of communication. And I have to add that some music from the 80s was great too!

Lois discovers that she has a real passion for photography. Is that a career that you once dreamed of pursuing?
Well as far back as I can remember, I had always wanted to be a writer. It's something that I have always thought about ever since I was a child. I used to shut myself away in my room and just write. And write. And write. When I was about eleven, I began writing my very own weekly serial called "Karen and Terry" about two best friends and their thrilling adventures (about as "thrilling" as watching weeds grow now that I look back on it). But they did have two really hunky boyfriends and the stories covered the girls' exploits and experiences, which included everything from bullying to kisses. Years later my grandmother kindly informed me that she had thrown them away because she'd wanted to use the winebox that they were stored in!

Another memory that springs to mind is that of a gorgeous old typewriter in a shop window. It was orangey-red and sat among all the high tech electronic ones, looking almost serene. I just had to have it! So, the day my Nan and I picked it up was one of the most exciting, ever (especially as she'd been making payments for it each week). Other kids were into dolls, I wanted a typewriter (as well as a doll) so I guess the clues to my dream profession were always floating about somewhere.

Can you describe a typical writing day?

On weekends and days off from The Day Job, I'm not happy unless I've done at least four hours of writing work a day. My head gets all mushy and my eyes become all blurry by about hour five though . . .

Do you have a few words of advice for aspiring writers?

Can't remember where I heard this, but it sums it up: "Success is 1 percent motivation and 99 percent perspiration." And the lovely Will Smith once said something in an interview in 2004 that stayed with me: 'Don't let your successes go to your head, don't let your failures go to your heart.'

Which writers have influenced you the most?

The simple answer is, I can't name a particular writer, but can list a few books that have for some reason done the following: influenced or touched me in some way, made me think (a lot) or simply had me laughing out loud—something that is pretty hard for me to do (with books, not in general!) . . .

Here's the list:

***The Lovely Bones* by Alice Sebold**

Wow, wow, wow. I had this on my shelf for a good few years before finally deciding to read it, because I knew I had to be in the correct place to really take it on. And I'm so glad I waited. What a beautifully written, thought-provoking and moving novel. Absolutely stunning. Even though there were a few harrowing scenes, I didn't want the book to end. I even found myself going over certain sentences because of how beautifully they were constructed. A particular scene involved the lead character coming face-to-face with an old family pet—and still, I can't get that lovely image out of my head.

***Kaleidoscope* by Danielle Steel**

I read this many moons ago, perhaps when I was a teenager, but have never forgotten how it made me feel. The suffering of the main character and how her experience differed to that of her other sisters' is brilliantly put forward. I rarely read books twice but I did with this one (albeit a few years later) because I wanted to experience it as an adult and see if it still had the same effect. It did.

***The Secret Dreamworld of a Shopoholic* by Sophie Kinsella**

I'm not going to admit to any similarities between myself and the main character. I will say this though: WHAT A FUNNY, FUNNY NOVEL! The scene when Becky pretends to be, I think Scandinavian (this was a few years back now), made me laugh out loud so much I thought I'd burst. Brilliantly funny.

***Romeo and Juliet* by William Shakespeare**

The original story of star-crossed lovers. Okay, at school I found the old English quite annoying (and much to the irritation of our poor English teacher, hilariously funny). But as a fully paid up member of the adult brigade, I'm now able to truly appreciate the beauty of this book and its simple message about love. Something that transcends time, race, and language.

***Scenes from a Sistah* by Lolita Files**

How much fun is this book? Very funny and very raw. Centers around the loves and lives of two best friends. Great stuff.

***Thirtynothing* by Lisa Jewell**

Even though the premise was very "boy meets girl," the ride was sooo enjoyable. Snuggling up to read this book was like unwrapping a huge marshmallow. A warm and fuzzy moment in time. Magic.

***Lord of the Flies* by William Golding**

During the guffaws and yawns of my classmates, I was secretly fascinated by this story of a group of shipwrecked young children and their emergence into savagery. Big Brother before the TV series! I suppose this book also allowed early stirrings of a fascination with psychology to emerge.

***A Day Late and a Dollar Short* by Terry McMillan**

This book deals with the raw complexities of a modern family. I especially enjoyed reading from so many alternate perspectives that differed wildly from my own. Which is why, this is one of my favorite Terry McMillan books. Go girl!

***Memoirs of a Geisha* by Arthur Golden**

Just a little bit . . . exquisite.

***The Best a Man Can Get* by John O'Farrell**

So funny, funny, funny—reading about the main character's honest and brutal account of first-time fatherhood. There's so many laugh-to-yourself (or be labeled a weirdo) moments, one involving a baby and a ceiling. Enough said.

***Blessings* by Sheneska Jackson**

I remember this being a lovely addictive page-turner, set in an American hairdressing salon. I finished it wishing and hoping there was a sequel. Must try and read this again one day . . .

***Oliver Twist* by Charles Dickens**

Another oldie but goodie. This novel dealt with street crime, child poverty, and domestic violence, themes that unfortunately are still so relevant today.

Was it easy to get published?

If you'd like to read the entire story, please visit my first blog, "Diary of an Unpublished Writer" http://www.upadiary.blogspot .com. I started it around 2002 and it basically documents my insane journey to publishing deal. The angst, the fears and then the joy . . .

What is the best thing about being a published author?

Readers telling you the book made them laugh and cry.

Photo by Laku Davies

LOLA JAYE was born in West London, grew up in South London and has also lived in Nigeria. She has a degree in Psychology and a Masters in Psychotherapy and currently works for the NHS as a counselor. In between writing and working, Lola likes watching reruns of *Dallas* and *The Sopranos* while avidly dipping into a huge tub of dairy ice cream. *By the Time You Read This* is Lola's first novel.

Find out more about Lola and what she's been up to by visiting *www.lolajaye.com*.